D1079535

About the Author

As a teenager Deborah created many stories, until two children expanded her creativeness to wall paintings, cardboard UFOs and tents out of bedding so her son and daughter could make up stories of their own. Until recently when a dream encouraged her to write again and thankfully *Passage of Destiny* is the end result.

Dedication

I'm dedicating this book to my loving parents, Joyce and Roland Fielding and my two children Simon and Laura, without whom, I would never have managed to find the time to put fingers to keyboard and create such a unique fantasy storyline or a bizarre group of characters. I'd especially like to thank my Son Simon for being patient during the many countless hours that I'd bounced various ideas off and then arm wrestle him into proof reading odd sections of a then rough manuscript, instead of what he'd rather be doing, playing computer games and going for walks. I'd like to thank my son and daughter for being a great source of material for two of the main characters in the book, for they have brought them to life. I would also like to thank my lucky stars for having got the idea, from a dream I'd had many moons ago.

Deborah Lynne Pearson

PASSAGE OF DESTINY

A CIP catalogue record for this title is available from the British Library.

ISBN 978 1 78455 655 6

www.austinmacauley.com

First Published (2015)
Austin Macauley Publishers Ltd.
25 Canada Square
Canary Wharf
London
E14 5LB

Printed and bound in Great Britain

CHAPTER ONE

At first glance, the remote valley looked the same as any other to the casual traveller, who might decide upon viewing it, that this seemingly ordinary countryside setting, whose initial appearance seemed antiquated and untouched by the passage of time was actually without a doubt an extraordinary sight to behold, as was the picturesque village situated there. Despite the valley's commonplace appearance, a recent display of sunsets, over the past several days had produced a formidable explosion of an alluringly provocative display of colours, and within one such sunset, a unique fusion of soft effervescent gases, flowing majestically across an almost cloudless sky, on what would normally have been, an ordinary summer's evening. These mysterious, multi-coloured wisps settle above the quaint diminutively styled village, sheltered within the obscured valley, located just a few miles from a small coastal shoreline.

The picturesque village was small, consisting of just a few houses and buildings, which included a post office, bakery, butcher's shop and the local pub called The Three Moonbeams. Residing in the centre of this peculiar village was a quaint little church, elevated on a slight hillside, where it caught the last remnants of the sun's vibrant colours upon its stained glass windows and warm dark stones, encrusted with fragments of blue crystal, surrounded by an ominous collection of hideously formed gargoyles, scattered amongst the stone work, where an excessive amount of rain-water could escape through the gaping mouths of these winged monsters, while they stood guard alongside their freakishly bizarre cousins known as grotesques.

Normally, these gruesome creatures would glare down menacingly, eager to snatch the unwary, but these were distinctively different, some peered over window frames, others climbed up the exterior walls of the church, and all but one were seen gazing up towards the stars. This one particularly unique creature, stood out amongst the rest, appearing somewhat relaxed and care-free with his legs hanging casually over the entrance way, sporting an unusual fringe covering one eye, while another displayed a devilishly, mischievous glint, with his hands resting on his knees.

Meanwhile just a short distance away, located somewhere on the opposite side of the valley, a singular medieval styled house stood, in desperate need of repair, concealed by an abundance of almost impenetrable foliage and narrow pathways, securely nestling within an overgrown and long forgotten garden. Within this, a profusion of shadows from an open fire danced gracefully along the inside walls of an upstairs bedroom, as the sun gradually began to set, and nearby a couple lay entwined on a large oak framed bed whispering words of undying love to each other.

An antiquated Moses basket was carefully positioned by the bed, containing a rare and precious gift, a gift created from fragments of stardust and an enormous amount of love, blissfully unaware that there was to be an end of one dream, and the beginning of another this night. Selemie could feel the end was near, and yet she did not fear it, as her dark eyes gazed lovingly into her husband's brown eyes, which were the colour of her favourite edible treat, called chocolate. Selemie knew this was not the end but the beginning, and like the rest of her race, she had accepted it, and embraced it into their culture long ago, back when the Universes were still young.

She could hear the beating of James's heart beneath her ear where her head lay, as both held onto each other, too afraid of letting go. Selemie was unique in every way, for she had the ability to evolve and move on, when her time was near, however, for Selemie and her people, it wasn't something you took for granted, because like everything in life, there was always a price to pay for this special gift, as they were only now finding out.

The decision to leave her new born child behind, a child born of an everlasting love, took a great amount of courage, courage she never knew she had. The mere thought of leaving her behind caused Selemie such pain and heart ache that it was almost impossible to accept. Leaving her daughter here on this strange planet, knowing it wasn't her daughters' time was an agonizing choice. Nevertheless, Melanie, their most beloved daughter was worth the sacrifice, their beautiful baby had been worth it all, and more, as another ripple of pain enveloped her mother's body.

Time was rapidly running out, while the spasms of pain were getting stronger by the minute. It was taking an enormous amount of energy and willpower for her to hang on that little bit longer, to spend as much time as possible here with her husband James and daughter Melanie, named after her great grandmother, remembered as a modern day free spirit according to James, who one day decided, to break free from the restraining chains of blue blood superiority and family tradition and start living a little, announcing that she was going to 'Bloody well enjoy life while she could and stuff family tradition'.

She would on many occasions visit the family home spending most of the time with James and his sister Rachel. His parents often classed her as the worst sort of eccentric a family could have, but reluctantly put up with it, and James loved her for it. He remembered with pride the look of horror on his parents' faces when his grandmother would arrive unexpectedly to one of their famous and highly sort-after dinner parties with a young man in tow, who worshipped the ground she walked on. There had been an artist, a budding rock star, several top male models, the odd actor from both the theatre and the big screen, but the most scandalous of all guests to arrive with Melanie Rosalyn Trevern, was an outlandishly dressed transvestite called Ruby. Ruby was one of James's favourites amongst many friends of his late grandmother; the memory of it would always make him laugh.

James gazed down at Selemie to find her smile swiftly turn into a grimace as the pain within his beloved intensified, and immediately he held her closer to him, sensing her need for their precious daughter, as he rested his head against hers, his light brown wavy hair resting against the straight ebony black hair of his beloved's, knowing deep within his heart that there was nothing he could do. Selemie's desire to hold Melanie was strong, to show her how much they loved and adored her, but unfortunately she could not, for as frustrating as it was for her, she had to wait a little longer. She needed this time to concentrate on what was to be her final journey. Time was rapidly running out, she knew it was a losing battle she could feel her inner life force struggling while it tried to use the last remaining ounces of strength to keep her alive, for as long as possible.

Any signs of pain and suffering were shown only by a slight twitch at the corners of her almost black coloured eyes, and the irregular breathing. They should have realised the dangers from the start, the risks to both her life and that of the baby had always been high. But unfortunately love has a way of closing its ears to logic and common sense, it bypasses all safe guards and protective barriers that surround the fragile heart, giving the person something so unexpected, so unique that once found, they feel invincible to the point where they are able to take on anything and win, but not this time. From the very beginning they knew it had to be a home birth, too many problems would have arisen, and the consequences would have been beyond their control, secrecy was vital, especially for Melanie.

At the far end of the room, by an open window, two friends gaze across the lush valley beyond as a dramatic display of gas clouds emerges through the flurries of the evening sunset. Charlie and George were both friends and trusted allies to James and his deceased grandmother Rosalyn, who was often known as 'Rosie'. Although eccentric in personality and dress sense, she was trusted indisputably.

Charlie who wore a tweed tailored suit with matching waistcoat and one of his customary flamboyant bow-ties, stood a good deal shorter than his friend George, who towered over him like an avenging angel. Unlike George, Charlie still had a full head of hair, and took great pleasure in teasing his friend about his baldness, but envied him his designer eye glasses and handlebar moustache. Both friends looked at each other worryingly as the sun descended behind the mountain tops at the opposite end of the valley, casting rays of burnished red, orange and gold across the sky, with a peculiar infusion of blue intermingled within it. But deep within this structured mass of tranquil beauty and calm, a sudden unexpected gathering of fury, abject misery and raw pain emerged, in the form of dark black, angry storm clouds. Shards of lightening streaked across the skies, destroying a vast portion of the unruffled beauty. A sudden infusion of wind, escalating at an extraordinary speed, caused chaos and destruction as far back as the next valley, producing a torrent of heavy rain.

George, being a well-respected and highly qualified doctor, monitored the pregnancy from the very beginning and had, in truth, performed an impossible task with the help of a miracle, a prayer and a dose of stubborn determination, to save Melanie, but, sadly, he could not save her mother. How could he save her when her whole anatomy was so different? She was after all a visitor here, an alien from another planet, located in an unknown Universe, but for all intents and purposes she was just like the rest of us fully-fledged humans.

James in the meantime continued to whisper in her ear, the unending and everlasting love he carried deep within his heart for her, as tears of misery slid unhindered down his face, landing gently on the bed covers he had so lovingly wrapped around her moments ago. 'How would I go on living without her? My very reason for existing is slowly slipping away from me, and I am powerless to prevent it' he thought with an aching heart as he held her close. Occasionally lifting his head to place a loving kiss along her brow, while concealing his desire to scream, shout and curse God, Earth and the whole damn Universe for this misery. Demanding to know why he could not have this small slice of happiness, he'd managed to take from life's Universal cake.

When they were together nothing mattered, everything else seemed so unimportant; Planet Earth, its occupants, and the entire Universe were of no real consequence to James. The love he felt for Selemie was a rare and special thing, and by some miracle he had found it, only to have it gradually slipping away from him.

He breathed in and could smell the faint scent of flowers such as roses and night scented stock that drifted in on a strong evening breeze from the garden below, where every Rose bush below had bowed their heads as if in mourning, for the loss of so special a friend, and if a rose could shed a tear, then they would surely cry for Selemie, as heavy rain drops fell like tears of sorrow.

James looked into Seli's eyes, a nickname he had given her at the start of their romance, and thought how lucky he had been in finding the other half of his soul. Never would he have believed it possible for him to find so rare a person as Selemie to love, and be loved in return for so short a time, but for James it had been worth it. He lowered his head once again so his lips might gently brush against hers, while he gazed at her thinking, 'She'd never looked more beautiful as she does right now.' remembering the first time they met, or rather bumped into each other at the observatory in Edinburgh five years ago, 'A life time ago.' thought James.

Seli glanced up at him knowing what he was thinking, and smiled at the telepathic pictures he was showing her, as she lifted her hand to gently touch his cheek before kissing him once again, while the pain of such a loss was becoming more profound every time he looked into her unusually dark eyes, knowing that his whole life was slowly slipping away from him, making it too difficult to breathe, deciding there was only one option left for him, and that was to go with her, because their love was just too strong to survive alone, 'Am I being selfish, cruel and heartless to my new baby girl?' he wondered, before concluding, 'Probably, but I wouldn't have lived a long and happy life without my sweet Selemie beside me, so I'll go and live with her in the next,' James announced to himself, bringing his wife closer to him. Selemie knew of her husband's decision, she understood it and could never judge him for it, maybe in time, Melanie, (who was being shielded from her parents' anguish by her mother) would understand why they left her here, and eventually forgive them.

Selemie glanced across the room at her two closest friends, and quietly asked, "Please look after little Mel. Tell her that we will always love her; we hope she will understand the reasons why we're leaving her here, and the importance that she remain here. Now that my end is near, I can see how vital her role will be in the years ahead. More than one life will be at stake, more than one will depend on her." announced Selemie calmly.

George and Charlie both look anxiously at each other, before moving a little closer to the bed when Selemie noticed Austin, her faithful companion silently enter the room, in the guise of a typical black and white Tom cat, and slowly make his way over to the Moses basket where Melanie lay sleeping. Selemie looked at Austin with eyes overflowing with love for her friend and asked, "We want her to stay here and live with you, Austin. To experience life on her father's planet and become the beautiful woman we know she will be, you are my companion and dearest friend, Austin, who will always have a special place in my heart. You can see what I see, so you know why she has to remain here with you. Please ... Will you look after our baby girl?" pleaded Selemie, feeling her heart breaking.

Austin stood at the far side of the basket, and with a single nod of his head agreed to Selemie's request, replying, telepathically, "I will guard her with my life, I will not let you down, you have my word," as he gazed up at Selemie, who with a brief smile replied, "I know you wouldn't, Austin, thank you, friend, your loyalties now lie with her. I can rest easy knowing that you are protecting her." she replied before turning to gaze at George, who was busy wiping away the perspiration from his forehead with his handkerchief, and asked, "Please bring little Mel here to me, so we can hold her for the short time we have left." George put Melanie into the waiting arms of her mother, while Charlie offered a solemn promise saying, "We pledge our promise to look after her, to give her the love and care you would've given her yourselves." before glancing across at George who slowly nodded his head in agreement, while the couple spent their last minutes playing happily with their daughter, collecting precious memories for their long journey.

James released a laugh at his daughter's determined attempt to suck and chew his finger, while Selemie lovingly stroked her daughter's head, covered in wisps of auburn coloured curls. Eventually they kissed their daughter goodbye, and reluctantly let go of the tiny hand that tried desperately to hang on a little longer. They smile having noticed Melanie's wide eyed look of determination as her hands try to reach out for them once more, when at the last moment Selemie placed the tiny pale hand of her daughter's against her own alabaster coloured hand, palms pressed together, and began to concentrate.

James wrapped his arms around his loved ones, placing a kiss on each of their heads, as a tiny beam of light left Selemie's hand, and entered Melanie's, while Charlie who hadn't the courage to speak because his voice was thick with pent up emotion watched, as George announced suddenly, "I'll take Melanie to my brother and his wife, they will look after her. They were unable to have any children of their own, and would cherish little Mel. They can be trusted." This he promised before turning away, giving the couple enough time in which to show their daughter how much they loved her. They remained together as a family for as long as it was possible, right up to the end, when the last fragmented beatings of their hearts sounded, while both held onto a single precious memory, an image of them holding their baby daughter, playing with her, laughing with her, loving her, as eventually at long last their hearts stopped beating.

Only the sound of a meowing cat broke through the heavy silence that filled the room, causing both men to turn, to find Austin sat on the end of the bed with his head bowed low and with tears falling onto the bed throw, tears he was unused to shedding, being a guardian, a highly skilled watcher, trained in the art of protecting the ones he cared for. He paid homage to a couple he would always regard as the bravest and noblest of people, whilst at the same time, observing George with sharp-eyed intent, as he lifted Melanie out of the arms of her parents to gently place her back into her warm cot.

Even now in death Selemie was able to shield their infant daughter, as a soft effervescent wisp of cloud surrounded the four poster bed. Its soft glow enveloped the occupants in a gentle embrace of warmth and light that filled the whole room, causing everyone to shield their eyes. Austin used his body weight to turn the basket around, sheltering Melanie from the bright light, before clambering up the side of the Moses basket, balanced precariously on his two back legs, so he could watch over his new charge knowing his task would have been far easier, had he not been in the guise of a flea-ridden old tomcat, a creature Selemie was fascinated with.

When at long last the bright light had eventually dissipated, leaving behind two small multi-coloured spheres of pure energy, gliding majestically towards the baby basket, where Melanie lay, reaching out her tiny hand to grab hold of the multi-coloured Orbs, before they could phase through the floor heading into what had once been the library, but what was now a room covered in a series of extraordinarily designed full length canvases, depicting a series of strange images not of earth, this is where they would disappear through one of the canvases.

While in the far distance a series of unearthly sounds were heard, drifting in on a blackened horizon, as the sun delivered its final bow. The eerie ghostlike sound caused the entire area to shake violently, as everything within a mile radius of the mountainside began to shake violently, distorting it unnaturally, transforming it into something altogether different, while the terrible sound of a creature's outcries from within the blackened mass, terrified both human and animal alike, endeavouring to escape the horror before it was too late.

When at long last the darkened mass dispersed, leaving behind a horror so terrible, so horrific, it had caused a complete transformation on the molecular level, changing everything into individual pieces of hard slate. Every blade of grass, each flower, tree and rock had been transformed, but even more surprising, was that every insect and animal alike who were not quick enough to escape this horrific outbreak of violence had been dramatically altered. The sounds of despair continued to echo over the surrounding valleys, putting fear into the hearts of the local people, as the area cleared enough to reveal a tall figure cloaked in black, standing bare foot in the centre of this massed destruction, barely able to hold himself upright as devastation and desolation attacked both his body and soul.

The stranger staggered under the heavy weight of grief as it racked his body, while his head bowed low, his arms by his side, and his fingers spread wide apart, releasing an energised force so powerful, it produced steam and smoke from every pour of his body. He slowly lifted his head, showing an almost pure white skin with tints of grey in areas and shoulder length ebony black hair that matched his soulless empty black eyes, making it evident that a greater part of this person had died that day, the better part of him, eventually he turned and walked away heading towards the untouched woodland forest beyond. With each painful step, the flesh on his bare feet bled from the lacerations caused from the razor sharp pieces of newly formed devastation. He was incapable of feeling any guilt or remorse for what he had created, while in his grief-stricken state, owing to the death of his beloved twin sister.

Then all of a sudden he stopped, placed the palm of his hand over his severely wounded heart, brought on, by the sudden, unexpected outpouring of wretchedness, and releases a sharp terrifying cry for help, before merging with the darkness, a tortured soul, lost, alone and grieving, all of which, were a dangerous combination...

CHAPTER TWO

The beginning of a new dream,

23 years had passed since the untimely death of Melanie's parents, leaving her in Austin's capable, highly-trained care who right now, appeared quite happy, stretched across a branch of a large oak tree, growing near the balcony of their attic apartment belonging to a Mrs Edna Grimes their landlady, whose residence was on the ground floor along with Max her grandson. 'The apartment like the house had character we love,' concluded Austin thoughtfully before adding, 'I've also taken a liking to this gnarly, old oak tree,' he admitted, gazing over the edge of the branch he was lying on. Remembering it was to be Melanie's 24th birthday in a few days, and as predicted, her friends were planning yet another surprise.

'I can't see what all the fuss is about.' thought Austin, before adding 'I'm going to be 200 earth years old, you don't see me making a lot of fuss about it.' he thought, swinging his back leg too and fro, as it dangled over the edge of the tree branch, giving it a friendly little pat with his paw, which was surprising considering his views on affection were that, it often complicated matters, especially when he had a job to do, which brought his thoughts swiftly on to Melanie, unaware that her pet cat was in actual fact a shape-shifting alien from another planet, who suffers with unpredictable mood swings and bad attitude, making him unique in the feline world, he would quite often lay in wait for his arch enemy, his nemesis of the trees he'd nicknamed 'The Red Squirrel,' who from day one of them moving into the area two and a half years ago, had plagued him relentlessly, a professional antagonist in the making.

'One of these days, he'll make a mistake and I'll have him,' thought Austin furiously with a swift flick of his tail, recalling how the red mischief-maker would appear without warning, knock him out of the tree, then vanish again before Austin could retaliate, leaving him dangling precariously over a branch. Austin cursed again saying, 'The red flea-ridden pile of fur.' whilst gouging out a chunk of bark with his claw, wishing it was the squirrel and not the tree he was attacking, and then thought rather gleefully, 'How delicious it would be, to suddenly appear in front of him, in my true form,' the thought made him quiver in anticipation. 'To see the look on the face of that flee-riddled rat of the trees.' he concluded satisfyingly.

If seen in his natural form Austin would be considered handsome, being part humanoid and part bat of about 5½ft tall, partly covered in smoky blue/grey coloured skin and fur, with a pair of sinister looking bright green eyes, a small pointed nose, a nicely shaped mouth containing razor sharp teeth. He had slim human-like hands and feet, with black tinted finger nails, lips and eyelids, as were the tips of his ears. His inordinately bright green eyes would, when provoked into anger, change to become a deep soulless black. His wings were large, beautifully designed and almost translucent in appearance, covered in unusual tattoo markings, an ancient form of writing, they folded neatly away down the centre of his back. He bore a short hair style combed back but with a unique twist, that of a quirky little fringe hung over one eye.

To look at him now, Austin had all the appearance of being an ordinary everyday black and white Tom cat, complete with a bright red collar and an annoyingly hateful bell Melanie had given him last Christmas, he would often wonder whether she knew it would irritate him to the point of madness, and that was why she bought him the damn thing in the first place. Austin was a highly respected Alien on his home planet, currently on a long term assignment, a job he took very seriously or at least he tried to, except for the interference of the female variety making his job as guardian ten times harder. Once chosen they would stay with them for the whole of their life time, and in turn watch over the younger sibling's as well, but they are more than mere servants or body guards, they are family.

With the agility of an expert Austin turned towards the balcony after one final look over his shoulder for his arch nemesis; the red squirrel, noticing several blackbirds, song thrushes and the odd escaped budgerigar arriving, to start their morning singing session, guaranteed to wake Melanie up as it did every morning, and annoy the hell out of poor Austin who would often say, as he made his way towards the bed, 'I hate their happy chirping, hopping from one branch to the other, no one should be that happy in the morning. I can't wait for the day when Melanie finds out the truth and I can be myself again.' he thought, while tip toeing silently across the duvet.

At the precise moment that his backside had hit the bedding Melanie opened her deep violet coloured eyes to the sound of bird song, with her long wavy hair the colour of vintage full bodied red wine, spread across her pillows like the rippling waves of an ocean. She turned to admire the early morning sunlight shimmering across her bedroom wall, in a psychedelic display of colour through the open doorway, while Austin scrutinised her closely and, like every morning, expected his usual hug and play, and would often roll over onto his back to perform the act of a playful kitten for five or so minutes, 'all for Melanie's benefit of course never my own' concluded Austin, as Melanie said with a slight laugh whilst climbing out of bed. "Good morning Austin." she uttered, determined to start the day early for once, at Charlie's book shop, the very one she used to visit every Saturday, while her parents did the weekly shop, having had a passion for stories and make-believe, and would often spend many hours listening to Charlie's wild stories of bold adventures in far off lands. Having learned to read and write at a very early age gave her the opportunity to create her own stories and experience them at night in her imagination, before storing them away in an old trunk under her bed, the very same trunk that had once belonged to Charlie, who mistakenly told her he used to keep his hidden treasure inside it, before retiring as a pirate of the high seas, at which point Melanie seized the special find for herself.

Very few people knew of her special gift, one of many gifts she had inherited from her mother, one such ability was to capture an image, a feeling or perfume conjured from her own stories, disguise them as a dream and play them back. She spent countless hours sitting on a small upholstered chair near the main desk listening to music from an old gramophone player, whilst looking through a stack of books Charlie had selected for her earlier that morning. Austin having hid beneath her chair, fed off scraps of food from Melanie's plate at lunch time, taking note how all the regular customers seem enchanted by her, and were often disappointed when their little ray of sunlight was not there. Melanie smiled affectionately while making her breakfast, thinking of her time spent in Charlie's shop as a child, as Austin watched her from the comfort of his favourite armchair.

Before leaving her apartment, Melanie made a vain attempt at showing Austin who was boss, by laying down a few ground rules, but as usual with Austin, it never filtered through. "I want you to be good now Austin and I'll see you tonight, OK?" Instructed Mel, firmly, but Austin merely flicked his tail and went to see what was on the menu, then grouched miserably at it being tinned cat food again and not what he hoped it would be, a nice bit of salmon or tuna he usually got from visiting old Mrs Grimes on the first floor later in the day.

On hearing the front door close and lock Austin went to have a snooze in his favourite arm chair, until it was time to pay a visit to the first floor, while thoughts of sneaking a packet of pork scratchings out of the cupboard came to mind, they were after all, one of his favourite snacks, but knowing Melanie may have already counted them changed his mind. His attention turned to their landlady, Mrs Grimes, or 'Edna' being a small, batty old woman with an eccentric personality a madman would envy, recalling one of the many stunts she'd pulled.

One of her many bizarre traits was embarrassing the local vicar, Reverend Hislop, a shy handsome man with a receding hair line and a kind smile. Who would always cross his fingers behind his back, while whispering a silent prayer whenever he saw Edna walking up the path of the church, with her mysteriously aloof Grandson, Max, in tow. Reverend Hislop would often appear agitated and nervous, at the mere mention of Sunday service and Mrs Grimes in the same sentence. He wiped the beads of sweat from his brow and wrung his hands nervously, whilst making a desperate attempt to reach Edna, who was undoubtedly the Antichrist version of Miss Marple. Having been on the receiving end of her outlandish eccentricities, and still receiving counselling, one incident stuck out amongst the rest.

The day in question had started out as an ordinary run of the mill Wednesday, when having just watched the film, The Exorcist on DVD with Max, Edna had suddenly decided that Austin, one of her tenant's pet cats, was in fact, possessed by demons and should be exorcized without delay, and so enlisted the help of poor Reverend Hislop in the performing of an exorcism, after first making sure Max was out of the house.

Austin was on rout to Edna's kitchen at the usual snack time, when he was grabbed, tied to the kitchen table, and forced to listen to the unusual rantings of Reverend Hislop, quoting various Latin scriptures while making the sign of the cross above his head, then forced to watch the Reverend with a degree of humour, as he placed a silver embossed challis filled with water, by the side of his head, altering his mood entirely, for Austin disliked water of any description, causing a sudden frenzy of razor sharp claws and teeth to appear out of nowhere. The straps that had held him down were torn to shreds, while Edna made an immediate escape out of the kitchen, leaving the poor Reverend trapped in her kitchen with a frenzied Austin.

The terrifying unearthly sounds echoing out of the kitchen were unnerving, seconds felt more like hours, before the front door opened and out staggered Reverend Hislop or what was left of him. Looking dazed and in shock, with scratches marring his flesh and clothing, and his dog collar hanging from around his neck by a thread. Barely able to stand unaided, the Reverend had to lean against the door frame for support, and eventually the garden fence whilst making a desperate attempt to get home, when Melanie found him. He placed an unsteady hand on her shoulder saying, with eyes wide with terror. "Bless you child, may God go with you." he uttered, meaning every word, as passers-by watched him perform the sign of the cross in front of her, before heading into the sanctuary of his beloved church...

CHAPTER THREE

Meanwhile back to the present day, at precisely eight-thirty sharp, Melanie had entered the book shop by the side door, a shop owned by Charlie, who while in his mid-eighties give or take a few years, possessed the gentlest of personalities which everyone admired, but equally a fondness for tweed suits, complete with matching waistcoats, and garishly designed bow ties Melanie bought him at Christmas or birthday's.

It was clear to everyone who entered the musty old book shop, that Melanie and Charlie adored the place, tending to each and every book, manuscript and historical parchment with care, delicately peeling back the ancient pages, to peer upon the precious words within, archiving old volumes and parchments dating back to a bygone age. The old book shop was undoubtedly a forgotten slice of history, untouched by modern technology, a time capsule filled with old light fittings, an old shop counter, an assortment of musty old chairs placed against the wood panelling that surround the walls, where a host of shelves protect a vast array of treasures.

Having taken off her coat Melanie hurried into the main area of the shop to find Charlie precariously balanced up a ladder, the very same ladder that, in her opinion, had seen better days, "Charlie! Get down from there!" Mel asked nervously while holding her breath, as Charlie turned to give Mel a red-faced cheeky grin, while pushing up his thin-rimmed glasses, before gathering a stack of books off the top shelf. Melanie's heart was in her mouth as her friend descended the ladder and rushed over to relieve him of his burden as he said, "I know, we agreed that you alone are to use the ladders Mel, but you see, I wanted to get a set of books down before the shop opened." he explained and hurried over to check the order book, casually stroking his chin as he started to reel off a host of jobs for the day, "We have two special orders from overseas, an order that's going to be picked up this afternoon at about three o'clock, oh! And I'd like to get started on reorganising the 'Rare Books' sections at the back of the shop," then paused before adding, "Would you post yesterday's order for me dear?" he asked before taking a stack of books to another area of the shop, leaving Melanie the task of hurrying to the Post Office and her favourite sandwich shop on the corner called Tess's Tasty Tarts Shop, for their usual sandwich selection.

A little later while hurrying out of the sandwich shop with their prepared lunches, having first dealt with the post office, she collided with a solid wall of warm flesh and strong hands that automatically reached out to save her from falling. Leaving her to gather what remained of her wits as well as her voice, as someone asked from above her head, "Are you alright?" Melanie, having cautiously raised her head, found herself held captive by a pair of the darkest eyes she had ever seen. She tried desperately to utter a thank you, while gazing helplessly into the stranger's eyes which seemed almost gentle, warm and unrestrained enough to will her into their darkened depths. The attraction she felt was instantaneous and full on, and it took every ounce of the will power Melanie had, to resist being fully absorbed into their blackened abyss. Suddenly without any warning, the spell was broken by the sound of a car horn, forcing her attention away from the strangers mesmerizing gaze, giving her the opportunity of a hasty retreat, leaving the mysterious stranger staring after her, while she fled into the book shop.

Once inside Melanie tried to ease the ferocious beatings of her heart as she removed her coat and hung it on the peg and went in search of Charlie, hoping he was not up the ladder again, knowing her heart would not take a shock twice in one day, but with luck found Charlie talking on the phone saying as he put the receiver down. "We have another request for a first edition Hamlet." he said excitedly while entering it into the order book, as Melanie replied, "The Post Office wasn't very busy this morning." she admitted, hoping a dose of book sorting would help her to forget all that had happened with the stranger.

A little later at around 11.30am, one of Melanie's dearest friend's, Sarah, burst into the shop in a whirlwind of over indulged excitement and strong perfume shouting, "Surprise!" and cornered poor Charlie in an embracing hug asking in her usual sugar coated like way, if he would allow Mel time to have lunch with her today. It was a disgusting display of sucking up on Sarah's part, as she batted her eyelids and kissed him on his wrinkled cheek, making Charlie agree to anything she asked. She had barely enough time to grab her bag before she was hustled out of the shop by her excitable friend and dragged into a quaint, little period-styled café, fully decorated to fit the Victorian era and called The Top Hat Tea Rooms. They placed their order with the waitress, who was adorned with a costume fitting the Victorian theme, and Melanie went in search of a table, luckily she found one upstairs near the front window, near an old cast-iron fireplace with the usual mixture of ornamental paraphernalia befitting the period of the quaint little café.

Sarah tried to keep her excitement under control throughout dinner, concerning the surprise planned for her friend's birthday, hoping Mel would try and coax it out of her, but sadly, her plans were thwarted when Melanie, stubbornly changed the subject by commenting on her delicious egg salad instead, and laughed having witnessed Sarah's disappointment, who asked dejectedly, "Aren't you the least bit curious Mel?, I would be." admitted Sarah, as Mel set down her coffee cup saying, "Of course I'm interested, but this time, I thought I'd grit my teeth and wait it out," Sarah was about to argue the point when her mobile phone rang, and she started a dialogue with the caller as the waitress moved away from their table. "No of course I haven't! I'm not stupid Lynni." complained Sarah rolling her eyes, whilst performing the sock puppet motion with her free hand indicating that this could drag on a little. Sarah paused briefly before adding, "That was last time, I'll not say anything I promise ok? We'll see you later tonight at Mel's ok? Right bye, Lynni. Oh! Mel says goodbye as well." she added, before signing off, to catch Mel's eye. "You know, I'm beginning to get the distinct impression she doesn't trust me," she uttered as Mel burst into laughter.

Half an hour later after an enjoyable lunch hour, Melanie hugged her friend goodbye and headed back to the shop and Charlie, who asked "Did you have a nice lunch?" Having just completed a sale's transaction when Mel joined him behind the counter, she replied, "Yes we did. They're planning another surprise, only this time Sal's managed to keep it quiet for once." Charlie looked impressed with Sarah's new-found will power. "You'll have to give me an update my dear, I'm buzzing with curiosity. Oh, and before I forget, I've given your sandwich to my old friend, Butch." he confessed casually with a hint of affection in his tone for the golden retriever, who looked wise beyond his dog years, but always appeared happy when visiting the shop. He wore a tatty old red scarf around his neck that had obviously seen better days, a scarf no one dared remove for fear of having their hand bitten off. Despite Butch's friendly nature with Charlie, his gruff visage and tendency to skulk in alleyways unnerved those who didn't know him, but he was friendly enough, especially during the lunch hour, when Melanie would often find Charlie sharing his flask of coffee and sandwich with butch. Then he would smuggle his little friend into one of the back rooms before locking up for the night, especially during the winter months.

The clock behind the counter had just chimed three in the afternoon, Charlie was busy humming a little tune whilst sifting through a box of second hand books he had just been given by one of his many friends, while Melanie balanced half way up the ladder at the rear of the shop, listening to the music on her I Pod, busy cataloguing the old books section.

She found that so long as she balanced her weight evenly on the rungs of the ladder, it would hold her without any danger, 'this was going to take a lot longer than one day, but there's an improvement' concluded Mel, as one of her favourite songs started to play, causing her to forget the fact that she was on a dangerously unstable ladder.

Her hips began to sway to an upbeat and catchy tune when the shop door opened, Charlie greeted his customer with his usual jovial flair and enthusiasm, while Melanie continued working, oblivious to the fact that the new customer was now her sole audience, leaning casually against the edge of the book shelf with his arms folded enjoying the show. Melanie sighed deeply and thought 'Damn! The clock's against me today' as the time approached four o'clock, and she decided a careful yet rapid descent down the ladder was needed, her rich auburn curls bouncing gently within the loose confines of the ponytail, while humming a little tune. Suddenly her foot slipped on the third run of the ladder, causing her to make a frantic grab for the securely fixed shelf, but she missed, and banged her arm as she fell.

Instead of landing in an embarrassing heap on the floor, she found herself suspended in mid-air, held at the waist by a pair of strong hands that guided her safely to the floor, with a slow and graceful ease. Melanie turned to thank her saviour the moment her feet had touched the ground, but instead found herself once again, held captive by the same pair of alluringly provocative eyes that earlier that morning, had left her incapable of either thought or speech. She never once believed in coincidence, destiny or fate of any kind, but this, this was something else entirely, she could feel it, sense it, and almost taste it at the back of her mouth, as she continued to stare into what felt like, the darkest depths of uncharted space.

The air was electrically charged, as a subtle barely felt breeze enveloped both her and the mysteriously alluring stranger, as did the delicate scent of grassy meadows and exotic wild flowers, while the intensity of his stare unnerved her. He slowly and carefully reached out to take hold of her hand, to cradle it between his own, and examine the bruise on her arm then rub the area with his thumb in slow easy motions, while his unyielding gaze merged their souls together, for what felt like an eternity before she found the strength to break eye contact with this compelling stranger and say, as the pain in her arm disappeared. "You have an uncanny knack of saving me today, whoever you are?" Trying not to notice his beautifully shaped mouth that made her lips tingle in anticipation, she thought; 'Ok so he's irresistibly handsome, enticing, with a whole lot of gorgeousness thrown in but that doesn't mean I'm gullible enough to fall for it. Oh! Lord, I hope he can't read minds.' she added, with a guilty blush on her cheeks, as she moved a strand of hair away from her face, while his lips twitched slightly and continued to look down at her from a height that was slightly intimidating.

Vian adored her wacky sense of humour and was captivated by her compellingly beautiful violet coloured eyes, the same pair of eyes that had haunted his dreams and possessed his heart, from the very moment he knew of her existence. Melanie was far more wary, and stepped back enough to gain much needed space between her and the stranger who stood before her tall, slim with short cropped dark brown hair combed back, along with an unusually pale complexion that made him stand out in a crowd, causing her to wonder where the hell he'd come from, for he wasn't local. Vian smiled and asked in a soft silky smooth voice, "Are you alright Miss...?" Wise enough to keep up the pretence of a chance encounter, despite the fact he already knew who Melanie was and her family history.

Melanie did her best to reply in her best customer service voice, having found the strength of will to resist the pull between them, and replied, "I'm alright now, thank you." then paused briefly before adding rather breathlessly, "I'm…" but had to pause. 'Come on Mel, get a grip for goodness sake.' she told herself sternly, as he spoke saying, "Call me Vian," before adding "It's not every day I get to play the hero twice in one day to the same girl, I'd call it fate wouldn't you?" he uttered with a slight curvature to his lips, but Melanie ignored the question, as she repeated his name several times in her mind before replying, "Again thank you...Vian." hoping for a quick escape, whilst trying to ignore the feel of his thumb as it brushed against her arm, as he asked, "May I call you Mel?" Then he slowly lifted up her hand to meet the warmth of his lips, taking Melanie completely by surprise.

The moment his lips brushed against the warmth of her hand produced a sudden unexpected surge of electricity that shot all the way up her arm, and found its way straight to her heart. The surge was so powerful, so intense, that it caused her to stagger back violently, as her eyes sought his in the hope of finding a reasonable enough answer to what had just happened. It was then that Vian's whole demeanour changed, for he slowly and purposefully walked towards her, manoeuvring her into the most darkened corner of the shop, as the desire to have his lips on hers overpowered him completely, to the point of insanity.

Melanie felt a sudden instinctual awareness, a type of dread and fear for what was about to happen, burning its way into her heart, while he guided her away from prying eyes, and their bodies brushed against each other hesitantly with their hands firmly linked, the combination of which, caused not only a sudden barrage of feelings and emotions to surge through her entire body, but a fusing of souls as well. The floral scented breeze gained momentum while she quietly begged him to stop, moments before his lips touched hers. It was a passionately intense kiss, a kiss so powerful, her feet almost left the floor.

An entire lifetime's worth of images flew by in seconds, showing strange destinations and new faces, faces she neither recognised nor understood, while the underlining sound of his voice inside her head uttering the word **'remember'** brought down the invisible barriers, barriers she never knew existed. Only the sound of Charlie's good-humoured voice breaking through the hazy fog of her mind, announcing he was about to close for the day, brought her back down to earth with an almighty crash. Vian reluctantly let her go, but not before whispering seductively in her ear, I promise you, we will meet again, my sweet Mel." he said in a meaningful tone before walking away, leaving her feeling dazed in a state of shock, slowly realising the horrifying truth that there had been a joining of spirits, a pulling together of souls, between her and the stranger, the like of which, she could still feel the after effects of even now, and would probably go on feeling for the rest of her life, or was she simply going crazy.

She had by some miracle made her way back to the main desk, feeling a little apprehensive for their next encounter. "Mel! My dear, are you alright?" asked Charlie, a little preoccupied while locking up the shop, after making sure his little friend 'Butch' was securely housed in the back room with the door open. "I'll give you a lift home tonight." he offered generously, knowing only too well that his car was the epitome of an old rust bucket, that by some miracle manages to pass its MOT with flying colours, named Betsy in memory of a pet horse he'd had as a boy. "Hello old girl." he said gently patting the dash board, as the engine sputtered into life as Mel got into the passenger's seat.

Melanie's apartment was the converted attic rooms from an 18th century house, it was the only one with an attached balcony, perfect for Austin to sunbathe on. The moment she entered her room Melanie was set upon by a mass of fur, claws and a whole lot of affection, "have you missed me?" She asked hurrying into the kitchen to prepare supper.

CHAPTER FOUR

After what felt like the longest week on record, Friday night had at last arrived, Melanie had been home for about half an hour when the doorbell rang and standing there in high heels and a cloud of strong perfume, were her two dearest friends waiting to be let in. The moment Austin realised who it was, he did an immediate about turn and headed off towards the bedroom, deciding to keep out of the way of what he considered were two of the most annoying humans he had ever come across. Sarah being the worst, standing over 6ft in height and a full time model, with blonde hair and a pair of smoky grey eyes that had helped her choose the right career move, which was surprising considering she had received a degree in theology (religious studies). Lynnette however was 5ft 6inch tall with a mass of thick dark brown hair, and eyes of the deepest blue, born in Paris, France, she now worked as a French interpreter/ translator for a private company in the city.

After a tornado of hugs and kisses, they hurried into the living room and practically fell onto the sofa in a flurry of high excitement. Sarah leaned down to rub her tired feet saying, ""We're giving you an early birthday gift tonight Mel, so go and get ready", "Right Lynnette?" she asked her co-conspirator, who said, "We are celebrating your birthday, so wear your hair down, OK? It shouldn't be tied up all the time, it's boring," demanded Lynnette Melanie having learned from past experience, went to get ready. Within minutes her bedroom looked like a bomb had hit it, with poor Austin sat in the middle of it, looking a little disgruntled and altogether put out, as the clothes continued to fly in every direction, finally settling on a multi coloured tunic styled top with matching sash belt, bought a few days earlier. 'It would look great with my white sequinned covered jeans and my black low heeled boots' she thought, and received a round of applause from her friends when she entered the living room, "You look beautiful, I think we're going to end up fighting the men off you girl." said Sarah as she headed for the door with her friends following. Austin observed them from his favourite armchair, their excitable chatter echoed on the stairwell as they made their way out of the building.

20 minutes later according to Sarah's watch, having chosen a high classed restaurant for their special occasion meal, looked on with a cheeky glint in her eye saying, "You'll love what we've got you Mel."

Melanie rolled her eyes at her friend's childlike glee, as Lynnette made a grab for her cutlery once the food had arrived and said "Let's eat shall we, I'm starving" and dived into her meal.

It wasn't long before Sarah noticed they were being watched and leaned forward saying "Oh would you look over there, they are without doubt the most handsome, good looking hunks of flesh I have ever seen in my life, one of them is smiling at me, he's giving me a cute little wave," she announced. "I think I may pass out or something" she admitted, as all three turned to glance across the room. Lynnette uttered "the fool waving at you with the silly smile on his face looks weird to me, so you should fit right in there Sal" and laughed at her own joke. Melanie was too overwhelmed to hear any joke, having realised she was staring into the eyes of the very same man that had invaded all her senses earlier that very morning.

Vian nodded his head in a show of acknowledgement, causing her to turn away from his overpowering gaze, only to find her two friends looking at her with genuine concern etched on their faces. Lynnette having reached across the table to take hold of Melanie's hand, asked "What is it? What's wrong?" she wondered, glancing from Mel to the strangers. Melanie picked up her wine glass, took a hearty swig in the hope it would help calm her nerves before she dared tell her story, or at least part it. They listened intently and waited for her to finish before they dared make any comment. "You know, it could just be a coincidence Mel, after all, there aren't that many decent restaurants open around here, plus, you're a good looking woman Mel, so naturally a man is going find you attractive" commented Sarah wisely with a reassuring smile.

Lynnette merely shrugged her shoulders saying "for all we know, it could be a boring business dinner, so do try and relax! This is supposed to be a celebration after all" giving her hand a reassuring squeeze. Melanie managed to produce a slight smile, which took a herculean effort on her part, knowing deep down within the pit of her stomach that this was, once again, more than just mere coincidence. You're probably right as usual" she agreed, as Sarah glanced unconvincingly at her friend saying, "We've always been there for you Mel. Although, now that I think about it, we didn't know each other until we met at University, so my using the word always isn't an accurate description" Sarah's hypothesizing was suddenly interrupted by Lynnette who uttered "can you please get to the point Sal, we're falling asleep" and helped herself to the bottle of wine on the table. Sarah having caught Lynnette's eye replied "what!? Oh right sorry, I get carried away sometimes, it could be as Lynni said, a coincidence. Right? So for goodness sake cheer up, or we'll all start crying, our make up will run, and this restaurant will empty quicker than a boring night at the Opera" she replied, causing Melanie to burst into a flurry of laughter at the mental picture and deciding she would not think of the man sitting on the opposite side of the restaurant.

Once the meal was over and the bill paid, they headed back to Mel's place for a night cap so she could open her presents from her friends, which consisted of a gold chain and earrings, a bottle of Melanie's favourite perfume and the latest Stereophonics and Robbie Williams' albums. Meanwhile having been forced into abject misery due to their untimely return, Austin slept in the bedroom instead of his favourite armchair by the fire that was currently being occupied by three coats, two hand bags and a pair of high heeled shoes, plus a strong dose of perfume. Austin paused to glance at his beloved chair as he experienced another bout of sneezing due to his allergies, caused by the newly sprayed perfume. Austin grumbled, as he headed into the bedroom to bury his head under a pillow, hoping it might block out the annoying din they were making.

Early the following morning Melanie Lay with her head resting on her arm, staring up at the ceiling, recollecting the unusual dream she'd had, while Austin observed the shadows darting across the ceiling from the rays of sunlight reflected off the glass, thinking of his time on the farm with Melanie, watching her grow up, alongside a mixed bag of oddities and farm animals, that had somehow found their way on to the farm. There was a horse called Pilot, an old hen called Gertrude who ruled the farm with an iron beak, a foul mouthed parrot called 'Double Dutch' who early one Spring morning appeared out of nowhere, and a fascist dictator in the guise of an old billy goat with no name, and finally who would ever forget the illusive boa constrictor named 'Stretch' who had the uncanny knack of escaping his specially built home in search of a snack, namely Austin, the thought of which even now, sent shivers down his spine. Once Melanie was trying to recover one of her school socks Austin had taken a sudden shine to, blissfully unaware of the fact that 'Stretch' had once again escaped his cage. Austin had plenty of time to hide his prize (a single pink sock), but as he rounded the corner at high speed with the sock firmly between his teeth, he suddenly without warning did an about turn, and came back again, flew past Melanie, dived over the settee, through the living room door and into the dining room, deciding that the safest place for him right then, was on the top of the enormous shelf unit, with the sock still firmly between his teeth, and he stayed there until 'Stretch' had been recaptured. Luckily, the snake was taken to the local zoo not long after that.

Meanwhile back to the present day Melanie was up and dressed for work in record time for once and having rushed through her breakfast and two cups of coffee, quickly lost her temper with Austin, who had decided a game of chase was a good way to start the day for any human. "Austin!! Give me those keys right now, before I lose my temper! I mean it Austin! I have to get to work!" Melanie shouted, trying to sound angry and not laugh at Austin's ill-timed antics. While Austin quoted one of his often used phrases; 'A watcher has to do what a watcher has to do' as the sound of knocks, bangs, thuds could be heard from within the small living room, as the battle raged on. It had taken well over ten minutes to pin Austin down, and a further ten minutes to tidy her hair, brush off all the cat hairs from her clothes and put on her coat before Melanie was ready to leave. She looked back at Austin, who was lying contentedly in his favourite arm chair, looking as if all was right with the world, 'No one would've guessed, that only a short time ago, an all-out war had broken out in here' concluded Mel, with a rueful look on her face, as she shut and locked the door.

Melanie hurried around the corner that would take her to her beloved book shop, but had to stop suddenly, due to the horrific scene that greeted her, for in place of her dear book shop, a raging inferno of flames and thick black smoke billowing out of control, filled the sky and surrounding area. Crowds of people watched in horror from behind makeshift barriers, while the fire fighters tried to control the fire, Melanie forced her way through the crowds screaming Charlie's name, while she fought off all those who tried to stop her. Eventually two policemen managed to subdue Melanie long enough for one of them to end up with a split lip, where Melanie's fist had accidentally hit him, before escorting her to their unmarked car. Once seated, the lead investigating officer introduced himself and his partner as Chief inspector Metcalfe and Detective Sergeant Milo, who held a clean tissue over his cut lip while he went in search of a cup of tea, leaving Melanie in the care of inspector Metcalfe, who offered the unfortunate young woman his freshly washed handkerchief out of his pocket, before he dared ask any questions. Being a seasoned officer of the highest calibre Metcalf was kind and gentle wearing the usual worn out suits that had obviously seen better days, with a matching pair of scuffed shoes and an untidy haircut. But D S Milo was tall, thin and impeccably dressed, with short cropped ginger hair, clean shaven, and eager to learn, which was why he chose Metcalf as his partner 2 years ago, and had never once regretted it.

Melanie watched the inspector through painful eyes asking "Charlie wasn't in there was he? Please! Tell me he wasn't, he can't have been in there?" she pleaded near hysterically. While Metcalf replied in a calm tone "We're not sure if Mr Riley was inside the building when the fire started, Miss Philips" and began taking notes, before asking, "Do you know if Mr Riley had any family at all? Any relatives we'd be able to get in touch with?" His instincts told him that she already knew her friend had been inside the shop when the fire started, as she answered in a whispered voice saying "I don't think so, Charlie never mentioned having any family" as she looked down at her hands, picturing one of the gentlest, kindest people she had ever known, and causing her to suddenly break down and cry, as Metcalf, getting out of the car, said "W.P.C Crawford will take you home and stay with you should you need her. Alright?" before closing the car door, as the car moved away.

Eventually the fire and subsequent death of Mr C. Riley were announced to be that of an accidental death due to an electrical fault, because of a substandard pre-war electrics and fuse box. Much later Melanie and her two friends were on their way to see a private solicitor at 'Templeton, Templeton and Grainger' based on the high street. It was a miserably dull, cloudy Monday morning that seemed to fit the mood of everyone. They were greeted by a Mr. L. Templeton the head of the company and shown into his private office. He was in his mid sixties a little taller than Melanie; with dark brown hair, warm brown eyes wearing a fresh white rose bud in his lapel, smelling of expensive aftershave, who offered Melanie a sympathetic smile saying "may I express my deepest sympathies and hope that the pain you feel is of short duration" guiding her to a soft upholstered chair near his desk, while her two friends sat on the matching sofa a short distance away.

Having sat in his slightly worn out leather chair, he opened the file in front of him saying, "Mr Riley must've thought a great deal of you Miss Philips, for he has left the entirety of his estate" and paused before adding "his estate consisting of the sum of £300,000 pounds in cash, and a piece of property with several 100 acres of land attached to you. You are now a very rich young woman Miss Philips. Congratulations." explained Mr Templeton, noticing the last remaining bit of colour leave Melanie's face. All she could do was look up at him and whisper "I had no idea, all the years I'd known him, and he never said..." concluded Melanie in a state of shock. Sarah and Lynnette glanced at each other in surprise, both equally as shocked as their friend, before hurrying to the drinks cabinet, for a glass of the solicitor's very best sherry. Melanie gulped the rest of her sherry before leaving, as Sarah managed to utter "What you need now is a holiday Mel, Mr Riley would approve I know he would" she said, as Lynnette said "Yes! Why not go and have a look at this house he left you". Melanie looked at her friends and replied "Alright, but the two of you have to come as well. OK?"

CHAPTER FIVE

Ten days and a whole lot of excitement later, on a warm muggy Saturday afternoon, Lynnette exited the taxi and staggered painfully up the overgrown garden path of Melanie's new house, grumbling "My feet are killing me! Please hurry up and unlock the door, so I can take off these painful shoes", while Sarah paid the taxi driver, before hauling the remaining luggage up the path, then setting it down by the front door to take a detailed look at Mel's new house, saying "Ooh nice place Mel, it definitely has character don't you think?" She said gazing up at the most beautifully designed house she had ever seen, when it suddenly dawned on her that they were now in the middle of nowhere, and uttered "We're going to hire a car while we're here, right? It'll be easier that way" she advised, as Melanie gazed up at the house with the peculiar feeling of coming home, while Austin peaked through the cat carrier, wondering when in the next century, she was going to release him from this dreadful contraption, while she cautiously unlocked the front door and went inside.

When at last he was allowed his freedom, Austin chose to ignore everyone around him, and went to explore the area, ready to take on anything that got in his way, although these days, he was a little more careful thanks to his experience with 'Stretch' the snake. Suddenly the sound of Sarah and Lynnette crash landing in the middle of the hallway loaded down with bags, baggage and spare body parts, having tripped over

Austin, was heard, followed by the sound of groaning from within the tangled mass of fake leather luggage and designer shoes, as Sarah uttered rather painfully "I think I've permanently broken something", "I don't know whether it's my back, or one of the things I've landed on, but right now, I'm hoping its Austin the rat" she uttered as a spasm of pain shot all the way up her back.

Melanie having observed the make shift war zone Austin had created, found it all rather amusing, and suddenly erupted into a spontaneous bout of laughter so much so, she had to hold onto the banister rail for support. Sarah having heard this glared up at her friend from within the tangled heap of arms and legs on the floor, as a sudden movement from under one of the many items beneath her caught her attention. This turned out to be Lynnette's head, popping out from under an overnight bag and coat, resembling a train wreck.

There was a moments silence before the hallway erupted into laughter while managing to untangle themselves, before taking in the unique splendour and architecture incorporated within the detailed carvings of the staircase, cornices and door frames. "My god!! Just look at that light fitting! Beautiful doesn't do it justice, does it?" commented Sarah, gazing up at what could only be described as breathtaking, "I've never seen anything like it, anywhere" answered Melanie before adding "Have you Lynni?" she asked inquisitively. Lynnette couldn't bring herself to say anything other than shake her head, while she examined the antique mouldings resembling tree branches, with unusual flower shaped lights made of etched glass and small gemstones encrusted on each one, while crystallised thorns made of jet were along every stem, and leaves made of green coloured glass, as were the light switches 'I hope it's insured?' hoped Melanie seriously.

When Sarah brushed lightly against the wall by the stair case it caused an aroma of wild flowers to surround her, resembling the spirit of a newly awakened ancestral ghost. "Oh wow! Hay Mel!! Come and check this out, the walls are scented!" Sarah said excitedly, as both Melanie and Lynnette hurried to investigate, "You're right!! The walls are coated in perfume, but why?" wondered Mel, when Lynnette being a self-professed expert on perfumes, stepped back with one of her hands resting on her hip saying "I cannot make it out, the perfume changes with each contact".

Melanie looked at her friend and asked the obvious question "How can a scent change?" feeling slightly perplexed, but Lynnette was once again at a loss. "I don't know, this is all very strange, maybe it's haunted?" concluded Lynnette calmly, as Sarah burst into a flurry of excitement at the thought of it being haunted saying. "Wow that's so cool! Let's go check out the rest of the house! We might find one in the bedrooms, or better yet the attic, if there is an attic?" She grabbed Mel by the hand to pull her through the door leading to yet another part of the house, leaving Lynnette the task of dis-entangling their entire luggage.

They spent the better part of an hour looking around the house, but one room stood out amongst the rest, having found the walls covered from floor to ceiling in what appeared to be painted panelling that resemble stretched canvas. Each panel had its own unique story to tell, showing images of a make believe alien world, filled to the brim with unusual plant life and strange looking creatures, scurrying through the undergrowth, obviously created from someone's wild imagination. Lynnette and Sarah both walked around the room to take a closer look, not quite believing what their eyes were seeing, but all Melanie could do was look into the eyes of an alien couple, stood in a loving and tender embrace.

Melanie stood transfixed by what she saw, unable to move, speak or even hear, and wondered, 'How could this be?' As another question rose to the surface 'Why in all of creation would I dream such images as these?' Suddenly her thoughts were interrupted by the waving of a hand in front of her face, it was Sarah, who stood in front of her. "Earth to Mel come in Mel, are you in there? Wake up. Let's go and see the rest of the house" she suggested, before heading off towards the dining room in a flurry of perfume and blonde hair, with

Lynette following, leaving Melanie gazing transfixed at the image of a couple that had somehow captivated her entire attention.

Later that same afternoon everyone was still reeling over what had been discovered in the library. Melanie while preparing Austin's salmon dinner said "it's nice knowing we don't have to go out to a well for the water isn't it? And the modern bathroom suit with a matching shower is a bonus! She said, as Austin hopped from one paw to the other in eager anticipation of the delicious salmon, "I agree" replied Lynnette, with a shudder at the thought of having to fetch water and boil it on a stove, while Melanie put Austin's dish down in front of him. "What I can't understand, is why Charlie never told me about this place? Why all the secrecy, I'm beginning to realise, I never actually knew him at all" Said Melanie frustratingly.

Lynnette glanced at her troubled friend. "We'll probably never know for sure Mel, so try not to worry too much about it ok? Charlie wouldn't want you to, would he?" she announced, as Melanie let out a deep sigh. "Your probably right as usual only, this seems to be a puzzle only Sherlock Holmes would take on, and solve, but then again may be not" she concluded, before taking another sip of her coffee. Lynnette noticed Austin's look of irritation while leaving the kitchen to go upstairs, and asked with raised eye brows "Is Austin ok?" Melanie gave an immediate reply saying "He'll be alright in a day or two... He's probably missing Edna our landlady" as the sound of Austin's bell hanging around his neck echoed down the stair well. Sarah held back a giggle. "Poor Austin, I almost feel sorry for him" she announced with a smile.

Later that evening Melanie read aloud the documents the solicitor had sent her, "The house was built around the early 1800s, and attached to the property are several acres of land and woodland, leading to shore line and private beach," she stated, the announcement of which, caught Sarah's full attention, who said, "There's a beach! Let's see?" she asked, looking over Melanie's shoulder to get a better look. "Wow! We'll have to go and explore it Mel." announced Sarah, getting more and more excited. Later that night while the rest of the world slept Mel began to dream...

CHAPTER SIX

<u>*Memories*</u>

This was the first of many dreams for Melanie, showing two moons above a strange new alien world, where the last rays of a burnished golden sunlight reflected off its surface, at the end of yet another day, for this mysterious planet. The warm evening air filtering through the cluster of trees, whose trunks were the colour of pure white, covered in an explosion of vibrant blue coloured leaves. Melanie found herself sat by a small stream of blue-green tinted water, where her unusually pale hand caressed a small cluster of tiny pink flowers, which seem to illuminate the entire meadow, with each touch.

The entire area was awash with activity, people of varying ages were enjoying the warm evening. Nearby a little girl barely able to walk staggered away from her mother, her eagerness to investigate the world around her was obvious, her tiny pale feet peeked out from under her tunic dress as she playfully stomped her feet, before sitting down to use her tiny hands to pat the clusters of flowers. Everyone seemed similar in both appearance and skin colour, consisting of a pale white hue with a light grey tint in areas of the skin, their eyes and hair colour were ebony black with a blue tint. Their need for vocal communication was not necessary, for they were able to communicate through the touching of hands. Children of various ages play nearby, with what appear to be a sphere like objects, the idea being, to keep it air born without the need of physical contact, use only telekinesis. Melanie's attention was caught by two children in particular, twins, a boy and girl of about six years old, the pull of recognition was strong as she watched them play.

At the opposite end of their Galaxy, a multitude of star constellations form a cluster, known as a Galactic belt, indicating the end of their own solar system and the beginning of another. Melanie cast her eyes all around her, 'I don't know where I am but it is an amazing place' she concluded, as she once again watched the little girl reach out her hands to capture the multi-coloured specks of star dust streaking across the night's sky. The child's interest was caught, by the sight of an illuminating glow worm slithering its fat hairy multi-coloured body across the ground, hoping to avoid the pair of tiny inquisitive hands, causing Melanie to laugh before she committed every single minute of her visit to memory.

CHAPTER SEVEN

Early the following morning at a reasonable time, Melanie awoke to the alluring aromas of a breakfast being prepared, and spent a good few minutes breathing in the delicious odours, before throwing back the covers, diving out of bed to find a single rose on the bedside table. 'Where the hell did that come from?' she wondered, before going to take a closer look. She picked up the rose, held it to her nose to breathe in the sweet scent, before going to find a container for it, prior to throwing herself in the shower, and within minutes, Melanie was on her way down to breakfast with Austin in hot pursuit, laughing joyously as she said, "I'm going to beat you this time Austin, you little rascal." when in actual fact, there was never any hope of beating Austin in a game of chase, but it was fun trying.

She flew into the kitchen like a mini tornado with a smile saying, "What's for breakfast? I'm starving." she declared exuberantly, surprising both her friends, who turned to say good morning. Mel hurried over to the table picked up her cutlery in eager anticipation of what was to come, for Lynnette known by all as the culinary expert, was doing the cooking and said, "You're in a good mood this morning." whilst serving the carefully prepared delicacy, before joining them at the table. "Did you sleep well?" she asked noticing how Melanie's face produced a radiantly happy smile as she replied, "Yes I did," "I had the most beautiful dream," she announced, busy tucking into her food with gusto, "I have a really good feeling about this place you know," claimed Mel enthusiastically, as Sarah and Lynnette both glanced at each other, before looking back at Mel saying, "we're glad you feel that way Mel, we knew it would do you some good coming here." before tucking into their breakfasts.

Knowing it was going to be a nice day, they opted for tidying the garden and hurried outside wearing shorts, t-shirts and hiking boots before going in search of the storage shed at the back of the house. Sarah's eyes lit up having spotted her favourite toy, "Ooh an electric lawn mower, move aside girls, I've always wanted to have a go on one of these." claimed Sarah excitedly, giving it an all-important once over before starting the motor and putting her foot down. Melanie and Lynnette dived out of the way when Sarah shot down the garden laughing hysterically. Melanie looked on in horror shouting, "Sarah! Be careful!!" while her friend manoeuvred the lawn mower like a woman possessed, and for the next hour or so, all you could hear was Sarah's infectious laughter echoing around the garden, and the sound of an angry cat, hissing and screeching at the machine that seemed hell bent on killing him.

Melanie and Lynnette having both decided to trim the over grown shrubbery at the front of the house while listening to music on a portable radio, breaking into the occasional song when a familiar tune started to play. Eventually after a gruelling session in the garden, the back door flew open and in staggered three exhausted young women, and if Austin's reactions were anything to go by, they were all in dire need of a shower. Twenty minutes later after a bracing hot shower, the need to raid the kitchen was overwhelming as Lynnette said, "I think it's your turn to cook Sarah.", "I did breakfast," she uttered, looking relieved, due to her aching arms and shoulders. Sarah or what was left of her, was sprawled across most of the table with her head on her arms half asleep mumbling, "Oh no!! Can't I cook tomorrow night, please? I'm bruised all over because of that bloody lawn mower, and it's all Austin's fault, the stupid flee infested rat, for having a one on one fight with the bloody thing, while I was still on it!" she uttered gloomily.

Austin lifted his head out of the dish of tuna, to stare at Sarah, with an almost smug look on his face, before carrying on eating, "It's your own fault Sal for chasing Austin in the first place. You shouldn't tease him like you do, you know it upsets him." explained Mel. Sarah managed to lift her head up long enough to make a statement saying, "Oh, but it's alright for that flee ridden rat on legs to tease me is it?" "Oh that's just lovely, now I know who my true friends are." she expressed disappointedly before laying her head back on her arms deciding to ignore everyone, until Melanie took pity on her and offered to cook. Immediately after supper they all opted for an early night, hoping that by morning the 'Deep Heat' cream would cure all muscle pain.

The following morning Melanie awoke to the sound of bird song and gave a huge stretch before noticing a rose resting alongside the first that had appeared suddenly during the night. Her alarm bells rang out. 'Either Austin's learned a new trick, or we're haunted by a ghost with a sense of humour' she thought, giving Austin a suspicious look while on her way to the bathroom. Austin snorted and slowly shook his head thinking, 'a ghost indeed'. Later that same morning, with the sun high on the horizon Lynnette let out a sigh of frustration saying, "Whose idea was it to go on this walk?" she asked as she sat on a large boulder rubbing her sore feet for the umpteenth time, "Don't be like that Lynni," announced Sarah, as she hopped from one boulder to another waving her arms in the air like a demented monkey, blissfully unaware of the glowering look her friend gave her before replying, "We should have used a car instead of my poor feet, it's easier." she grumbled. Melanie smiled while listening to the banter between her two friends, as Sarah then replied, "Investing in a good pair of walking shoes is a must Lynni." Melanie edged her way around the large boulder saying, "Come on you two, let's explore a little further." and walked off ahead of them. Sarah leapt off the last boulder. "Be right with you Mel!" She yelled adding, "Hurry up Lynni a spaced out slug's faster than you." she said jokingly, disappearing through the undergrowth, leaving Lynnette hobbling after them.

Eventually they found an idyllic stream, "Let's rest here shall we?" suggested Melanie sitting near the water's edge to trail her fingers through the cool water, when Lynnette as if by magic produced, a bottle of wine and three plastic beakers out of her rucksack, while Sarah made daisy chains while humming a little tune, reminiscing about their University days. Melanie sighed contentedly saying, "Austin would love it here you know." she said looking up at the sunlight as it filtered through the trees. Lynnette glanced at Mel suggesting, "why not bring him the next time?" Then paused briefly before adding, "On second thoughts perhaps not, he'll hate being in the cat carrier again." "Dare we chance it?" she enquired, Melanie let out a big sigh of disappointment, "You're right. Although he might actually follow us of his own accord, or I could carry him." suggested Mel, as Sarah added her own sudden idea saying, "This stream might cut through your property Mel? Why don't we follow it and find out?" surprising her friends, who replied, "Great idea Sal!"

A little while later while crashing her way through the thick vegetation with the help of a long stick, Sarah took a glance over her shoulder at her two friends saying, "You know, I feel like Chris Bonnington the great explorer, on a journey into the unknown...exciting isn't it!" Only to come across a mystery of her own, concerning some old stone pillars, placed at regular intervals around Melanie's house, standing about 8ft in height, old and weather-beaten, displaying symbolic markings carved deep into each stone structure. From the moment she saw these unusual stone structures, Lynnette was struck with an unnerving idea "I don't like it, this feels similar to the Wicker man films? Ya know, weird ceremonies and such, this whole area feels wrong to me Mel" she said looking around nervously. Sarah agreed saying after a brief pause for thought, "She's right Mel, I've heard lots of stories about these small out of the way places you know. These villages steeped in old traditions and folk law, for all we know we could end up being sacrificed to an ancient medieval god or something." letting her imagination get the better of her as usual.

Melanie's laughter echoed through the forest as she replied, "I wish you two would not get so carried away with such silly notions. Next you'll be telling me you've seen a bloody witch or something. You were just as bad in University." suggested Melanie, as Lynnette then added, "Yes well, if I see anyone looking at me with an odd look in their eye, then I'm out of here cherie," she announced with a stiff-shouldered resolve, as they came to a sharp bend in the stream, that would take them in the opposite direction, but fortunately, an old wooden bridge gave them easy access to the far side of the brook, that would eventually take them home. "Hey! Mel!" shouted Sarah, "All we need is a troll under the bridge, and we're all set to act out a fairy tale or two!" She said laughing. Lynnette having heard this idea turned to say, "I think you should be the troll cherie! You would fit right in" and laughed, as Sarah looked over her shoulder saying, "Very funny Lynni, I'm laughing on the inside." as they all headed for home.

Later that same evening, a modern feature length episode of Sherlock was being shown on TV. The mood was made suddenly more intense by the arrival of a mysterious figure lurking in the darkened shadows of an eerie corridor who began to follow the girl, who used her hands along the walls to map her root. They could hear her heavy breathing as she neared the end of the dimly lit passageway hoping to find an escape. Melanie and her friends gave a sharp intake of breath and unconsciously leaned forward in their seats, as Sherlock Holmes and Dr Watson entered the scene. All three friends were ignorant of the fact, that their living room door had opened and in sneaked Austin. Sarah sat with a piece of fruit inches away from her mouth, fully immersed in the TV program, when suddenly without any warning, as a gloved hand grabbed the girl from behind, Austin leapt on them from behind the sofa screeching like a demented banshee.

Chaos reigned for the next few minutes, as cries of fear and shock echoed throughout the whole house, which very soon turned into pure unadulterated fury, as a variety of inanimate objects were flung in Austin's direction, in the hope that at least one of them would hit him as he made a dash for the door, skilfully avoiding all incoming missiles, but paused briefly at the top of the stairs, while his eyes held a glimmer of pure pleasure. 'Getting one up on the girls I will miss when we have to go back' he admitted, releasing a deep heavy sigh of disappointment. Meanwhile back in the 'war zone' that had once been the front room, tempers were nowhere near as calm, "I'm going to ring your cat's neck Mel! I'm warning you!!" promised Sarah, all the while wishing it was Austin she was hitting and not a stuffed cushion. "Calm down Sal, I thought it was funny, and you've got to admit he had perfect timing, you would almost swear he planned it." Lynnette admitted, wiping the tears from her eyes, only to end up laughing all the more, and Melanie joined in. Sarah glared at the pair of them in exasperation, as her lips began to twitch before she herself laughed.

A little later when Melanie entered her bedroom, she found Austin laid on his back, with his legs in the air, mouth open and tongue sticking out to one side, sound asleep, until he sensed Melanie had entered the room and turned to rest his head on his two front paws to watch her lose the battle and fall asleep. Like a scene from a classic horror film, a shadowy figure entered her room, with yet another single red rose clutched in his pale hand he placed it alongside the others, before daring to touch her with the back of his hand, brushing it lightly against the silken cheek, as a lingering kiss upon her lips was a temptation he could no longer resist, while whispering the words, "Sleep and remember, my beloved." he uttered softly before leaving. Austin settled down to sleep, listening to the comforting sound of Melanie's soft breathing, as the start of yet another dream began:

CHAPTER EIGHT

Memories

In Melanie's next dream, an odd assortment of furniture was scattered haphazardly around a room she now stood in. She unconsciously slid her hand over a spherical looking object on a nearby table, activating a soft style of music, as someone entered the room. "Ah, your back, it's about time." announced the voice. Melanie gave a start having turned and found herself staring into the eyes of a large humanoid looking bat-like creature, it was the last thing she expected to find in her dream, or could this possibly be a nightmare, she wondered?

His overall appearance made her stagger back slightly as she turned to face him, noting how his body was partly covered in dark blue fur and skin tones, with a matching pair of large wings folded down the centre of his back similar to a bat. He had all the characteristics and physical stature of a human, as well as the facial similarities, and was obviously upset about something, as he headed off into another room mumbling under his breath. Do hurry, the others have already finished." he claimed impatiently. She followed him into another room to find a whole section of the room completely open, causing her to gasp in both awe and amazement at the breathtaking view beyond the boundaries of the house, for there before her, stood a huge waterfall, they call 'Yoltana', with its green tinted waters flowing down the naturally formed rock face that would, on occasion, produce a sudden flash of pink as it travelled down the pure white crystallised rock they call Geniea.

Melanie stared at the view from the balcony, feeling drawn to the waterfall, thinking 'Why does it feel so familiar here, wherever here is?', as a flock of tiny birds with multi-coloured wings flitted from flower to flower, growing beneath the spray of water. A creature resembling a mongoose scurried through the undergrowth, its white fur-covered body, fluffy black-tipped tail and inquisitively bright red eyes were unusual, like everything around here, for she was standing in the first of many dormitory dwellings, which when combined, became a crescent moon styled domicile of stepping stones, cushioned delicately around the waterfall, as various families went about their everyday lives unaware that they had a visitor amongst them. For although Melanie, was living a mystery like no other, she wanted to know why? Why her?

CHAPTER NINE

The following morning Melanie woke up to find her room bathed in early morning sunlight, her gaze settled on Austin who lay watching her intently, "Morning Austin!" She said as Austin rolled off the end of the bed, and headed towards the door, while Mel gathered a fresh set of clothes, before heading into the shower. Having decided they were to go sightseeing Melanie chose the safest option, a pair of jeans, an aqua coloured blouse with flowers, and sequins across the front, plus a comfortable pair of walking shoes, with her hair down, secured by a colourful head band to match her top.

Having arrived at the Lake later than scheduled Lynnette noticed a poster advertising a Music extravaganza pinned in the corner of a shop window, starting tomorrow night. Sarah glanced at Melanie, "I hope it's not an old wooden shack with one light bulb in it, and a transistor radio, cos that would be beyond disappointing." moaned Sarah, as Lynnette suggested. "Let's get tickets, it'll be fun?" Melanie and Sarah both agree to the idea, indicating that an immediate need to visit all the fashion shops on the high street was imminent before heading home, Austin paused in mid stride at the far end of the hall and watched them arrive loaded down with bags.

Later that night the moon cast a mysterious glow over the entire valley, producing a series of strange shadows across the walls of Melanie's bedroom, giving it an almost eerie feel, and all the while Melanie slept. Her rich dark auburn coloured hair spread across her pillow, resembling a spilt bottle of burgundy wine, while Austin sat at the bottom of the bed waiting for the visitor's arrival, who, having approached the bed, looked down at his beloved for what felt like an eternity. He reached out his hand to gently pick up a strand of her hair, then weave it through his fingers thinking 'The colour is so unique, so rare, just like her' as the intense battle for her to know the truth, was almost unbearable, but he had to allow the inherited dreams take their toll. He clenched his hand hoping it would control his emotions, when an impatient voice inside his head said, "Hurry up Vian!!", "How much longer are you going to be?" his friend asked, as Vian let out a long sigh of frustration saying, "Be patient, We should have left you at home." but the voice replied, "You need me, you know you do." replied Raan.

CHAPTER TEN

The following evening having arrived at the dance, handed in their tickets to a man called big Eddy they hurried into the main dance hall, where Lynnette turned to her friends saying with a theatrical flair. "Tonight girls, we have fun! Ok?" noting Sarah's eagerness to dance, by the sway of her hips as she said, "Enough talk let's dance!" and hurried onto the dance floor. Melanie hesitated at first before being frogmarched onto the dance floor by Lynnette. The only drawback was the figure hugging black dress Sarah had persuaded her to wear, but thankfully you could not see your hand in front of your face, so her embarrassment was lessened somewhat.

Most of the music tracks were a mixed bag of the old and new, when Melanie shouted, "I need to go to the ladies, I won't be long ok?" and hurried off the dance floor, down the corridor and into the solid form of the last person she ever expected to see here, or anywhere else. Melanie's heart raced out of control as she stared into Vian's eyes who offered her a slight smile while he steadied her saying, "We are destined, to keep bumping into each other, wouldn't you agree?" he asked curiously, but Melanie was quick to reply, "No I don't!" she said stepping back a few paces before adding, "this is more than a coincidence, why are you here? Are you following me, is that it, if so why?" she asked in a no nonsense tone.

Vian starred completely captivated into her beautiful violet coloured eyes, noting how the golden flecks seemed to sparkle brighter, due to her extreme annoyance of him being there, as he replied, "You have a very suspicious mind if you think we're following you," he uttered incredulously. Melanie knew something fishy was going on and said as much, "Oh! I think I have every right to be suspicious where your concerned Vian, and who the hell is 'we', may I ask?" she asked in a firm tone. Vian continued to stare at her for a few moments longer before responding, in a sudden change of subject. "I like your dress Melanie, it's very nice. Where I come from, women don't usually wear the colour black, or wear anything quite so figure hugging. I could get used to seeing you like this." he said with a slight smile that unnerved Melanie somewhat.

Melanie narrowed her eyes suspiciously, with her hands planted firmly on her hips, trying to control her temper as she uttered, "Never mind the damn dress! We were talking about you, about why you're here? So stop changing the subject." She declared, standing her ground, as Vian replied, "You're a stubborn little thing. A trait I'm not sure I like." he said seriously. Melanie did her best to keep a hold on to her patience by taking several deep breaths before saying, "You're being evasive on purpose aren't you? Why? What are you hiding? You wouldn't come all this way to find me for no reason at all, so tell me!!" she asked determinedly, and panicked slightly when Vian took a sudden step forward and responded with, "Do you dream Melanie, at night, while you sleep?" he asked her suddenly, taking her completely by surprise once again.

She could not say anything at first as her tongue was firmly fixed to the roof of her mouth, but eventually with a huge amount of effort, she managed the thought: 'How did he know about my dreams?' she wondered, as she enquired in hushed tones, "What did you say?" while all colour drained from her face. Vian took another step towards her saying, "You do don't you Mel, you dream, what do you dream sweet Mel, tell me?" he asked looking deep into her eyes with an intensity that alarmed her. Realising she was standing in front of the ladies wash room, she made an immediate escape, but not before giving him a piece of what little there was left of her mind saying, "don't know who you think you are, or where you came from, but I don't have any intentions of answering your questions, so if you'll excuse me, I need to go and freshen up." and hurried into the ladies room.

Once inside, she collapsed against the door using it for much needed support, trying to calm her frazzled nerves, 'Did I really say that to him?' she asked herself, as she went to look at the person in the mirror she no longer recognised. "Why are you letting him do this to you? You silly girl, he's a stranger you met outside a sandwich shop for goodness sake. So get a grip girl." she told herself, before turning to leave, knowing instinctively that Vian would be waiting for her. She straightened her shoulders and opened the door, and managed about five steps, before he did the only thing he could do, and that was to yank her into his waiting arms and kiss her passionately.

That was how her friends found her, both echoed Melanie's name in surprise. "Aren't you going to introduce us to your new friend Mel?" they asked not quite believing what they were seeing, as Vian released her, but stubbornly held onto her hand, and took pity on her embarrassed state by introducing himself to both Sarah and Lynnette. "Melanie and I have known each other for a while now and are great friends, aren't we?" Mel faced him, suspicion evident in her eyes as she thought, 'What's he up to?' while Lynnette looked him up and down, saying, "You're a sly one Mel, he's dishy." noting how tall, dark and handsome he was before daring to ask, "Do you have any more like you at home?" Vian smiled saying, "No. But I do have cousins, their standing right behind you." he replied.

Everyone turned to look at the new arrivals, while Sarah in utter disbelief whispered, "I don't believe you sometimes, Lynni." while Lynnette merely shrugged her shoulders, while being introduced to his cousins. The first cousin stood well over 6ft tall in height, and went by the unusual name of Tarak; an austere, serious looking guy with an unwillingness to smile for anyone, wearing dark shoulder length hair with an unusual dark red tint running through it, and a very pale complexion. Sarah took one look at him and thought 'An obvious loner' having sensed the guys need for solitude. Whereas the second cousin, appeared quite opposite, more approachable, easy going and a lot more fun who went by the name of Raan; He was tall, slim like the others, and again, a pale complexion, short cropped dark brown coloured hair to match his eyes, wearing an overly friendly smile and a teasing glint in his eye that meant trouble. Lynnette cocked her head to one side and thought 'I can see you're going to be nothing but trouble' then with a curve of her lips she added 'I like that', as Raan winked at her.

Tarak considered Vian with a troubled expression as if to ask, 'what the hell are you doing?' But all Vian gave was a telepathic reply of 'as usual, you worry too much Tarak' and turned back to focus all his attention on Melanie. Tarak who had a tendency to take life way too seriously had good reason to, remembering the last time Vian told them to relax and not worry; the causing of an impending star implosion in a nearby solar system was not taken lightly. Ok! So they were young siblings at the time, but that didn't erase the seriousness of it or of them standing before the High Senan, waiting for punishment to be served. The High Senan was their equivalent of a leader. Vian was too preoccupied to note his friend's turmoil, he was too busy watching Raan's solid gold performance in front of the ladies.

Sarah grabbed Raan by the hand and dragged him onto the dance floor, while Lynnette not wanting to feel like the proverbial gooseberry, took a reluctant Tarak to the bar for drinks. Leaving Melanie alone with Vian, 'Lord Help her' she thought, whilst attempting some small talk, "So, what do you do for a living?" She asked him curiously while watching the dancing, "I don't. There's no need," he replied sincerely in his usual calm manner. "That figures." she said in a tone laced with sarcasm that made Vian turn his head to look at her with raised eyebrows, but he didn't reply.

Moments later Raan hurried over with Sarah who asked casually, "Are you all here on holiday, or is it business?" Tarak was the first to reply saying, "You could say a little of both." he said vaguely, making it obvious that they had just been given the sort of answer any secret service agent would be proud of, when the D J suddenly announced the next few songs about to play. Sarah's eager voice shouted out, "Quick. hold this for me!" And thrust her drink at Tarak before dragging Lynnette and Raan back onto the dance floor. Raan had a further eight girls dancing around him, and was loving every minute of it. Tarak groaned in despair as his eyes went skywards, praying that what he was witnessing would eventually be a bad dream, and not his halfwit of a friend. Later that evening it was the touch of Sarah's hand on her arm that brought Mel back to the here and now, telling her she wanted to go home, having had too much fun and too much drink, that brought an end to an interesting evening, and it wasn't long before Mel drifted back into dreamland...

CHAPTER ELEVEN

<u>*Memories*</u>

In this particular dream, she found herself sat in the middle of the floor with two small children, twins, a boy and a girl of about nine or ten years old, both had short black hair, pale skin and a pleasant temperament. Sitting between them was a tank filled with water, taken from the waterfall at the back of the complex, filled with a host of tiny creatures swimming contentedly inside the tank, she leaned forward to find miniaturized jellyfish, emitting an electrical charge of coloured lights with each movement, guided by the twins tiny hands that brush against the side of the tank, guiding them into a merry little dance. The twin's excitement was infectious, when having sensed someone behind her, she turned to find the very same bat like creature putting a large bowl of food on the table.

Knowing it was meal time both children hurried to finish their school project, by gliding their hands gracefully over the container of jellyfish at a faster pace. Melanie stared in disbelief as the entire tank of jellyfish transformed suddenly, into a single life form, she stared open mouthed thinking 'wow!' As the boy made his way over to a musical orb on a nearby table, and after several attempts finally found the one tune he wanted, something with a faster beat. His sister smiled at him and automatically joined hands with him to have a conversation while they ate. Melanie watched in silence while the sister threatened to hit her brother with her spoon, due to his constant teasing. The deep ingrained connection to the children, especially the girl was strong, as it pulled on her heart strings, when the creature with very little humour, grabbed her by the arm and guided her into a chair at the table, picked up her spoon, handed it to her in the hope she'd eat her meal. But to Melanie's horror, the food she was about to eat wriggled its way around inside the dish, an assortment of bright coloured plums. Melanie stared at the nightmare in front of her thinking, 'If these things have a heart beat then they can forget it, I'm not eating any' she promised, while the bat like creature stood over her like an avenging angel. The twins looked on in confusion while devouring their meal, and with reluctance Melanie guided a wriggling portion of food onto the spoon and into her mouth, when all at once, the texture of it changed, becoming almost fury, the shock of which woke her up:

CHAPTER TWELVE

Melanie opened her eyes to find the moon still up and the tip of Austin's tail in her mouth, and spent the next several minutes spitting out cat hairs, while hurrying into the bathroom for the mouth wash, giving Austin a cold hard stare as she went. Austin wasn't the least bit intimidated, from his spot at the far end of the bed he listened to the gargling sounds from within the bathroom. Having returned she brushed away any remaining cat hairs from her pillow, before settling down to slowly drift back to sleep.

Later that morning she woke up to find Austin's intense gaze staring down at her, waiting for his usual ten minutes of tummy tickle, and although she shouldn't indulge him because of the trick he pulled the night before, she did anyway. The sound of someone moving around was intermingled with the odd swear word in French, having accidentally stubbed their toe while en-route to the bathroom. Melanie looked at Austin saying, "come on Austin, let's get up.", Twenty minutes later Melanie and Austin were very much surprised to see Lynnette stood by the cooker making breakfast when they entered the kitchen, "Morning Lynni." said Melanie, while preparing Austin's favourite meal of tuna deluxe complete with pasta and vegetables, seconds before Sarah bounded into the kitchen, like a whirlwind of expensive perfume and shower gel, sending Austin's allergies into overload for the next few minutes, who peered at Sarah through streaming eyes giving her one of his nastiest looks, while Sarah said a rather chirpy, "Morning all." before adding, "I think it's going to be a great day, don't you?" and helped herself to coffee. "You're in a good mood Sal." commented Melanie whilst emptying the packet meal into Austin's dish. "I'm in a fantastic mood Mel cos we're meeting the guys for dinner today, isn't that great! We were getting on so well last night that I thought why not. What do you guy's think?" she asked, a little late in the day.

Melanie spun round so fast she very nearly sent Austin's meal skywards. "What did you say?" asked Melanie in an incredulous tone, as the dish she was holding hovered precariously above Austin's head, containing an ample portion of his favourite food that at any moment would be on the floor. Sarah caught Melanie's eye saying, "I didn't have time to tell you last night Mel, Sorry!" and paused before adding, "Besides, I doubt Lynni would remember anything from last night. She'd had too much to drink." explained Sarah. Lynnette turned to face her accuser and merely shrugged her shoulders saying, "We were having such fun last night plus, you were too busy pawing your new best friend, the weirdo with the overfriendly smile and the cropped black hair, what's his name Randy, Ron, Rooney, Ricky?" wondered Lynnette, not really giving a damn what his name was. Sarah replied, "his name is Raan you dolt, and he isn't a weirdo." she uttered in his defence adding, "he's just a little odd that's all." This left Melanie deep in her own thought as she said half-heartedly, "Right!" while setting Austin's food dish down who dived into it with gusto, before looking up at Mel with a large piece of tuna sticking out of his mouth, looking both funny and cute in equal measures. Melanie laughed giving him a loving pat on the head, before joining her friends at the table hoping she would be able to eat some of the breakfast Lynnette had prepared.

The pre-arranged meeting place was to be by the lake at 12.00 noon which was the exact time that the hire car pulled up in a nearby car park. Vian and Tarak stood overlooking the lake in private conversation, while Raan sat precariously on the backrest of a park bench with his feet resting on the seat, while his hands were open around what appeared to be a stone suspended in mid-air, he brought one of his hands into play by moving it in a circular motion above the stone, causing it to spin at a tremendously fast pace, while in suspended animation, the stone was moving so fast, that it eventually altered its natural form and structure, creating an entirely new entity. Tarak having glanced over his shoulder, saw Melanie and her friends approaching from the car parking area, and went to interrupt his friend's game playing.

He held out his hand, took immediate control of the stone, saying, "We have company Raan." he said calmly, as Raan released the stone, hopped off the bench and looked over his shoulder before putting his hands in his pockets. Sarah rushed over in a flurry of excitement saying, "Hi guys!" and immediately linked arms with Raan. Melanie although nervous moved instinctively closer to Vian, with her hands tightly clasped in front of her. While Vian gazed deep into her eyes, noticing how her violet coloured eyes brightened somewhat when he held her close, causing the golden flecks to sparkle like diamonds. He gazed even deeper and could see the endless amount of knowledge, hidden deep within the dark recesses of her mind, begin to unlock. It was thanks to her mother's unique DNA that made it easy for Vian to re-awaken Melanie's subconscious mind. What he did not realise or expect however, was the shear stubbornness and strength of will she had inherited from her father and the people of planet Earth, fighting with him every step of the way.

He knew Melanie was a unique challenge, but it was a challenge he was determined to win, her fiery temper and determination made him smile, and although her temper and tenacity had initiated the re-awakening of her life force, seeing this for the first time, left him feeling completely and utterly spell bound. He knew of his race's ability to genetically pass down stored memories from their mother, grandmother and great grandmother and so on, which prevented the possibility of things being forgotten over the passages of time. This had in a small way happened to Melanie, her mother's memories had been safely locked away. Melanie having felt an emotional and physical change gradually increasing, had to know the reason why, "What's happening to me Vian?" She asked boldly while the others lingered behind.

Vian glanced across the water for a brief moment before he replied. "What do you think is happening?" he asked, feeling her slight hesitation while she took a deep breath to say, "I don't exactly know, I'm a little confused about a lot of things lately, that's why I'm asking you, but you know something, I know you do. So I'll ask again, what's happening to me, why me, what's so special about me?" she asked seriously. Vian gave her a teasing glance. "You tell me, why do you think this is happening, why you, and not somebody else?" he replied teasingly, waiting for Melanie's response.

But Melanie's temper erupted suddenly as she stopped walking, turned to face him saying, "You're not helping me very much Vian. Giving me a question as an answer isn't going to get me anywhere now is it? Come to think of it, you were just the same last night." "I'm more in the dark now than I was at the beginning" she said, getting angrier by the minute. And as much as he enjoyed provoking her Vian knew now wasn't a good time to say anything. He glanced at her saying, "I promise you, we will talk later, but right now, why don't we go for a walk along the river bank?" Melanie took a deep breath knowing she wasn't going to get any answers from him right now. "Alright" she said with a determined glint in her eye. But the problem they then faced was that their hire car was still in town by the lake, so they left Vian and Mel at home, while the others went to pick up their car and returned a little later. Melanie waved goodbye as the car disappeared around the corner and said, "Let's go into the kitchen, I need to give Austin his dinner, he gets grouchy if I'm late getting any of his meals ready." she explained, before adding, "Now that we're alone, I'd appreciate some answers to the ever growing list of questions," she asked trying to sound in control, when deep down she was the exact opposite. Vian held her gaze as he said, "I knew your Mother, you might say we grew up in the same area, before she came here and met your father." then paused briefly before adding, "Your mother's name was Selemie, your father was James Andrew Trevern. They met at the Royal Observatory in Edinburgh." he uttered trying to gauge Melanie's reaction. She repeated their names over and over in her mind, while gazing into her coffee cup saying, "You're talking in past tense, so I take it their not alive any more right?" she asked hoping that it wasn't true. Vian merely nodded his head in answer to her question while Melanie, having glanced at him asked, "What happened?" Before turning her gaze back to her now luke warm cup of coffee that her hands were wrapped around while her entire body shivered, wondering where Austin was as Vian replied, "It was during child birth, your birth, that complications arose, resulting in Selemie's death." Once again he paused before adding, "and unfortunately your father died soon after." he uttered with a barely audible voice.

Melanie lifted her coffee cup to her mouth wishing it was brandy, and asked, "Couldn't the hospitals do anything for her even back then? Surely they would have been able to save her, it's not the middle ages Vian, I can't believe they couldn't do anything to save her." uttered Melanie, frustrated. Vian hesitated before answering this particular question, knowing he was treading on unsafe terrain. "You have to understand Mel, Selemie wasn't from around here, she wanted you to be born here in this house, the hospitals would've asked too many questions." He then paused before continuing, "Everything humanly possible had been done, within the confines of the house. Your uncle George did everything he could to save your mother, it was a miracle you survived." he explained calmly. Melanie considered what Vian had told her before asking, "Do you know what she looked like? My mother I mean.". Vian merely shook his head saying, "I'm afraid I don't, but I could show you something else." he offered and got to his feet, held out his hand hoping she might have the courage to take it this time, for she had resisted previous offers. He waited while she nervously tucked a lock of her hair behind her ear, before reaching out her hand to gently place it into his. Vian could sense how nervous she was and uttered gently, “Trust me Mel, it will be alright.” and guided her out of the kitchen and into the panelled room.

CHAPTER THIRTEEN

Having entered the room, Austin observed them from the top of the stairs. Vian turned on several lamps saying, "This was your mother's favourite room, she would spend many hours in here." he said with a slight smile, Melanie was clearly puzzled by this and confused, asked, "I thought the house was Charlie's?". Vian's reply was quick, "It had been in his family for generations, and as he was the last in his lineage he decided to give the house to your parents, as a wedding gift. Your mother fell in love with the place as soon as she saw it, he thought very highly of her Mel, classed her as a daughter. All the alterations were made by your parents, or rather you're mother." He paused before continuing, "Selemie had a unique artistic flare, wouldn't you agree?" he asked, whilst looking at the intricate art work on the painted panelling.

Melanie glanced at the panelling for a brief moment before turning away saying, "Charlie must have loved my parents very much, to give them this house, and yet..." commented Melanie before adding, "He never once mentioned them, all those years I spent in his shop. The questions I could've asked, the stories he could've told me, all that wasted time!!" she asked in a fit of frustration and betrayal. Vian stood near the window with his back against the glass looking surprisingly calm and relaxed saying, "Both Charlie, George and your adopted parents thought it best to wait until the time was right, until you were of an age to understand. It's not as straight forward as you might think, in time you will understand my meaning." he concluded calmly, which was starting to annoy her a great deal.

She gazed at the exquisitely painted panelling that surrounded the room, as she slowly reached out her hand to gently touch the images of people, places and plant life that seem so familiar to her. But the instant her fingers brushed against the delicate art work, her hand started to tingle and become warm, and for just a brief moment the images began to move, shimmer and slowly come to life; the leaves on every tree performed a slow exotic dance, as the gentle sound of everyday life began to emanate from within the panelling, filling the room with an unusual array of sounds and smells. Then suddenly a little girl stepped out from behind her mother. Melanie smiled as the child waved with unabashed excitement, offering Melanie one of her best smiles, showing off her two milk teeth, before shouting her version of the name Melanie out loud. She stumbled on unsteady ground before landing on her bottom looking far from pleased with herself, but her mother gave her a gentle hug and within minutes, the child was laughing again. Melanie stared in amazement not quite believing what she was seeing, as her confused mind tried to produce a rational explanation.

Meanwhile in the furthest corner of the image almost out of view stood a couple, mature in age, showing obvious signs of nervousness and anxiety, their unease clearly evident as they smiled at Melanie tentatively with their arms around each other, realising they were now looking at Selemie's child, their granddaughter for the very first time, without the need of an imaging orb which Austin used to supply at regular intervals. Amarah pressed a hand to her face hoping it might control her emotions, while her husband Tenzin comforted her. Melanie, having seen them, took a single step forward unconsciously aware that they were her grandparents. Vian felt the sudden change in Melanie's emotions and waited for her reaction, as she continued to stare at the couple she recognised from her dreams, then without looking at Vian she asked, "The dreams are real aren't they? The places, the people everything is real isn't it? It has to be, right? Either that or I'm slowly losing my mind, in which case, I'll be needing a padded cell." she concluded trying to stay sane for as long as possible, according to Austin, who was currently on the other side of the door with his ear pressed against it.

Vian responded saying, "You're not going mad Mel, and it's no magic trick I can assure you." "All you're seeing is real." he assured her calmly. Melanie sat down on one of the chairs without taking her eyes off the image of her grandparents, desperately trying to keep her mind on rational thoughts, if that was at all possible. "Are you trying to tell me that my parents are from another planet? That they are in fact alien? Because if you are, then I'm going to tell you to leave my house right now, and take your crazy ideas with you, and might I suggest you try a stronger dose of meds, because the ones you're taking aren't working!" she uttered tactlessly, Vian held her gaze saying, "Your father was human Mel. It was your mother who wasn't born here, she was and still is as you humans put it an extra-terrestrial from another world." he informed her, before coming to stand in front of her adding, "Like myself, Tarak and Raan who are also alien. Your mother was and still is a close friend of my family, and thought of very highly amongst our people for her bravery and courage." he said earnestly. 'I knew it,' thought Melanie, as she gazed into his ebony coloured eyes, 'I knew there was something different about him.' and then said aloud, "You've just informed me that you're an alien from another planet, how the hell am I supposed to react to that? How on Mother Earth do I begin to try and understand all this! No! I don't believe it, this is crazy and you know it!" she stated angrily whilst pacing up and down in front of the painted panel, forgetting all about the fact that she had an audience, "How am I to understand it with a rational mind Vian? I don't know what to think any more." Melanie said with a heavy sigh wishing Austin was here.

Vian smiled at her and replied, "I don't think you've fully understood my meaning Mel, your mother was alien, so naturally, you are part alien yourself... are you not? Think about it Mel, all the unique abilities you had when you were a small child, and still have. Gifts no other child had, haven't you ever wondered why you were the only one to have these abilities, why none of your school mates had them?" he asked with an incontrovertible composure Sherlock Holmes would have envied, that was slowly driving her crazy, whilst she listened to his nonsensical ravings. She had to stop pacing suddenly and stare at him in shocked surprise, as a host of images buzzing around inside her head, flash backs from her childhood, a childhood she shared with Austin, her friend, her confident and family, came back to life. Showing the pictures she would create and bring to life in the privacy of her bedroom, which felt so natural and normal to her.

She remembered the days she would get up early, prepare a small packed lunch filled with an apple, two home made jam sandwiches, a packet of crisps, plus a packet of pork scratchings for Austin, who always went with her, whenever she headed down to her secret hiding place, a place everyone knew about but pretended otherwise, that happened to be an empty stable box, in the far corner of the barn, where some of the bales of hay were stored. They would spend many hours in there, alongside an old hen called Gertrude, who owned the barnyard, alongside an old horse called Pilot, a donkey called Maddie, she would read her prized collection of story books to her animal friends, and bring all the characters to life with her magic touch. But whenever she asked why she was so different, they would always say, the Angels made her special, and that one day she would know why.

But the honest truth was that there were no angels, only aliens, beings from another planet, it was all a lie, a damned lie! She didn't know whether to freak out or pass out, and right now, either one sounded good. Although thinking back, it did make a lot of sense, that her parents would never take her to a doctor or the hospital, and would always ask her Uncle George to come by and see her until she'd turned eighteen, when he suddenly without warning, moved back to Canada. The realisation of such a huge lie hit her full on, as the tell-tale signs throughout her childhood resurfaced causing her mind to scream out loud 'Oh my God, I'm an alien, a freaked out alien!!' she cried over and over in her mind, as the image of her grandparents on the canvas moved forward, but Vian held up his hand to prevent and reassure them. While Melanie stood staring at her hands, hoping they might show the slightest indication of her being more alien like, but looked quite normal. She didn't feel alien, she was still Melanie Rose Philips right? Wondered Melanie, 'although technically, she was in fact, Melanie Rose Trevern / Philips / Alien' she concluded, as an almighty headache started to form inside her head. Vian laughed having seen the thoughts buzzing around inside her head, as anger fuelled Melanie's eyes and her temper when she turned to look at him saying, "Oh! You find it funny do you? Well it's not every day a person's life is turned upside down by a complete stranger. I don't know what the hell to say, think or even feel thanks to you! I need time to process all this!" she admitted while brushing her hair out of her eyes and making her way towards the door, hoping to make a quick exit from this headache infused nightmare, but Vian stopped her with a hand on her shoulder. "I know it's a lot to accept all at once, but I hope you'll understand the reasons why." he concluded in earnest.

Melanie turned to face him saying, "I know they meant well Vian, and strange as it may seem, I do understand why they kept this a secret until now. After all, telling me that I'm part alien isn't quite the same as telling me I'm part Greek is it, I'm not angry with anyone, I'm just confused and a little muddled about it all at the moment, I need time." and offered him a slight smile. Vian took hold of her hand saying, "I'll give you some time, spending time with your friends is important to you, so enjoy your holiday, but I hope you will allow me to see you again in a day or so?" he asked, with a degree of hope.

Melanie led him to the door saying it was alright, as they could hear the sound of a car, and knew instinctively that it was the rest of their party returning as the car came to a stop. Both watched the playful antics of their friends who were slowly making their way up the path towards the house, while Tarak looked skywards with a tormented expression wishing he was anywhere else but here right now. Melanie couldn't help but feel a little sorry for Tarak, but kept her laughter in check, as Raan turned his playful attentions on him, teasing him mercifully near the open door way, until Tarak gave his friend a look that gave more clout than words would ever do, telling him to back off. Raan held up his hands in a vain attempt at surrendering, while his eyes held a glimmer of mischief and humour.

CHAPTER FOURTEEN

Later while in front of the television Sarah asked, "My feet are killing me. Could someone give them a rub...Lynni? Be a dear and rub my feet?" she asked pleadingly. Lynnette did not bother turning away from her task of setting down the tray of hot drinks and replied, "We all have painful feet, but unlike you, we suffer in silence." and hid her smile, when she heard a groan from Sarah, who was attempting to rub her own feet. Lynnette while ignoring Sarah's endless chatter about nothing, asked her friend, "You're quiet Mel, anything wrong?" she wondered.

Melanie knew she'd have to limit the information she gave, and so having taken a deep breath said, "I was told some information about my real parents today Vian knew my mother's family, they grew up together." she said as the room fell deathly quiet apart from the clock ticking on the wall, and Sarah was the first to speak. "Umm... Don't take this the wrong way Mel but, are you sure he's telling you the truth?" she uttered seriously. Lynnette nodded her head in agreement, astounded by Sarah's foresight, something that didn't happen very often, adding, "You are a very rich woman now Mel. For all you know they could be con men. You have to be careful now." explained Lynnette taking the cups into the kitchen to wash. As Sarah asked full of curiosity, "What did he say exactly, about your birth parents?" Hugging a cushion in her lap at the far end of the sofa, waiting for her friend to answer,

Mel began to recount where her parents had met, and fallen in love. She didn't want to go into detail about her mother's lineage, for she didn't quite understand it herself yet, so how on Earth would they,Why don't we go to the observatory tomorrow, do the guided tour bit and have a look round?" suggested Sarah, adding, "We're not that far from it Mel, what do you think?" Melanie liked the whole idea of following in her parents footsteps, and agreed that they would go tomorrow. Lynnette didn't mind one way or the other, so long as they took the car.

Early the following morning with the sound of music playing inside the hire car, heading towards Edinburgh with Melanie and Lynnette sat in the front, Sarah lay across the entire back seat fast asleep, because any time before 10am was still night time according to Sarah. They arrived at the Royal Observatory in Edinburgh, found a good parking spot and headed towards the main entrance, leading into the East Dome, containing a non-working Inchreflectol.

Melanie's thoughts of her parents were interrupted by Sarah. "Hey Mel, guess what!" said Sarah excitedly, as she raced over to grab her by the arm. "One of the guides has invited us to the star gazing event tonight in the West Dome, some of the sights will be out of this world, do you get it? Out of this world! Please say we can stay and see it?" pleaded Sarah beseechingly trying in vain to keep her excitement under some sort of control, but failing fast.

Melanie took pity on her friend and replied, "Alright we'll stay, but only if Lynni agrees as well." Sarah wasted very little time in hurrying over to Lynnette, wanting to be the first to tell her their plans. Melanie watched Lynnette's mouth pucker as her hand rested on her hip before nodding her head in agreement, and received a huge hug from Sarah, who hurried off to tell Tristan the good news. Lynnette's eyes rolled skywards having caught Melanie's eye, both friends thinking the same thing, that Sarah just like Peter Pan never grew up. Tristan, one of the guides came over to introduce himself and offered them a little guided tour and history lesson of the East

Dome. It wasn't long before Melanie felt the pangs of hunger and suggested they go for something to eat in the centre of Edinburgh, and do the tourist bit. Lynnette was already making her way down the stairs and out of the main door, a clear indication that stargazing wasn't her thing. But Sarah wouldn't leave until arrangements had been made to meet Tristan later.

Immediately after dinner while having a little walk around Edinburgh, before heading back to the Observatory, Melanie glanced through a shop window at a Scots Guards outfit for pets, and could immediately picture Austin in one. She thought how cute he would look and went ahead and bought one. The problem was getting it on him, but just as the idea popped into her head, it very soon popped out again, due to past experiences concerning Operation Bath Time. When Melanie decided to give Austin, her pet cat his annual bath, that was when things turned nasty, she'd arranged the help of her two friends:

1 Corner Austin in the bathroom.

2 Get Austin into the bath.

3 Once the mission is complete withdraw to a safe distance.

4 Then apologise to the neighbours.

However an hour and ten minutes later, the flashing glimpse of a black and white object leaving the house at high speed was spotted, leaving behind Lynnette's partly mummified body in the now completely destroyed shower curtain, with her two legs dangling over the edge of the bath along side Sarah. While Melanie was wedged between the toilet and the hand basin, unable to quite comprehend what had happened, vowing never to give Austin a bath again.

Melanie took another look at the outfit she bought, having arrived back at the car saying, "Wouldn't Austin look cute in this outfit?" she asked holding up a Scots kilt complete with sporran attached to a vest style harness. Lynnette wondered if Mel was in her right mind for suggesting such an idea, when

Sarah uttered, "You're not actually going to get that on him and live, are you? Remember the last time we tried getting Austin doing something he didn't want to do, I still have the scars." admitted Sarah. Lynnette interceded saying to Melanie, "We all do, you're on your own with this one." as Melanie replied, "Maybe your right, he'd only end up tearing it to shreds," she concluded, returning to the Observatory where they found Tristan in the reception area, waiting for them.

Having returned home a little later than planned, they found a disgruntled looking Austin sitting on the rug waiting for their return. The look he gave was one of extreme annoyance, Melanie bent down to give him a gentle pat on his head, which he avoided while heading towards the kitchen and his empty bowl, "Austin's not very happy with me." said Melanie deciding that some fresh salmon might sweeten him a little. Melanie lay in bed recalling their day out at the observatory where her parents met, recalling some of the secrets that were being kept from her, secrets that could have changed her entire life around, and gradually as her eyes began to close, her last thoughts before drifting off to sleep was of Austin, her beloved cat, who would always forgive her come morning after is usual belly tickle she concluded. Within moments she began to dream:

CHAPTER FIFTEEN

Memories

Once again Melanie found herself back in dream world, regarding the chaos both twins were causing, while dashing to and fro gathering various objects, before taking them out onto the balcony at the rear of the house, overlooking the magnificent Yoltana waterfall. Surprised at how much time had passed since her last dream, for the twins were now the age of average teenagers, both of whom, beckoned Melanie over as they dashed outside. She observed the boy setting up at various intervals, tiny pale pink oval like objects the size of a computer mouse along the transparent railing, making sure to point them up towards the stars.

Whereas the girl and her father were busy setting up a collection of bright blue spherical shaped orbs the size of goose eggs along the balcony ledge, while in quiet contemplation the bat like creature arranged plates of food on a small table by the entrance, giving their neighbours the occasional glance before giving a nod of acknowledgement. It was obviously an important event, if the behaviour of the servant was any indication, this was no ordinary run of the mill picnic. Every family on every balcony busied themselves, and the most burning question on Melanie's mind was 'why?' she wondered, as her hand was gently held by Tenzin...Whose unfamiliar name appeared suddenly in her mind, a name she somehow recognised, as did the person she unknowingly inhabited, who went by the name of Amarah! Their palms were pressed together while he asked telepathically, if she was alright, before he placed his hand against her abdomen, making her realise that she, or rather Amarah was carrying another child.

Amarah while offering him a loving smile, informed him she was well, and that he shouldn't worry so much. He kissed his wife's hand, whilst guiding her over to join the rest of the family and their relatives, who were standing in a circle waiting patiently. The twins were busy sharing a joke or two until their servant gave them a look threatening dire retribution, if they continued this show of disrespect at such an important event. 'So…he was more than just a housekeeper then,' concluded Melanie as he exited the balcony with an air of self-importance while everyone on every balcony joined hands, palms pressed together at waist height, their faces tilted up towards the night's sky with their eyes closed.

Melanie followed suit and was immediately swarmed by a host of images in her mind's eye, images so powerful, that every person there could feel its raw naked power pulsating through their entire bodies, gradually becoming more solid and more real, eventually forming a cloud of multi-coloured translucent mist. Enthralled by the sheer vibrancy of it all, as the Yoltana waterfall was suddenly engulfed by speckled light and energised water, prior to merging itself with the coloured mist, and ascending towards the stars away from the waterfall and into the upper atmosphere, forming a multi coloured light show.

Melanie watched the start of what was to be a 'Lunar Eclipse' as it moved behind the Orianas and Amarii moons, in an aura of soft tranquil colours, before reaching its destination as the suns rays looked out from behind both moons, while the illuminated mist settled on the Erievna rings: 'made from tightly formed fragments of dark shards of granite left over from the planetary collision a millennia ago' and although invisible until the start of the annual Lunar

Eclipse of the sun, it was an amazing sight. 'How is this possible?' wondered Melanie while opening her eyes, to see for herself this miraculous wonder, thinking, 'please don't let me wake up yet, I want to see more' she pleaded, as the planet continued to reveal more of its many secrets.

But finally as everyone began to move away from the gathered circle, leaving Melanie alone to witness the twins hurrying into the house, with all of their carefully gathered equipment clutched in their arms, almost knocking over a tray of drinks their servant was carrying, who having carefully set down the tray hurried in after them, to give them a piece of his mind. Melanie followed, if a little apprehensively, to find the servant being hugged and kissed apologetically by the twin sister Selemie...'Her name was Selemie! And her twin brother was Taban!' Their names, like that of their parents, appeared from the dark recesses of her subconscious. She noticed the servant's face glow with embarrassment before making a discreet exit, leaving the twins examining their scientific equipment, and occasionally joining hands to discuss their findings in private, whilst sharing a joke or two...When suddenly a noise was heard in the far distance that sounded like her name being called getting louder and louder saying:

CHAPTER SIXTEEN

"Austin you skunk...Get out of the bloody way, before I put you in the bin outside!" said Sarah who approached the bed before shaking Melanie's shoulder, "Aren't you ever getting up? Its nearly lunch time, come on. I want to go somewhere today. It's beautiful out there, let's not waste it" Sarah said in a tone of pent up frustration. Melanie smiled before opening one eye, "Alright I'll get up, give me a few minutes. Have a cup of coffee ready for me in the kitchen." replied Mel, while Austin who was sat on the bed next to her snorted in disgust as Sarah skipped out of the room and down the stairs, singing one of her favourite songs. 'It's enough to make you want to hurl. It's disgusting, she ought to act her age.' thought Austin as he rolled onto his back waiting for his early morning belly tickle. Later Melanie was in the kitchen finishing her coffee, along with a warm French bread roll Lynnette had at the ready within minutes, suggesting, "How about we go for a walk, we could revisit the stream at the edge of the clearing, and take Austin with us?". Sarah rolled her eyes and moaned out loud at the mere mention of Melanie's nightmare of a cat coming along. But Lynnette loved the idea for some strange reason.

Their day out was perfect as far as Sarah was concerned, who lay on her back with her sun hat covering her face snoring as she slept. Lynnette was leaning against a fallen tree reading a book, while Melanie sat at the water's edge mesmerised by the sun light reflected off the water lapping against the river bank, as images of her previous dream flooded her mind, reliving every image, hearing every sound and feeling every emotion. She reached out her hand to allow the rippled water to caress her hand, while her thoughts continued to wander, 'Whenever I dream, I feel the empty ache in my heart becoming whole again', she concluded then paused. 'Is it wishful thinking to want to belong there, and be a part of it?' she thought as she slowly shook her head in a show of annoyance.

Austin grunted and flicked his tail angrily while he listened in on her thoughts thinking 'on occasions such as these, rare though they may be, I do have to bow down in defeat, and realise how utterly stupid she can be in her way of thinking' he concluded as he curled his upper lip in frustration adding 'If only I could talk,' he thought 'I'd give her a piece of my mind, I can tell you' while looking over his shoulder at Sarah and producing a devilishly evil grin, as a plan started to form in his mind.

He slowly and carefully made his way towards the unsuspecting Sarah, making sure Lynnette was still absorbed in her uninteresting book, while with a swagger in his walk the closer he got to his prey, you could almost hear him laugh under his breath 'The timing has to be right' thought Austin as he all at once, leapt into the air and landed on Sarah's stomach causing her to gasp in both pain and shock, as she whipped off her favourite sun hat to see what the hell had hit her, while Austin lunged for her hat, gripped it between his teeth and ran off with it, with a furious Sarah hot on his heels, acting out a slap stick comedy sketch. Austin then with pinpoint accuracy selected the exact spot for stage two of his plan, as he suddenly spat out the sun hat, did a swift about turn, leapt high in the air and knocked Sarah completely off balance. High pitched screams could be heard seconds before the sound of a solid object, hitting the water with an almighty splash was heard, 'That went well,' thought Austin with a smug smile on his face whilst hiding amongst the tall grass at the far side of the clearing, watching Melanie and Lynnette pull their soaking wet friend out of the river.

The wanting to commit first degree murder was evident, as Sarah sat in silence on one of the blankets, using a second as a towel. ‘Poor Austin’ thought Melanie, trying desperately not to laugh, as she turned to find Lynnette’s shoulders shaking with laughter, “Go on and laugh at my expense. But let me tell you this, if I ever get my hands on your cat any time today Melanie Rose! You’ll be kissing him goodbye, because I’ll ring his bloody neck! He enjoys tormenting me like this; he’s no normal run of the mill cat, that’s for sure he’s Satan!!” announced Sarah, as she headed for home with Lynnette’s help, leaving Melanie bringing up the rear, with Austin smiling smugly. ‘We ought to do this again sometime’ and skipped home.

CHAPTER SEVENTEEN

It was early the following morning; Melanie was sat on one of the upholstered chairs in the panelled room. It was the first time since her introduction to the room, that she had dared enter, and what surprised her the most was the fact that she was able to do this on her own, 'Well, not exactly on my own' she thought looking across at Austin, who was perched on the chair next to her looking unusually pleased with himself. She reached across her chair to lovingly stroke his head before turning her attention back to the ornately painted panelling.

Her palms itched as the urge to touch the panelling became a temptation she could no longer resist. She clenched her hands in a vain attempt at self-control feeling nervous for what might happen, but found herself leaving her seat walking towards the wall opposite. While Austin sat unmoved in his chair, observing her intently thinking 'this will be the ultimate test for my Melanie, the first step down a long path to future happiness, all it…' Then paused and held his breath, as Mel reached out her hand to gently touch the canvas, when a voice at the door said. "Mel! Are you in there?" Asked Lynnette curiously, startling both Melanie and Austin before the door opened and in popped Lynnette's head "Oh! My God Lynni you scared me half to death. Do you want to give me a heart attack or something?" declared Melanie nervously, while pressing her hand over her frantically beating heart.

Austin gazed at Lynnette thinking 'you stupid brainless French twit, of all the idiotic dim…' and paused his rantings to leap off the chair and out of the room, to prevent him doing something he would regret, concluding that 'a puppy dog has more brains than her', as her overly chirpy voice said, "Breakfast is ready ma petit", before heading back into the kitchen, leaving Melanie standing in the middle of the room feeling disappointed, as the sound of chaos echoing from within the shrubs growing under the kitchen windowsill caught their attention.

Sarah looked at Mel saying, "I see Austin's his usual charming happy self this morning." finishing off her coffee before helping herself to a second cup, "I can't understand it, he seemed happy enough first thing this morning." replied Melanie puzzlingly, propping her elbows on the table, as a sharp voice shouted, "Elbows off the table!!" ordered Lynnette from her place at the sink, "You're like an old mother hen, you know that don't you?", said Melanie as she swiftly removed her elbows. Austin entered through the kitchen window, and taking a quick look around, went to inspect his dish. Having noticed several clumps of foliage sticking out from under Austin's collar Melanie turned to remove them, while Sarah glanced over her coffee cup saying casually, "We haven't heard from Vian and his friends, I wonder what their up to?". Lynnette gave Sarah a stern look. "Why would we want to see Vian and his friends?" she asked, as Sarah replied, "Oh! Lynni, you are hair-brained, you think the silliest things." and carried on laughing.

Lynnette turned to face her accusers saying, "You have some need to talk chérie", as Melanie asked, "I thought you'd found you're Mr Right in Tristan, Sal, the star gazing buff?" it was then that Sarah turned starry eyed while resting her head on her hands saying, "I have.....Well I think I have, he's so dreamy don't you think? In a clean cut kind of way, with the dreamiest smile." she uttered, as Lynnette and Melanie both rolled their eyes. Austin felt sick to his stomach. Sarah asked, "What are we doing today girls?" She wondered, as Lynnette replied rather hurriedly, "I have to go back to London.

Something to do with work I'm afraid." she explained. "You do?" asked Melanie, adding, "Well, I'll go with you, I need to pick up a few things from Edna's." she explained, and headed out of the kitchen.

Later that same day at around 11:45 give or take a few minutes, Melanie pulled up outside her friends workplace and asked, "What time shall I pick you up Lynni?" Lynnette hopped out of the car saying, "I don't know yet, I'll have to let you know, ok?" giving Melanie a cute little wave before hurrying into the building, as Melanie set off for Mrs Grime's boarding house. Edna was waiting as Melanie parked her car, "You're here at last! I thought you'd never get here. Come in, come in and I'll make us a nice pot of coffee." she offered, and led Mel by the arm, down the hallway and into the kitchen where two cakes were cooling on a wire rack. "I thought you didn't like coffee?" enquired Melanie curiously, "Normally I don't, but I'm determined to win the baking competition at the church fair this weekend. The old trout down the road will not win this year" promised Edna while straightening her thin shoulders. Melanie smiled knowing the 'old trout' was poor Mrs Conley. Edna glanced over her shoulder at Melanie while washing a sink full of pots saying, "It's quiet around here now you're gone Melanie, and I never thought I'd hear myself say this, but I miss that little trouble maker of a cat Austin. He made life interesting. I bet he's been nothing but trouble hasn't he?" she commented with a hopeful glint in her eye. Melanie put down her empty cup and replied, "I think he's missed you actually, why don't you come for a visit, stay for a few days. I'm sure you're tenants can cope without you." The old girl eagerly accepted saying, "I won't be able to come until after the fair, but how does next week sound to you? Say Thursday?" suggested Edna as Melanie wholeheartedly agreed, knowing it would improve Austin's mood seeing her again. Edna then said, "Oh! I almost forgot, a few days ago a stranger came looking for you, said he was family, he looked quite upset having missed you." Edna noticed Melanie's surprised look as she asked, "Really? Did he leave a name and address by any chance?", as Max, Edna's grandson appeared in the hallway, his curiosity had finally got the better of him.

Max was of average height, slim with wavy dark blonde hair and long fringe, hiding a pair of amazingly bright blue eyes. He was unconscionably shy amongst strangers, except for his mates. Edna shook her head in disappointment, glancing curiously at the stack of mail she'd carefully looked through earlier in the day, by holding it up to the light. Max hurried to open the front door saying, "I'll help you with your stuff if you like?" he offered, brushing away the dark blonde wavy hair out of his eyes, as Melanie thanked him. With all the boxes now in the car, Melanie asked how he was, having noticed the dark rings under Max's eyes and his paler than usual complexion. He leaned against Mel's car saying, "It's these damned headaches, they're getting worse. Nothing seems to work, they are slowly driving me mad." he admitted rubbing his hand across his eyes. "Come and visit me with Edna on Thursday, a change of scenery and all that." Melanie suggested hoping he would say yes.

Max glanced at Melanie saying, "Ok I will." and smiled before adding, "That means I can still go to the gig on Saturday, 'The Slapping Sallies' are the hottest chick band around. I can't believe Darren managed to get hold of tickets? Although, his family being filthy rich might have something to do with it." he said with a wink. Melanie lent against her car saying, "Lucky old you, tell me how it goes, ok? I want all the details." she said, as Max added, "Jason's recent split with his partner Robert is one of the reasons we're going, it might cheer him up, and of course there's Ziggy." announced Max, while Melanie frowned in confusion asking, "Ziggy?" Max shrugged his shoulders saying, "Yeh I know, his mum was a huge fan of Ziggy Stardust, and named her son after him, poor Devil." They spent several more minutes talking about a variety of topics before saying their goodbyes, and Melanie went to pick up Lynnette after receiving a text from her saying she was ready.

Having at last arrived home, Melanie opened the front door and shouted, "Hey Austin I'm back" while putting the boxes down, as Lynnette rolled her eyes saying, "I think Austin's getting fat.", "You should put him on a diet." she concluded, noticing the slight podgy stomach. At the mere mention of the word diet within Austin's ear shot, the atmosphere changed almost immediately, as an object flew across the hallway at high speed hitting its target head on, which happened to be the back of Lynnette's head, before landing on the floor by her feet, causing her to almost drop the box she was carefully bringing in through the front door. Melanie and Lynnette both glance down at the object by their feet, and then at each other, realising it was one of Melanie's teddy bears from her collection. Lynnette then uttered, "I always said your cat was strange, Melanie Rose and I think this proves it, don't you?" Melanie picked up her teddy, placed it back where it should be, puzzling as to how he did it.

Meanwhile, upstairs in Melanie's bedroom, Austin marched back and forth, clearly upset and insulted at being called fat, 'Fat? Me?' he thought, 'She dare call me fat? The French Troll with little to no brains. I'd love to go back down there and show her who she's dealing with.' concluded Austin as he stomped his paws across the floor wishing it was Lynnette he was stomping on. A devilishly wicked gleam appeared in his eyes, as he hurried over to the bay window to watch the sun set over the mountains, realising how much he'd missed stretching his wings and going for a fly in the moonlight. The sudden overpowering urge to rebel shook him to the core, he hopped onto the iron railings, transformed into his true self, and took to the air above the clouds, stretching his large ornately sculptured wings before initiating a series of weaves and darts around each low flying cloud, with the odd somersault for good measure. He did not realise a car had pulled up behind Mel's, with Sarah and Tristan inside, both noticing something flying above their heads, as Sarah's high pitched screams echoed across the valley and both made a desperate dash towards the house.

Melanie and Lynnette both opened the door allowing two terrified people in, who having snatched the door out of Melanie's hands, slammed it shut and locked it for good measure. Leaving Melanie and Lynnette looking at each other with puzzled expressions, as Mel asked, "What is it with you two, what happened? Seen a ghost or something?" Sarah turned her terrified eyes towards her two best friends saying, "Or something is right. It flew right at us, this ugly looking Vampire bat like thing... Well! From now on, I'm not going anywhere outside this house after the sun's gone down, Lynnette can take out the rubbish, it'll probably like you more than me Lynni." claimed Sarah, as Lynnette stuck her tongue out at her friend. Melanie was determined to have a look, and so with a firm hand removed Sarah, unbolted the door and opened it, to find Austin in mid lick of grooming himself before sauntering in like a visiting royal, as Lynnette carefully set down her makeshift weapon.

CHAPTER EIGHTEEN

Memories

On this particular visit to dream land, Melanie awoke in a strange bed as the bedroom door opened and in walked her what? 'What do I call him?' Melanie asked herself thoughtfully, looking up at the housekeeper. After all, he didn't fit any of the housekeeper or servant titles on Earth, or resemble anything like an old English butler. 'I wonder if his name's Jeeves, now that would be funny' she concluded thoughtfully, as he said, "Do hurry up Amarah, It's all well and good Tenzin giving you a longer rest period, but he should realise, that it's your cousins' joining ceremony today, and there is still a lot to do. Taban and Selemie are impatient and eager to get there." he said whilst shaking his head in exasperation before leaving the room to go and check on the troublesome twins.

Reliving her mother's childhood through her grandmother's memories was turning into a wonderfully unique experience for Melanie. She looked down and smiled whilst lovingly rubbing her swollen tummy, when the feel of a tiny hand reaching out to her through the flesh that separated them caught her completely by surprise. She looked down and smiled saying. "Not long now little one, you'll soon be with us." she promised walking over to a panelled wall in her Grandparent's bedroom. She waved her hand across it causing it to magically disappear, allowing her access to a selection of clothes, footwear and so on.

She walked into the main room of the house, to find the ever faithful servant standing over Taban with his arms folded, while he supervised the clean-up of an ornament that had been broken. Taban waved his hand over the broken pieces of crockery causing it to glide onto the dustpan next to him with little to no effort, 'They use Telekinesis, that's interesting' thought Melanie, watching as the expressions of disapproval left the servant's face, 'I think he takes life and his job a little too seriously. I wonder if he has any kind of fun at all' Melanie wondered. She sat between her grandfather and uncle during dinner, and the oddest thing of all, was of her staring into the face of a teenager, a teenager who was to be her Mother. 'I wonder what a head shrink would make of it all' she thought, as each family member joined hands, to wish each other a day of good health, before selecting some of the food that was laid out on the table.

Eventually after what felt like a rushed breakfast the family left to attend a joining, Melanie looked up at the cloudless mauve and pink coloured sky, to see a portion of the planet's rings as Munastas turned on its axis. 'Oh, wow!' thought Melanie feeling a little in awe.

The journey took nearly an hour on foot, through sparse woodland and rocky terrain, and at first glance, it didn't look like much, until you gazed down at your feet to realise that this was no ordinary ground they were walking on. At first you are standing on solid ground, then you are standing on thin sheets of clear transparent crystal, made from bed rock and geodes, (which are coloured crystals forged deep within the planets inner core). Melanie stood transfixed at the world beneath her feet, as Tenzin's discreet tugging of her sleeve got her attention.

Everyone welcomed each other with a joining of palms at the meeting place, and it didn't take long for Melanie to pick out the couples who were to join, or as we would call 'married', but this was a joining on a much deeper level.

Melanie could feel Amarah's hand being lifted and joined with Tenzin's, as he pulled her closer to him to place his free hand over her swollen tummy and kiss her, showing her images of their own joining. Melanie could feel the love they had for each other, and felt humbled by it, as Selemie rushed up to Amarah and immediately joined hands with her mother showing her how excited she was to finally be of an age to witness a joining. Taban however showed less excitement, but it did give him the opportunity to meet up with some of his friends from the scientific exploration club, and talk shop.

Standing on either side of a narrow path leading down to the joining circle was the familiar figure of their servant Jeeves, standing amongst many others of his race. Their wings were fully open and their arms were down by their sides with their heads bowed low, 'Each was distinctly different in, height and build I see' Melanie concluded, as her entourage passed by. Ten couples in total were chosen, and each one began to separate from their family members, to go and stand as individual couples in front of an elderly man known as the joining elder, wearing a black full length robe covered in symbols, and it was as the sun light caught the robe that the colour appeared almost dark blue not black, while his long white hair touched the floor. Standing on either side of him were two boys, both of whom had pure white hair, but wore pale blue robes.

Having followed the rest of her family, Melanie positioned herself within a standing ring covering a quarter of a mile, and waited for the joining elder to begin, while chanting a silent lament over and over, as the elder began to speak aloud to the couples about to be joined. Each couple joined palms and faced one another. Melanie watched transfixed as a splattering of bright green coloured water hit the underside of the crystal floor below her feet, while at the same time high above their heads, the planet's rings began to glisten and shimmer brighter than usual, releasing what appeared to be tiny flecks of luminescent residue, a powder. The lament got louder and louder as the liquid below their feet seeped through the floor, while each couple moved closer to each other, absorbing the lament echoing inside Melanie's head. The merging of both the luminescent powder and green water, produced an unexpected release of thick green cloud, that began to move around the group in a slow serene dance, so that you could no longer see the joining couples, while the lament continued to get louder and louder, causing a sudden build-up of energy behind the families involved. This sudden surge of energy had a quality like no other, arching its way over the heads of each family member, hoping to join with the green mist.

Meanwhile deep within the hazy mist that shielded each couple, while the bonding grew stronger and more substantial, Melanie was left feeling unexpectedly overcome with fear, as the images of what had transpired between her and Vian in the book shop all those weeks ago, caused her to panic and hyperventilate. Recognising for herself the magnitude of what had just happened in the joining ceremony, for a similar event had happened between her and Vian, 'Oh my God! Please no. Please someone tell me it's not true. He couldn't have performed a joining, not with me. I don't want any sort of joining, surely I have a say in this' she screamed out loud in her mind, feeling very much alone and afraid as she gradually began to leave her grandmother's body, and that of the dream or was it a nightmare?

CHAPTER NINETEEN

Melanie awoke with a terrified start and sat bolt upright in her bed, covered in perspiration and breathing heavily, praying the dream wasn't real, while Austin stared at her with a look of clear understanding, seconds before he climbed into her lap, 'The things a watcher has to do' he thought before adding 'she was just the same as a little girl, she would often wake up after a bad dream, and the only way she would go back to sleep, was if she cuddled me in her arms.', 'I hope none of my family ever hears about this, I'd be the joke of the Universe' while purring contentedly from his awkward back breaking position within the tight confines of Melanie's arms. But the only thing it did do was give him a bout of cramp down the right side of his body, as the sound of pain induced grunts and the tinkling of the bell hanging around Austin's neck, echoed out of the bedroom window.

Early the next morning on a cloudy and somewhat cooler day, Austin wondered if anyone noticed the missing piece of French toast, while he smacked his lips adding 'I'll say this for her, she's a good cook' he concluded, climbing the fence leading to the dense woodland beyond. Watching while Sarah and Tristan went for a walk along the river, Lynnette meanwhile went to answer her ever growing list of emails, as Melanie made several vain attempts to put up the three bird boxes they'd found in the shed, 'All right, so I haven't used a hammer before, it shouldn't be too hard surely' she concluded, whilst carrying a set of step-ladders down to the bottom of the garden with an air of determination.

Half an hour and a lot of thumb hitting bruises later, the sound of a hammer echoing through the trees was heard followed by the words, "Ouch! Damn and blast it, that hurt!" cursed Melanie whilst standing at the top of the ladder hugging her throbbing thumb, and Austin shook his head in amusement at Melanie's expense thinking, 'someone please tell me, why? Why, would she want to put up bird boxes around here? What would be the point? All she's done so far is hit everything except the nail, including her thumb. I hope she remembers she's up a ladder.' he thought. The hammer must've hit the trunk of the tree several more times, before the sound of Melanie's voice echoing across the valley shouting, "Ouch damn it all to bloody bleeding hell! I'm getting sick of this!" announced Melanie's increasing annoyance and rising temper. She was unaware that Lynnette was walking towards her with a visitor in tow, a man, but to Austin this was no ordinary man.

"Mel! There's someone here to see you!" shouted Lynnette hurrying down the garden. Melanie looked over her shoulder asking, "Really! Who is it Lyn..?" But her voice lodged in the back of her throat leaving her speechless as the stranger approached her. She recognised him immediately as her uncle, but couldn't quite believe he was here, while Lynnette glanced from one to the other clearly puzzled by their reactions.

Taban struggled fearlessly with his inner demon, as he stared into the eyes of his twin's offspring. He could have located her at any time whether she knew it or not, for they were and still are, deeply linked because of her mother's DNA. Twins are after all, very rare on his home planet, with good reason. The bond between both twins are exceptionally strong and dangerously unpredictable, should one twin break contact or die the second twin could become sporadically volatile and dangerous to everyone. It was an unbreakable rule on his planet that both twins must not have their own joining, due to the link with the other twin.

Taban continued to gaze into the eyes of the young girl, who even now, stared back at him with a look of instant recognition, indicating to him, the start of her dream initiation, but by whom he wondered. Melanie stood rooted to the spot with a deep feeling of maternal love for this person that had encircled her heart, so much so, she found her feet moving of their own volition, down the ladder. She knew without saying a word that he was Taban her mother's twin brother. The blood coursing through her veins had a will of its own, she wanted to throw herself at him and hug him fiercely, show him she was happy he had found her at last, but what would his reaction be if she did, for there was a sense of fragility about him, a part of him was fragmented beyond repair.

All this time Austin was in a state of nervous tension, due to the shock of seeing Taban again after all this time. It might also have to do with the prospect of him transforming into his true self in order to protect Melanie should things go from bad to worse. The predicted looks of horror and instantaneous terror from Melanie and Lynnette, should they see the real Austin was almost too much for him to risk, as he looked from one to the other. Taban stood unmoved. Oh! Yes, she was his sister's daughter alright there was no denying it, he could feel his sister looking back at him, and the most surprising thing of all was that it helped calm him, as he slowly lifted his hand to gently touch her cheek but didn't dare, and so lowered it again, "Hello Melanie, at last we meet. I'm Taban your uncle." he said in a quiet clear voice that sounded distinctly odd and unrecognisable to him, and yet, he didn't know why. Melanie took a tiny step forward saying, "I knew who you were the moment I saw you, I'm Melanie. This is Lynnette one of my best friends and my ever faithful pet cat Austin. Everyone. This is my Uncle Taban, my Mother's twin brother" she said with a smile that broke all records in the happiest smile competition.

Austin knew the second before it happened what Melanie was about to do, and stood up on all four paws preparing for the fastest transformation ever made by any watcher. He took a deep breath and held it as Melanie flung herself at her uncle to hug him, taking her uncle completely by surprise, it took every effort Taban had to remain standing and not land in an un-dignified heap on the grass, as the demon within him began to stir the moment his arms circled his niece. He was shocked beyond words to hear her sobbing quietly into the nape of his neck, whilst she clung onto him as if her life depended on it. Taban had never in all his life had to deal with an emotional wreck in the form of a niece, but if he was anything at all then he was a fast learner.

Suspecting he was having a major heart attack, Austin's legs gave way from under him, while Lynnette stood at a discrete distance, finding it all a little too much to handle, using her handkerchief to wipe her eyes and noisily blowing her nose. Melanie lifted her head to gaze into her uncle's eyes with acute embarrassment while attempting to wipe away her tears. Taban gave her a reassuring smile as he gazed into the pair of violet, tear-glistened eyes and asked, "Are you alright now?" Melanie's cheeks blushed fiercely as she replied, "Yes. I think." while Lynnette having pulled herself together replied, "I would suggest we have a bottle of something to celebrate, but it's too early even for me. So I'll go and put on some of my special coffee. ok?" and hurried off to get things started, leaving Melanie, Taban and the ever watchful Austin following.

When Sarah returned from her long walk with her new boyfriend, they were greeted by the sounds of loud voices from within the front room. Both looked at each other wondering who had come to visit and went to investigate. The first thing that caught their attention was the selection of biscuits and coffee on offer, and they wasted little to no time in giving out brief introductions before diving into the food. As Melanie glanced at her uncle asking, "Where are you staying? Is it close?" whilst putting her empty cup down on the table, "I travelled straight here." answered Taban casually, as Sarah laughed. "Well in that case, you can stay here with us there's plenty of room, isn't there Mel?" explained Sarah, before taking another bite from a biscuit. Melanie, having caught her uncle's eye, pleaded, "Please say you'll stay?" while Taban felt Austin's' piercing gaze burning through him like a laser, before he eventually agreed to stay.

Melanie watched her uncle head down the narrow lane going nowhere in particular except to put a few belongings together, before she impulsively grabbed hold of Austin and started dancing with him laughing giddily. Austin was not amused at being cuddled and kissed within an inch of his life, but he went along with it anyway, for this was the first time his sweet Mel had been truly happy, except for Christmas time, but that didn't really count. To see her so happy was worth all the agony, discomfort and sheer embarrassment she could bestow on him. Having entered the front room Melanie came face to face with three sets of eyes, all of which looked at her with blank expressions. "What?" she asked obviously confused, even Austin didn't expect this kind of reaction.

Then all of a sudden it was like the charge of the light brigade, as poor Austin found himself being crushed and suffocated to the point of passing out by the sudden onslaught of Melanie's friends. All attempts of escape had failed, but he did however, manage to stick his head out long enough to take a few much needed gasps of air, for all four of his lungs, while the pain barrier was at the point of no return as the group hug continued...

CHAPTER TWENTY

When Taban eventually returned with his meagre belongings, the spare room at the end of the hall had already been prepared. Melanie took Taban up to his room, noticing how he resembled the actor Christian Bale, "Oh Wow!" she said out loud, "a Christian Bale look-alike for an uncle, who would've thought?" she concluded, realising she'd actually said it out loud. She slapped her hand over her mouth, as her cheeks went red with embarrassment. Even Austin who sat on the end of Taban's freshly made bed, blushed, as a sudden query entered his mind asking, 'Do cat's blush?' he wondered to himself casually.

Taban stared at his niece for a brief moment before bursting into laughter, it was the first time in what felt like an age that he had done this, and he continued to laugh before he dared speak, "I don't know who this person is you speak of but, I should thank him and you, it's been a long time since I have laughed." he said as the barriers around his heart were lowered for the briefest of moments.

Melanie was for the very first time able to see the raw knife-edged pain, anguish and loneliness her uncle carried with him, like a scar that never healed, making her more determined to be there for him now. Melanie wasn't the only one able to see Taban's pain, Austin was able to see it as well, he could also see Melanie's determination to help and thought 'Oh great, this is all I need right now, Melanie's nurse maid routine on an unstable element' but his thoughts were interrupted when Melanie said, "My friend Edna's arriving on Thursday for a few days, she's quite an eccentric but we like her. Oh! She's bringing her Grandson Max along as well, he lives with her." she explained, as she scooped Austin off the bed and headed to the bedroom door sensing her uncle's need to be alone for a while. Once at the door she turned and said in a happy tone, "Lynni's cooking tonight, as it's her turn, so it's bound to be great she was taught by her uncle who was a French chef I believe, anyway it'll be around 5.30ish. Ok? Umm..." she paused momentarily before adding, "I'm glad you're here." she said smiling like a Cheshire cat as the door closed behind her.

Taban stared at the closed door before walking over to the window, to suddenly grab hold of the window frame and hang on to it as if it was the only thing anchoring him to the here and now. He could feel the creature within him becoming stronger and more impatient with each passing day, and he knew the reasons why, but keeping it restrained for so long a time was the ultimate test of his superiority and control, a control he was slowly losing. Meeting Selemie's daughter for the first time went far better than he thought it would, she was a surprise, a genuinely pleasant surprise. He couldn't remember the last time he'd actually laughed, it felt strange, but good, while bowing his head as a sudden onslaught of memories penetrated the deep recesses of his mind, showing him the last time he had actually laughed. A slight curvature of the mouth appeared while remembering some of the happy times of long ago.

Later that night after everyone had gone to bed, Melanie went to investigate the panelled room. Austin watched her climb out of bed, put on her dressing gown and novelty Tigger slippers Sarah had bought her last Christmas, and head towards the door saying in a hushed tone, "Stay here Austin, I won't be long. Ok?" she instructed, as Austin hopped off the bed 'Like hell I'm staying here, this is as big a moment for me as it is for her!' he thought defiantly and was by the door in a flash, only to find it locked and thought, 'If I'd got a decent set of legs, I would kick something.'. He knew there was only one option left for him, and that was to transform into his true self, unaware that a bleary eyed Sarah was making her way down the stairs.

The moment her feet reached the bottom step, she looked up to find herself face to face with the real Austin, the large bat like creature she'd spotted a few nights ago. A high pitched scream bounced off the walls and Austin's sensitive ear drums, prior to him being set upon by a pink frilly edged umbrella, receiving several hits to his head, one across his back and two across his shoulders, before retreating from Sarah's good tennis arm. Melanie stumbled out of the panelled room, as her friend shrieked, "The monsters in the house!!" as she was on the verge of a full on melt down. "I saw it with my own eyes! It had large wings, glowing eyes and dripping wet fangs! Like something out of a horror film!" declared Sarah to her friend, who looked somewhat sceptical. There followed the sound of running feet and a thud, a gasp of pain and several swear words in French, as a foot clashed with another chair leg, and hair resembling a bird's nest belonging to Lynnette appeared, realising there were enough people dealing with Sarah she went back to bed as Sarah said adamantly, "I know what I saw, it was about my height, blue grey in colour with an Elvis quiff for a fringe." she announced, before heading back to bed.

The following night Melanie was at long last able to go down and visit the panelled room, while the entire house lay still and quiet. She tiptoed down the stairs with Austin following close behind her. Once inside the room with the door firmly closed, Austin climbed up onto a chair having realised he'd see a lot more from there and waited in eager anticipation. Melanie meanwhile having taken a deep breath walked over to the panel in the wall, and stood there for a good ten minutes, gaining enough courage to imitate the same movements Vian had done. Austin was beginning to think she'd lost her nerve, but let out a huge sigh of relief when she finally lifted her hands.

Melanie could feel a slight tingling in her hands as the depictions within the wall began to move and slowly come alive, it was so beautiful, and so vibrant, reminiscent of a two way mirror, revealing a colourful countryside scene, showing a grassy hillside with tall trees covered in tightly compacted flower buds, that were about to open at any moment. In the distance the Orianas and Amarii moons orbited the planet Munastas, while the celestial rings surrounding it were clearly visible. She could experience all the smells, sounds, feelings of everything depicted within the panelling, causing her to wonder, how was it possible?

Nearby a large group of naturally formed blue rocks that had broken through the solid crystallized glass floor, revealed a small opening in the floor. As the sun began to set, casting a final glimmer of sunlight onto the planet's rings and producing a sparkle like never before, the flowers on every tree began to open, flowers that were huge in size, at least a metre wide and within their centres, clusters of seed pods no bigger than walnuts. The sound of popping indicating the seed pods release, was heard. It was a race against time for a successful reseeding, allowing the roots to penetrate the soil. However some were not so lucky, for they are the favourite food of the local inhabitants they call the Zinies, who live in the paradise below ground, a paradise known as Erievna.

Melanie sat on the floor with her arms around her legs watching the picture unfold, as hundreds of flying creatures, no bigger than a tennis ball appeared out of the opening. They had fluffy wings the consistency of frayed candy floss, tiny claw like arms and legs, huge dark brown eyes, and a tiny mouth. They were highly inquisitive, mischievous and very cheeky little creatures, that would on occasion, take the seeded fruits from the hand of any passer-by if they had a desire to. They are a cross between a capuchin monkey and a mongoose only cuter. This was the only time you got to see them above ground, when it was harvest time, which usually lasted for about five days or so. They were acrobatically skilled in flying, enabling them the easy task of capturing the seed pods before they fell to the ground.

Groups of mothers with babes in arms sat close to the opening, teaching their youngsters the art of harvesting the flowers and seed pods. Some of the older children would attempt to capture them, the nearer they got to the ground, making it a type of game or competition. Melanie smiled having seen a dad land near his partner and child, offering his beloved infant a single seed pod to hold for him, and although the seed pod was almost as big as the infant, it would not let go. The infant gazed adoringly at its father with love shining in its eyes, as he once again took the air. Time seemed to fly as Melanie continued to gaze into the panelled wall, but she would not leave until the harvesting had ended, and the area was quiet. Having realised the fact that she had sat there for over 4 hours, with the evidence of it painfully obvious in a numb bottom, she staggered up to bed with Austin following her with a bemused look on his face.

Over the next few days, Melanie and her uncle enjoyed each other's company, with Austin close by. They would talk about the farm, Melanie's adopted parents, Selemie and James her biological parents, and Austin. Taban did feel calmer here and more at peace with Melanie and her mad cap friends, and of course Austin, the terror of the county. But it was during the night-time that Taban feared the most. That was when the creature was most powerful and more difficult to control, it was a constant battle, for the creature within was clever, shrewd and cunning in its methods, but most of all ruthless. It carried within its black heart a deep rooted hatred for Selemie, for leaving them on this hell hole of a planet. In its sick and twisted mind of reasoning, merely existing was not enough, it claimed to have found a way out, a way that would soon change everything, but it would not say any more than that. Taban stood by the window looking out across the early morning sunrise trying not to think of the hellish nightmare that was about to become very real…

CHAPTER TWENTY-ONE

Thursday morning had finally arrived and as hoped, it was going to be a warm sunny day as was the forecast for the whole of the next week. Lynnette was busy preparing a celebratory meal for the evening, while Melanie and Sarah prepared the spare rooms for Edna and her Grandson Max, who would be arriving at the station at about 11.35am according to the travel times, with Edna insisting that they would be making their own way to the house via a taxi.

Max and Edna boarded the train on time, and spent the next five minutes getting comfortable for their long journey, and it wasn't long before Edna had finally drifted off to sleep with her head resting on Max's shoulder. This gave Max an opportune time to allow his thoughts to drift while gazing out of the train window at the passing scenery. He had felt a deep rooted connection to Melanie the moment he saw her, but had never said. He gazed down at his grandmother's sleeping form and smiled, thinking 'She's a crazy old eccentric, with an insane sense of humour' and yet she understood him far more than anyone else ever did, and the fact he would go to the ends of the Earth for the crazy old bat said a lot in his book, and the old girl knew it and quite often exploited it, using it to her own advantage. All the varied and colourful attempts at emotional blackmail she'd used made him chuckle under his breath.

It was the local Vicar he felt sorry for the most, for he was absolutely terrified of her. Max had never seen anyone quite so on edge or nervous whenever he came face to face with her, you'd think he'd come face to face with Satan. 'No wonder he was losing his hair the poor guy' he thought with a chuckle under his breath, yet the one he was looking forward to seeing the most was Austin, Mel's madcap feline, 'He has got to be the weirdest cat on this planet' concluded Max before adding 'Not many cats would sit for hours in front of a TV watching films or computer games whilst eating pork scratchings, what cat does that?' wondered Max, who, having inadvertently gazed deep into Austin's eyes, sensed instinctively that there was more to this cat than just fur, claws and fish breath, concluded Max. He was so absorbed in his own thoughts, he was ignorant of the fact that he was being watched by a group of men sat on the opposite side of the train. Their piercing gaze seemed to penetrate the very core of him, while he unconsciously placed his hand over the scar on his chest, as he slowly with no will of his own, turned his head to find them staring at him. He shifted nervously in his seat thinking 'What the hell are they looking at' opting to ignore them and take in the scenery, while listening to the music on his iPod.

After an hour of train travel a voice on the intercom announced they would be arriving at their destination. Knowing Edna was about to vacate the train the conductor hurried to inform the driver. Once off the train Edna double checked the number of cases she'd brought, which always totalled three. While Max carried a large holdall full of clothes and a backpack for his laptop, which he slung over his shoulder, while brushing the hair out of his blue eyes to take a look around the platform while waiting for Edna. His thoughts were halted suddenly when he noticed a group of passengers offering to help Edna with her luggage. Edna turned to find three pairs of dark almost black coloured eyes staring at her, all with dark brown almost black shoulder length coloured hair, except for one, who had short cropped dark brown hair and a silly looking smile on his face. It took Edna a few seconds to find her voice. "We're heading to the taxi rank, so grab a bag and follow me." she announced with authority, handing each of them a suitcase before marching off through the station, leaving both Tarak and Raan looking at each other with raised eyebrows as a sharp edged voice said, "Stop wasting time and hurry up!" ordered Edna. Vian hurried after this apparent friend of Melanie's with a degree of trepidation. According to Austin's detailed description it must be her, with Max bringing up the rear.

A private hire car was on hand in which Vian and his friends offered Edna and Max a lift as no taxis were available. Edna looked Vian straight in the eye and asked rather boldly, "You're not the bloody mafia or a hit squad are you? Because you'll get nothing from us sonny, so be aware!" she uttered, but accepted the lift anyway and told them the address. "Well! That is a coincidence isn't it Tarak?" said one guy to his friend before adding, "That's our destination as well. Small world isn't it?" claimed Raan, with a cheeky grin as he put an arm around Max's shoulders in a sudden show of buddy-like friendship that made Max feel decidedly on edge, while the only thought on Max's mind was, 'Oh great, this is going to be a seriously weird holiday.' before climbing into the back of the hire car to find two of them sitting on either side of him, as an overly friendly voice said, "I'm Raan, that's Tarak and the other one is Vian. And you are…?" enquired Raan curiously with raised eyebrows.

Max observed them through his long fringe thinking, 'They all have the appearance of professional hit men.' and followed it with an another thought, 'And as for this Raan guy, he seems the most dangerous of the lot, his smile hasn't fooled me one bit.' he concluded noticing the degree of unspoken communication going on between the three strangers, as he reluctantly gave them their names. Vian being the designated driver for the day was as Max predicted, criticised on his driving skills every step of the way by his co-driver Edna. Max pulled out his iPod and before he had a chance to place both ear pieces into his ears they were very quickly snatched out of his hands and popped into the ears of both Tarak and Raan, who turned the music up to a higher setting hoping it would drown out Edna's voice. Max looked from one to the other in amazement and received a sudden hug from Raan who said, "I can see we're going to be great friends Max." and laughed enthusiastically at the thought Tarak had sent him. Max was unconvinced by this idea and thought, 'Yeh right, said the spider to the fly, right before it devoured him.' feeling even more on edge, as Vian received a good telling off for not stopping at a red light for Edna never did. Vian immediately put his foot down hoping to reach Melanie's house in record time, and if he had anything to do with it they would.

They must've broken every world record in driving to finally park outside Melanie's home, and by the time Melanie and her friends had opened the door Edna was heard saying, "With your driving skills sonny, you're definitely not a member of the Mafia, you're one of the bloody goon squad...That was terrible driving...I've seen a blind man do better!" announced Edna, pausing in mid-sentence having seen Melanie, and rushing over to give her one of her special hugs adding, "Melanie my dear, I've brought your friends along who gallantly gave us a lift in their car. Nice boys, but their driving leaves a lot to be desired I can tell you. Now, let me have a look at you, you're looking well", exclaimed Edna beckoning Max over with a wave of her hand to begin introductions to Melanie's friends.

Max took one look at Lynnette and was instantly bowled over by her French accent, and she wasn't too bad on the eye either. Sarah was bubbly and a lot of fun, currently dating a nerdy type called Tristan, and then there was Taban, Melanie's uncle, who, while standing in the back ground sent out vibes that made Hannibal Lector seem like a pussy cat. The vibes Max got from him were not good, not good at all, from the moment he looked into his cold dark eyes, his heart began to race out of control, and he had difficulty breathing as Taban's presence here frightened the hell out of him. His inner voice was urging him to run, leave now, and get away, but the loyalty he had for Edna forced him to stay. Austin was to Max's disappointment not here, and when asked where he was, Melanie suggested he was out chasing the local wild life, when in actual fact, he was gazing down at them from the upstairs landing, having noticed the look of fear in the boys eyes when they saw Taban.

Melanie turned to Max saying, "It's good to see you again Max, I hope you'll enjoy your time here with us. How are your friends?" she asked curiously, surprising Max who replied, "Oh Ziggy and Darren are ok. Jay's still working on his Cybernetics degree, so we don't see much of him these days." he said, glancing at Vian and his friends out of the corner of his eye through his long fringe. Max's enthusiasm for his friends lit up his face, and Melanie was happy to see it as she suddenly remembered the gig. "Oh, I've just remembered. How was the Slapping Sallies gig? It must've been great!" she asked excitedly, knowing how good the rock band was.

Max's body language said it all as he replied, "Oh man!! They were out of this world. They're one of the hottest rock bands this side of the Solar system. Ziggy's got the hots for the bass guitarist, and got a slap in the face when he said she could strum his guitar any time." explained Max as both he and Melanie laugh at his friends' expense. Raan nudged Tarak in the ribs giving him a playful wink, showing him the images he'd snatched from Max's memory, showing all the fun they could have at one of these live gigs, causing Tarak to unceremoniously shake his head, knowing only too well what Raan was thinking. Edna's fascination was caught by the unusual ornate light fittings and carved staircase, which gave Melanie the opportunity to offer Edna and Max a brief tour of the house. Alone at last, Max went to lie on his bed, hoping that the headaches he suffered on a daily basis, wouldn't be as bad as they usually were, listening to Melanie's excitable chatter to Edna before making her way back down the stairs, almost bumping into Vian in the process who had been waiting for her for what felt like an age.

How long they stood there gazing into each other's eyes, before she had the courage to pull away she didn't know. "I was beginning to think you'd decided to stay away, or is it my uncle's sudden arrival here that's brought you back?" she asked with a steely glint in her eye. Vian knew Melanie better than she thought he did, and so decided to lighten the mood a little. He held her gaze and said while leaning against the banister rail, "You needed time, time to accept what is real and honest. Time to accept who and what you are, I thought a mere two days were not long enough. You've attempted to open the vortex in the panelled room and I'm glad of that. This tells me, you're accepting the truth about yourself, although, I suspect you've always known, deep down in your heart who you really are. But there is still yet more to discover." he suggested truthfully. But before Melanie could reply, Vian covered her lips with the tips of his fingers saying, "Now isn't the time, you'll find out soon enough." he said, and promptly pulled her into his arms and kissed her, having sensed Edna's desire to come down to the kitchen for a much needed cup of tea. Melanie was totally unprepared for Vian's sudden passionate embrace, giving him the opportunity to delve deep into her memories of the last few weeks, eager to see everything she had seen, and be a part of what she had experienced, as the sound of Sarah's voice from within the kitchen saying, "Austin you rat, you're a thorn in my side! You know that don't you? If I find out Mel's been feeding you extra food the moment our back's turned, there'll be trouble, and get off the bloody table, go on, get down you useless hairy lump." ordered Sarah. Vian released Melanie's lips and let out a heavy sigh of frustration, at the precise moment that Edna appeared at the top of the stairs, and wasted very little time in commenting, "Oh!...I'm sorry dears, have I interrupted a romantic interlude between two star crossed lovers?" said Edna cheekily, before adding, "Melanie Rose you little devil, you never said a word about having a boyfriend hidden away down here. Well that's nice I'm pleased for you, really I am, although I think you could've done far better than him dear, although beggars can't be choosers I suppose, and on the plus side he's no strain on the eye is he?" she said, turning to face Vian as her mood changed suddenly, "Let me tell you something buster, if I find out you've hurt my angel in any way, I'll hunt you down like the dog you are, ok?" she said, and then tapped him gently on the shoulder, before heading off in search of a pot of tea.

Melanie's shocked gaze followed her friend's departure, but the gentle touch of Vian's hand stroking the side of her face caught her attention, she turned her head to find Vian looking at her in a way that made her toes curl, knowing he had the ability to break through all the barriers protecting her fragile heart, and that terrified her. Vian could sense her unease and whispered, "Be calm my beloved. Be calm." he uttered as her heart began to relax adding, "You're friends truly love you, and I'm glad." he said while leading her towards the kitchen having sensed her need for a distraction.

CHAPTER TWENTY-TWO

Taban stood at the top of the stairs watching Vian and his niece leave, as Max exited his room, and paused having seen Taban, asking rather cautiously, "Are you heading down stairs as well?" he asked, making sure to avoid any eye contact with this seriously weird uncle of Mel's. While Taban having sensed the boy's unease thought it best to take things slowly, after all, it's not every day you finally get to meet your own destiny, in the form of a young boy.

A boy whose path had crossed his only once before. Memories of that fearful night came flooding back like an adrenalin rush, increasing the frenzied, overpowering, rush of emotions, emotions he had tried so hard to control, that even now, through the overwhelming torrents of emotional warfare, Taban could still sense the hurt in the boy's heart, a heart that was crying out for love, a love that had died in a supposed car crash, all those years ago, back when Taban tried to save both his mother and her unborn child. Both felt the deep inherent connection between them, but the boy hadn't recognised it for what it was. It was a connection Taban had hoped would never see the light of day, for the boy's sake at least, but Taban knew like everyone else that fate can be a strange and unpredictable thing.

The following day, as predicted by the cheerful weather man, was turning out to be a good one. Everyone decided to go to the beach and according to Edna, she was to drive, due to Vivian's inept driving skills, "My name is Vian." he corrected coolly, while Max and Raan laugh at his expense. With the food Lynnette had so lovingly prepared securely placed under one of the seats, Edna shouted impatiently from behind the driver's seat, "Do hurry up, we're wasting daylight here!" looking like a retired spinster's version of a Hollywood starlet, wearing a candy floss pink coloured outfit and sunglasses, with a matching bow on her walking stick. Max having already climbed into the car was busy glancing through his music list on his iPod, with his fringe hanging over his eyes hiding the dark circles, having spent most of the previous night wrestling with his headaches, he didn't see the point of dressing up and so wore his usual, a pair of dark cargo jeans, trainers, a favourite top with a trendy design on the front and a hoodie. Sitting on either side of him were Raan and Melanie's uncle Taban, with Raan being his usual cheeky over the top self, listening to Max's music with his arm around Max's shoulders, swaying from side to side to the music. Max laughed under his breath thinking 'This guy is seriously weird' but just went along with it.

Edna watched her Grandson through the rear view mirror and smiled, having realised from past experience, how rare it was to hear Max laugh. She thought back to when he first arrived on her door step four years ago, claiming to be her grandson. It was one Wednesday morning, when a barely heard knock sounded on her front door and there stood Max, quiet, withdrawn and hesitant, Edna soon changed all that. When Edna realised the possibilities that he could very well be her grandson, it was like a gift from heaven, so far he had told her very little of his life in foster homes and orphanages, but what little he did say, made her heart ache for him. She didn't care if Max was or wasn't her true blood kin, for she had over a short period of time, grown to love him anyway.

Meanwhile sitting in the passenger seat next to Edna, Tarak was trying desperately to focus on anything other than Edna's ceaseless nattering, he'd even put up with Raan, who on a daily basis had him questioning 'What had gone wrong? Where had the fun filled attitude come from? None of the others had it, so why Raan?' Pondered Tarak puzzlingly whilst gazing out of the car widow wishing he was anywhere else but here. Edna glanced across at Tarak saying, "Now watch and learn Terry, I'll show you how you should drive, I learned during the war, back then you had to learn quick, especially when you're driving a tank." she admitted casually. It had taken Tarak a few seconds to realise the old girls error concerning his name, leaving him wondering what a tank was. As Vian exited the house carrying Austin in his cat carrier closely followed by Melanie, who'd won the argument half an hour earlier about bringing Austin along. She climbed on board, sat next to Vian at the back of the car nearest the window with Austin's cat carrier securely strapped in, and announced they were ready.

Everyone looked uneasy as Edna straightened her shoulders, adjusted her hat and sunglasses and announced with glee, as her foot hit the accelerator pedal. "Hang onto your knicker elastic kids, this could get rough." The multi carrier took off as if the devil himself was after it. Austin was catapulted to the rear of the cage suffering all the effects you'd normally feel in a wind tunnel at NASA while everyone else held onto any part of the main structure of the vehicle they could, until Edna applied the brakes, sending out a billowing dust cloud at the edge of a narrow foot path. After several minutes of extreme nausea, while the driver, having opened the door, jumped out buzzing with energy and vitality a lot would envy, the other passengers felt the complete opposite.

If an alien could feel travel sick then more than one of them was suffering with it now, Austin looked dazed and slightly shell shocked, as he was helped out of the cage by Melanie who likewise, looked a little pale. Once out of the cage Austin sat on the grassy bank gathering what was left of his wits, as the world continued to spin, thinking 'Never again is that bloody woman getting behind the steering wheel of a car. I'll kill her first and leave her body at the side of the road to rot, better yet, I'll transform and give her a bloody heart attack the crazy old trout but, knowing Edna, she'd think it was hunting season and come after me' he thought, giving the old girl the evil eye, as she seemed eager to be off, but the rest of the group were not so eager. It had taken them a good few minutes to gather both their wits and the supplies needed before heading off to the beach. Austin went on ahead of them to scout the area, when he heard Edna saying, "If you drop that box Ron, I'll hit you with my walking stick!" as another voice replied "My name is Raan not Ron" and Edna's high pitched voice announced, "That's what I said!!" before marching off ahead of them. Max laughed thinking, 'I was right, this is going to be one freaked out holiday."

They were over half way down the narrow over grown lane, when a wild rabbit shot out in front of Lynnette and Melanie, with Austin in hot pursuit not realising until it was too late, that he was on a direct collision with Lynnette, or to be more accurate her legs, and she landed in a ditch on her backside. She eventually staggered to her feet saying, "One day, cherie, I will microwave your cat. I warn you now!" she promised while attempting to walk with Max's guiding hand. Melanie attempted a smile as Taban asked, "Do things like that happen often?" he asked curiously, as Melanie replied, "All the time, Austin takes great pleasure in playing tricks on people. The problem is, it can get him into trouble, but he's harmless really." explained Melanie, trying to sound believable. Then as if by magic, the area opened up to reveal a secluded beach, partly made up of sand and pebbles, with a thick weather-worn set of wooden steps cut into the side of the rock face, allowing easy access to the sand, sea and a small wooden hut, nestled against a sheltered part of the cliff face.

Having already reached the bottom step with Austin close behind her Edna watched while Sarah and Tristan quickly removed their clothes, leaving behind a trail all the way down the steps. Melanie laughed having witnessed Tristan grab hold of Sarah and toss her into the sea. Austin climbed onto the roof of the hut and kept a close eye on the seagulls or as he would call them 'flying rats'. Edna meanwhile went to investigate the interior of the rickety and slightly dilapidated wooden hut, and within minutes, she came out carrying a stack of deck chairs and shouted, "Instead of looking like a bucket load of fish out of water, make your selves useful for goodness sake." "Anyone would think you'd never seen a bloody beach before!" she said to Vian, Raan and the others, noticing Taban slowly making his way across the sand to where her grandson Max was leaning against a large boulder listening to his music. Max looked up in surprise as a shadow was cast over him and after a moment's hesitation moved over a little, allowing Taban the opportunity to sit down.

At the opposite end of the beach Melanie had persuaded Lynnette to change into her beach wear and was at present racing her to the sea where all the fun was happening. A short distance away a cautiously subdued voice said, "I wouldn't want to say anything out of turn at this sensitive moment, but you have to admit that Melanie Rose Trevern is a surprise to us all isn't she?" admitted Raan, holding back a grin as his and four other sets of eyes follow every move Melanie and Lynnette make, as they race across the sand laughing hysterically, before Raan himself darted off into the beach hut.

Having abandoned his music Max cautiously made his way to the sea shore to sit on a dry patch of sand to watch the live show. Taban found it highly amusing the images racing through the boys adolescent mind, most of which, were obviously not for the faint hearted 'Should a boy so young have such thoughts about a woman?' wondered Taban with a slight blush to his cheeks. Raan having hurried up to his friends saying, "I'm enjoying our holiday. You have so much fun here." he said heading off towards the sea, wearing what appeared to be a pair of lime green swimming trunks and a shocking pink coloured swimming cap he had stolen out of Sarah's bag, to keep his hair dry. Taban uttered, "Next time, I suggest you leave your friend at home." and went to get a small bottle of still water from the food boxes. Raan grabbed hold of Melanie and tossed her playfully over his shoulder into the sea. Austin watched from the roof of the beach hut, making a vain attempt to hide his laughter, having witnessed Raan in a shocking pink and green outfit, while Edna choked on her tea after the sudden flash of florescent pink and green flew past her on what was to be an unforgettable day out at the beach for everyone.

CHAPTER TWENTY-THREE

The following morning over a nutritious breakfast, Sarah's over-enthusiastic voice was educating her friend on a topic close to her heart, "Did you know, that when we look at the sunlight we're actually seeing it eight minutes in the past? Oh! And do you realise that if I click my fingers like this, the light would've circled the Earth seven times, it makes you think doesn't it, and it's a well-known fact that we're all made from the fragments of dying stars or more accurately nuclear waste, it's in our genetic makeup" commented Sarah wisely, as she lifted up her cup for another top up from Melanie, whose turn it was to be mother. Melanie let in a breath of air. "Sarah, don't you think it's a little too early in the day for a lesson in astrophysics? It is for me. I'm still recovering from our day out yesterday." admitted Mel, Sarah looked at her best friend feeling a little hurt and dejected. "Don't you find it at all interesting? I do. I never realised how small and insignificant I'd feel, in comparison to our little spot in space, it puts it all in bigger perspective." she uttered, having realised she carried starlight inside her.

Melanie smiled at the look of love emanating from her friend's face, knowing it wasn't space dust she was interested in, it was Tristan. "I do find it interesting Sal, and have done in all our meal times, but not now ok?" asked Melanie, before adding, "Where is Tristan this morning? I haven't seen him." she said, sitting opposite her friend at the table. Sarah's face fell as she replied "He had to go back to the Royal Observatory in Edinburgh, he couldn't have any more time off, but the good news is that I'm going to visit him next weekend." Melanie nodded her head while eating her cereal. Just then the kitchen door opened and in staggered Max still half asleep, asking for food, and hot on his heels was Edna, who mumbled a good morning before heading straight for the tea pot and her pack of ultra-strong breakfast tea, and wouldn't say any more until she swallowed a couple of sips, obviously Edna wasn't a morning person. Sarah glanced in Max's direction asking curiously, "Did you enjoy the day at the beach yesterday Max?" while Melanie prepared his and Edna's cooked breakfast. Max nodded his head saying, "It was interesting." and left it there. Edna having heard this reply, lifted her head out of her half-filled cup of tea and said "Interesting, that's not what I'd call it. I have to say, some of your new friends are odd, very odd, but according to my grandson, I shouldn't be too judgemental of other people. I should accept the world for what it is." she claimed, still not quite believing it.

Melanie and Sarah both looked at Max with raised eyebrows, amazed that he could be so forward thinking, when a voice from the doorway added, "I agree with Max…He has a very wise head on a pair of young shoulders wouldn't you say". Everyone turned to find Taban standing directly behind Max, with his hands resting on his shoulders. Max glanced nervously over his shoulder having felt the hands tighten briefly, before Taban removed them to sit opposite the boy, having sensed the boys unease at his presence.

Edna, having inadvertently caught Taban's gaze for just a brief moment, witnessed something cold, unsympathetic and cruel emanating from the very depths of his soul, causing her to have second thoughts about letting Max stay. She watched Taban take an unusual interest in the list of music Max had on his iPod, and listened to the comments he made about Max's taste in music, which resulted in her grandson laughing. A voice interrupted her worried concentration. "Are you alright Edna?" asked Sarah full of concern, having noticed the colour drain from Edna's face. Edna cleared her throat. "Fine, just fine." she replied whilst taking several sips of her tea, when in truth, she wasn't fine at all, as a sudden feeling of foreboding settled in the pit of her stomach, causing her to lose what little appetite she had as breakfast arrived.

The rest of the day was quiet, everyone doing their own thing, but staying close to the house. Sarah and Lynnette thought it a good idea to teach Max some basic aerobics in the back garden while the sun was out, forcing him away from his precious laptop and iPlayer, and even though he tried every trick in the book to get out of it. He eventually lost the battle, but loved every minute of it, after seeing the tight fitting outfit Lynnette had on which left nothing to the imagination. He did not realise that the whole thing had been a ruse to get him out of the way while Mel and Edna planned his birthday surprise, with a reluctant Tarak forced to act as look out from behind a curtain in one of the upstairs windows only...

Tarak was not the only one watching Max, for at the far end of the upstairs landing, hidden within the shadows by a window stood a solitary figure, observing Max with a rapt intent as Max suddenly fell over, in a vain attempt to copy an aerobic move the girls had performed. While our secret observer remained unseen by everyone, apart from Austin, who could sense its presence and thought it prudent to watch from his vantage point in the trees, close enough to witness the figure moving away, after Austin's attempt to telepathically link with it had failed. The ability to block a watcher was rare; Austin knew you had to be powerful. Just then the patio doors opened and out walked Melanie wearing one of her aerobics outfits hoping to join in on the fun. She gave Sarah and Lynnette a sly wink, indicating that everything had been completed satisfactorily, before sitting opposite Max facing the house, listening to Edna moving around in the kitchen, banging the odd pot and pan preparing the dinner, announcing to all who listened that she was going to do Max's favourite, a medium chilli with rice and flat bread, complete with a side salad.

Raan was busy sifting through other people's wardrobes looking for something to wear, and was presently in Max's room admiring his varied T shirt collection, and found the perfect one to wear. Within minutes he flew out of the patio doors with an air of the theatrics, wearing a T shirt saying 'EVEN ON A BAD DAY I AM WAY COOLER- on the front and on the back it had -THAN YOU! and wore a bandana around his head, a pair of sunglasses and cargo pants shouting, "Hey guys!" while Edna, who was in the process of setting up the table on the patio, damn near dropped the tray of wine glasses, having seen what greeted, her asking, "What are you supposed to be? May I ask, because I sure as hell don't know!" stated Edna, looking him up and down over the rim of her glasses, while slowly shaking her head.

Meanwhile back on the work-out mats Melanie and friends looked on in amazement, as Raan hurried across the lawn shouting, "I'm here at last guys!" Austin looked stunned, 'What the...Hell, is he wearing?' he wondered, as Max, having looked over his shoulder, recognised his T shirt and rose to his feet saying, "Hey! Wait a sec that's…" but his protest was cut short when Raan replied in an overly friendly tone, "Ah.... here he is, the kindest person I have ever known; for lending me this outfit, except for the sunglasses and bandana of course." "I found them in one of the other rooms." announced Raan with a smile, before giving Max a bracing hug around the shoulders, adding, "From now on, I will class you as my honorary friend, isn't that great!" But before Max could respond, Raan held up his hand saying, "No, you don't have to thank me Max, we're friends after all." and walked away. Edna snorted in disgust saying, while her grandson stared open mouthed, "Shout everyone for dinner please, somebody!" as Raan, Max, Lynnette and Melanie rushed towards the table and Austin hid under the table licking his lips thinking, 'I wonder if there will be any leftovers?"

CHAPTER TWENTY-FOUR

Later that same evening, as the Grandfather clock chimed the hour of 2am, Melanie was on one of her nightly visits to the panelled room and hot on her heals was Austin. They entered the room and moved to the opposite end of the panelling, which surprised Austin. Until now, she had only ever opened the same panel Vian had opened, but not tonight, tonight she felt bolder, more daring. She waved her hand across the panel in the far corner of the room and to her surprise it opened, giving her access to a stack of hidden shelves, and on one of the shelves were several wrapped parcels, two Orbs, a sealed Box made of Crystal with symbolic writing embellished on it. Melanie reached out a tentative hand for the biggest package and with care, took it over to the small sofa by the window, and opened the crystal box to find a book, and not just any book, it was a diary. She opened the book with Austin sitting by her side, and on the very first page were the words written in gold leaf saying:

FOR OUR PRECIOUS DAUGHTER MELANIE ROSE

Her hands shook as her fingers traced the words written in gold, while her heart beat faster than a speeding freight train, taking her a few minutes to pluck up the nerve to turn the page, for fear of what she may find. Staring back at her in full glorious colour, were photographs of her parents, who stood arm in arm outside the front door of this very house, 'They look so happy' thought Melanie, tracing the outline of their faces with her fingertips. "Now I know what my parents look like, especially my mother, I've always wondered." she admitted to Austin, who gazed at the photograph with a multitude of memories rushing through his mind, and an unbearable ache in his heart. He looked up at Melanie having heard her say admiringly, "She was truly beautiful don't you think?" Austin's answer was to rub his head against her arm, as she continued to turn the pages one at a time, finding more photos of her parents, plus the occasional poem and verse of love on the opposite page. Along with photos of George, Charlie, her uncle Taban and a woman she'd never seen before, concluding it had to be Roselyn, her biological grandmother. One photograph had her father pulling faces at her mother causing Melanie to smile even though her heart was aching.

The last photo showed her father James, attempting to carry a very pregnant Selemie in his arms, and playing the fool. This particular photo was the saddest of all for Melanie, for it was immediately after this during her birth that both her parents died. Melanie turned the page once again and found two verses written by her father which read:

I LOVE THE WAY

I love the way a single kiss can make our souls take flight and your eyes light up, whenever you're close to me.

I love the way you smile and two dimples appear, for me and me alone, while the colours in your hair come alive, whenever it's touched by the warm sunlight.

I love the way you are when the very first flowers appear at the start of spring, announcing it as a truly magical event.

I love the way you mystify me on a daily basis, and you're my very own mystery, that I have yet to solve.

I love the way you've changed my life around, giving it meaning and purpose. But most of all, I love knowing that you have been waiting throughout time itself for me, and me alone.

James

Austin moved closer to Melanie giving what comfort he could, having seen her wipe away her tears, before she was able to read the second love letter from her father which read:

MY SELI

I've managed to capture a rare speck of starlight that had fallen from the skies above, and hold it close to my heart, her name is Selemie.

I don't deserve this rare jewel that has found its way to me, and yet I know, I will treasure her always.

She is more precious than anything the whole of creation can bestow, for she is a vital part of me. She is my every breath, my beating heart, my absolute.

She is my reason for living, without her, I am nothing. I feel empty inside when we're apart. I feel soulless and lost without her, for she is the better part of me.

We will have a lifetime together, here on Earth or in our next life and beyond, for we were meant to be.

Fate brought our hearts together, and it will be fate that keeps us whole for all time and beyond....

My beloved Seli,

James

Melanie could barely see through the flood of tears that fell on the pages of the book. To love someone so deeply, so absolutely, as her parents had done, was her undoing, 'If the letters are anything to go by, it must've been a love so powerful, so strong that surely, it controlled you, as a person' thought Melanie with conviction.

For within the letters from her parents Melanie could hear the controlling influence in their relationship. 'It sounds as if it's a condition you need a rehab clinic for, would this happen to me and Vian? Is it happening now?' Melanie wondered turning the pages, showing yet more photos. One was of her mother in the latter stages of pregnancy looking tired and ill, with concern etched on her father's face, and underneath each photograph, a few lines were written undoubtedly by her father. She knew it was her father who had written them for he stated the fact that her mother struggled to write the English word, but she had in due course succeeded, for she found a solitary letter written by her, with hand drawn symbolisms around the edge. Austin having seen this remembered that 'Selemie adored the symbol of love we use, the red painted love heart' as he read the letter written by Selemie and James, shortly before they died. It read:

WISHES

Our Daughter, so tiny and new is sleeping now as I write this letter. I know my time is near, though I wish it was not.

To watch her grow, smile, laugh and play would be a cherished thing indeed.

To tell her stories, tell her of her family history, her heritage and loved ones is a wish not granted me.

We leave her here, not alone, for our truest friend is near, though she'll not know it yet. Never is there a friend more loved by us than he.

My heart tells me we should take her with us, but that could never be, for she will be needed here. I know this to be true.

Time is a thing of mystery, and it will show her all. It will open the gates of her mind where the secrets, memories and love from her past are kept.

She will I think, understand in the end.

Austin turned his head away to hide a single tear that fell from the corner of his eye, landing on the soft upholstered seat he now sat on. He could hear Melanie's thoughts; sense her feelings and emotions, which would undoubtedly keep her awake throughout the rest of the night. He was in truth, unsure whether it had been a good or a bad thing, her finding this book. But he was glad however, of one thing, that she now had images of her parents and their life together, but at the same time cursing them, for it had made things far more complicated. Austin let out a huge sigh of disappointment and regret, for even though he loved James and Selemie, he was in fact angry, for his job had now become a lot harder, 'What is it the people on this planet say, one step forward and two steps back, it feels more like fifty two' he thought angrily. Melanie heard Austin sigh and decided it was time to go back to bed, taking the book with her saying, "Come on Austin, let's go to bed." "I'm a little tired now" she admitted while picking him up and make her way back to her bedroom.

She could feel him rubbing his head against her neck in that loving gentle way, showing her he was there for her, and that he loved her. It reminded her of the many hundreds of times he used to be the same loving jester when she was a little girl, and as she turned her head to place a kiss on his head, she whispered, "I love you too, my Austin." as Austin gazed up at her thinking, 'Austin, you sentimental old fool, you're doing it again, you're getting too soft in your old age. It must be the climate or something.' he concluded half-heartedly, as he snuggled up to Melanie in bed watching as her eyes began to droop and within minutes she was fast asleep.

Austin tiptoed up to the book, closed it with his paw and gripped it between his teeth, then place it on the pillow next to hers, knowing she would look for it as soon as she awoke. Then with a heavy heart Austin hopped off the bed and slowly made his way across the room towards the patio doors, that lay open enough for the night air to flow in, and there he sat gazing up at the stars in the night sky, knowing he had plenty to think about, and plenty of memories to look through, for sleep was the last thing on Austin's mind right now. Once again, he let out a heavy sigh, while looking over his shoulder at his charge, before turning back to look up at the stars once again. Melanie having been asleep for about an hour, before he eventually made his way back onto the bed, as once again she began to dream:

CHAPTER TWENTY-FIVE

<u>*Memories*</u>

A selection of soft music played at the opposite end of the complex as crowds of people began to gather, before heading towards the music. Above her head Melanie could see the Orianas and Amarii moons in full colour, nestling against the all familiar sight of a pink, mauve and lilac tinted sky, with streaks of yellow speckled clouds strewn across it. 'What a beautiful place' thought Melanie as she suddenly found herself amongst, what appeared to be a garden party of some sort, noticing Taban as a young man, who having seen his mother rushed over to speak to her, and join hands in a private conversation saying, "I would like to leave and continue with my studies, I'm at a crucial stage right now. Would you allow me?" he asked hopefully, Amarah smiled at her son who was now a lot taller than her and replied, "Yes you can go.", he gave his mother a loving embrace before hurrying off to his science lab to study, as a huge number of girls observed him leave, whilst whispering to each other as girls do, but he didn't seem to notice.

Amarah spent several minutes greeting friends, neighbours and people she knew before spotting Tenzin her husband with their two daughters Selemie and adorable two year old Arisiisafely nestled in the arms of her father, who was attempting to teach her the art of communicating with her palms. But the little angel would have none of it, indicating that she would rather hit him with her hand instead, for it was more fun, Selemie was now a beautiful young girl who was trying in vain to hide her laughter, even the ever faithful Jeeves had to look skywards and smiled, knowing how much of a handful Arisii has been from the very moment she had arrived.

It was obvious to Melanie that, out of all the children born of Tenzin and Amarah he liked Arisii more. Tenzin spotted Amarah approaching and he visibly relaxed, as she relieved him of their youngest daughter Arisii for a while, before moving over to a soft patch of grass intermingled with clusters of lemon flowers. Amarah sat Arisii next to her on the grass, allowing her the chance to play happily with the flowers before saying goodbye to Selemie, who headed off to join the other dancers with the group of other girls her age. It was only then that Melanie noticed them wearing a type of costume, with clusters of flowers just above their ears. The costumes were made of soft draped fabrics that shimmered softly in the sunlight. Every member of the group, held an Orb in the palm of their hand, which seemed to sparkle a delicate soft lilac, resembling that of an expensively rare jewel about the size of a hens egg, and hanging around their waists was a belt, of similar colour to that of the Orb.

Everyone grew quiet while each Orb was placed in the centre of their forehead. On immediate contact with the skin, it suddenly transformed, moulding itself to the users face becoming a beautifully designed mask, covering the whole face. Arisii looked up shouting her sister's name at the top of her voice, waving a flower in the air, halting the proceedings. Selemie wasn't the least bit concerned about the fact that her baby sister was holding up an all-important event, forcing her to leave the group and rush over to her family, to accept the gift of a single flower from Arisii. Selemie gave her little sister a brief kiss before tucking the flower into her belt and rushing back to the group, which was waiting patiently for her return.

Once in position with the other dancers, Selemie gave Arisii a quick wave, as the music started. Arisii looked up at her mother full of smiles, before turning back to watch her sister dance, clapping her hands throughout the entire show. The dance was a celebration of sorts, a graceful happy dance, filled with the joys of being alive, performed every two earth years of our calendar. Each dancer performed with the grace, elegance and poise of a professional ballet dancer, each one gliding effortlessly around her partner, twirling, rotating, weaving around each other from one end of the clearing to the other, before repeating the dance, with their palms touching, as they glided around each other. Around their feet were thousands of freshly picked flower petals of various colours that without any warning, lifted off the ground to slowly rotate around the dancers, to the rhythmic sound of the music, shielding the dancers from the audience.

It was an enchanting vision of beauty, almost hypnotic. Even Arisii sat still long enough to watch her big sister dance, rocking to and fro to the soft music. Nearby a group of children attempted to copy the dance, each child wearing their own make shift mask while they danced. Selemie and the rest of the dancers moved faster, as the scattering of flower petals rose higher and higher before eventually disappearing. When the music stopped they, with a press their fingers to the forehead, deactivated the face mask. Selemie then offered it to Arisii to play with, who began filling it with flowers, grass and anything else she could get her dainty little hands on. Selemie rewarded her baby sister by saying, "You are the smartest little sister on the planet." earning her a sloppy kiss from Arisii while she continued to fill the face mask with treasures, before climbing into the arms of the watcher and falling asleep, before heading home...

CHAPTER TWENTY-SIX

When Melanie returned to the real world with the sound of bird song drifting in through the patio doors, she slowly opened her eyes to find Austin gazing down at her, waiting for his usual few minutes play before breakfast, for even a top ranking watcher has to have a little fun. Melanie noticed the diary resting on the pillow next to her and sat up, eager to look through the book left to her by her parents. For Melanie, the diary was helping her to understand her biological parents a little more.

She examined every photograph in great detail, tracing each one of them with her fingers as if, by doing this, it would help her commit them all to memory. She was at last, able to read the letters her father wrote without bursting into a flood of tears. She could hear her friends waking up as she turned yet another page, showing a photograph of her parents standing with their arms around each other, outside the local church in the village on their wedding day. 'They look so happy together' concluded Mel, as she lovingly traced their images with her fingers.

It was through this close examination that she noticed an all too familiar figure standing alongside them, realising deep down in her heart that it was him, she was sure of it, 'It was Austin!' she concluded before tucking a strand of hair behind her ear, hoping she wasn't seeing things, 'No! It's impossible, it can't be him' thought Melanie bringing the book closer for a better look. The same look, the same glint in his eye, the same curl of his upper lip when he got a little frustrated, it was definitely her Austin. But the next thought to enter her mind was, 'How old is Austin? It's impossible for a cat to live that long, no normal cat, that's for sure' she concluded while examining the photograph more closely.

It was then that realisation hit her, and hit her hard as she thought 'He's an alien, like my mother! Did he come with them? Of course he came with them you silly thing, think rationally for goodness sake' she reprimanded herself silently, as she cautiously lifted her head to look Austin straight in the eye, as if for the very first time, and likewise he stared right back at her, with a look of complete understanding, almost as if he knew what was going through her mind. Time stretched like an elastic band before she dare lift her hand to gently touch the side of Austin's small cat like face, but at the last minute decided not to, asking, "Who are you, who are you really Austin? I thought I knew you, but I don't know you, do I? Should I be afraid? Although, if you were set on hurting me you would've had better opportunities before now, nevertheless that doesn't stop me from being a little uneasy." explained Melanie calmly, while her heart was at the point of giving out.

Austin gazed long and hard at the photograph, hoping he'd somehow find an answer to the problem he now faced and thought rationally 'Well, Austin old pal, the time has come. It's now or never', he concluded as he turned, hopped off the bed with the morning sunlight beaming in through the patio doors, and closed his eyes, before transforming into his true self, right in front of her. Stunned silence weighed heavy for a good few minutes, while Melanie recognised him for who he was, as all of a sudden, she went cold with shock and started shivering.

Austin was by her side within an instant, holding what appeared to be a glass, containing a shot of whiskey. "Have a bit of this, apparently it's good for shock." he claimed calmly, cupping the back of her head, forcing it back and pouring the whole lot of it down her throat, before she could even ask how he got the glass of alcohol without leaving her room. The sudden burning at the back of her throat caused her eyes to water, as a bout of coughing ensued for several minutes, while the book from her parents lay forgotten on the bed beside her and she attempted to say, "Who...Um, are you, exactly Austin? What should I call you? I... I don't even know where to begin…" she admitted, as she impulsively got to her knees in front of him to look at him, before lifting her hand to gently touch the side of his face, noticing his fringe and impulsively flicking it. She remembered some of the special moments in her dreams that involved Austin, before sitting back on her heels.

She cradled one of his hands in hers, taking in the soft blue/ grey coloured skin and fur, while tracing the long black pointed finger nails with one of her own before letting it go, to slowly lift her eyes saying, "I know you're still my Austin and that you care for me, otherwise you would not be here…Would you? But I have to ask, would you have stayed with me voluntarily, if you had not been asked?". Austin having never taken his eyes from hers replied, "Without hesitation!" and with that reply, Melanie burst into tears. Austin didn't know what to expect once she knew the truth, but it certainly wasn't this, a sobbing fragile creature, he instinctively cradled in his arms without hesitation, rocking her to and fro whilst stroking her hair and whispering words of comfort in her ear, having seen Melanie's adopted parents do it, hearing her mumble the words, "You never left me." she uttered with a heart breaking conviction, as Austin pulled her closer to him, letting her know in his own sweet way that he would always be there for her.

Melanie could feel the sudden influx of warmth his wings had generated flowing through her, remembering a moment in her dream when, he had done the very same thing to a little girl called Arisii, the thought of which, produced a laugh as she hugged him a little tighter, as Austin thought, 'Now all I have to do is hope her friends take it just as well, while at the same time, keep it from the rest of the human race, it shouldn't be too difficult.' he said unconvincingly. Melanie pulled away long enough for her to wipe away the tears clinging to Austin's fur, laughing guiltily saying, "I am forever soaking people with my tears, it's pathetic really." Austin grabbed her hand. "It doesn't matter. My body heat will dry it soon enough, what I would like you to do however, is get back into bed and then we will talk for a little while." instructed Austin gently, yet firmly.

Melanie thought to argue the point, but one look at his face was enough to change her mind, he dragged a soft upholstered chair closer to the bed, and got comfortable, and knew exactly where to start. Having interlocked his fingers across his chest Austin began his story. "We had not long arrived here on this planet when your parents met, by accident, at a place called the Observatory in Edinburgh. Selemie's childlike curiosity was endless when it came to your little planet, she loved it, and as for your parents: the moment their eyes met, we all felt it, it was as if a bolt of lightning had suddenly struck all of us. I remember the day very well; little did I realise, that from that moment on our lives were going to change dramatically.

"Throughout your parent's somewhat unique relationship, it was Taban your uncle, who was suffering the most, we all of us knew of the torment he was being subjected to every hour of every day, being your mother's twin, but we could do nothing, only your mother had the power to make such a decision. Twins on our planet are seldom born, because of their abnormally strong connection to one another, none of them can ever perform or go through a bonding ceremony, or have children. Although, to give Taban credit, he tried hiding the consequences of this relationship remarkably well, we knew the misery and pain he suffered with on a daily basis, but like us, he could do nothing once the relationship had developed and that worried us greatly. Eventually your uncle's life had become so tortured and unbearable, that ultimately, he started to keep his own council, and isolated himself from us. For the first time in my life, I was afraid, afraid for both him and us." he confessed uneasily, as the memory of that time brought beads of sweat to his forehead.

Austin paused for a brief moment before continuing his tale saying, "Selemie having felt this, could no longer allow her twin to suffer, and had decided to leave your father and her life here and go back home with her twin, when something unexpected happened, something that changed everything, something so monumental in our eyes that even now, I still cannot believe it, and that was you Melanie. She was going to have a baby. The moment your uncle detected your imminent arrival, he did the unthinkable, he broke all contact with your mother and disappeared. How he survived on this planet without his twin I do not know. How he managed to break the connection between him and your mother is a mystery to all of us. Even I have to admit, that the love your parents had for each other was unique and special." admitted Austin.

"Eventually over a short space of time we gathered some trustworthy friends, two of whom were George and Charlie, before moving down here. Selemie had fallen in love with not only the house but the valley and the people as well. Charlie allowed your mother to pretty much do what she wanted with the house, and I think your mother loved that bit the most. I have to confess to the fact that, as soon as I saw your father I didn't think too well of him, but he did love your mother." confessed Austin.

He paused before adding "Apparently having chosen not to join the family firm, his family practically disowned him because of it. All except his batty old grandmother, called Rosalyn." Just the mere mention of her name was enough to produce a look of utter disgust on his face, and he then added, "I met her once, strange woman, definitely strange, and to this day I'd swear that one of her guests was actually a man dressed up as a woman." he uttered and paused long enough to ask, "Why do you people do that?...Never mind, I don't want to know." deciding ignorance was bliss in this case.

Austin relaxed in the upholstered chair and crossed one leg over the other, giving serious thought as to what to say next, while he slowly stroked his pointy chin. "The panelled room was something your mother felt passionate about, and set to work converting the old library into what you see today. Selemie was missing her family, and this way she could keep in touch with them on a daily basis, especially her little sister Arisii." he uttered. Just the mere mention of her name brought a smile to Austin's lips and a warm glow to his heart, as he then said, "Arisii had on many occasions asked to come and pay a short visit here but, both her parents and the high Senan himself had decided against such ideas due to her age, and as you might gather Arisii didn't take it too well. But the law is the law, which we all live by." claimed Austin, remembering the number of times she had begged and pleaded to come here.

Melanie wrapped her arms around her legs and smiled, as she too remembered the cute little fireball called Arisii. 'She must have been a real hand full for poor Jeeves...oops, I mean Austin.' thought Mel, laughing silently, as Austin cleared his throat noisily to get her full attention, ignoring the name she used before continuing his story. "Your parents had some happy memories of their life here, but as you people say, all good things come to an end. We just, didn't expect it to happen the way it did." He gazed out of the window as images came flooding back, images of that fateful night so long ago.

"The reccurring dreams you have, are not some make believe fantasy of your own making, they were transferred to you by your mother moments before her death. It is how they remember passed loved ones. People that are no longer with us, your grandmother Amarah will have the images, memories of her own mother, grandmother and great grandmother and so on, stored deep within her own mind, it is an endless circle of life" claimed Austin who then added, "Some memories are transferred to memory orbs for safe keeping, allowing the family access. We hold them in the palms of our hands; no doubt you've seen how they communicate with one another by the use of their hands?" Melanie nodded, waiting for Austin to continue. "Well it's just the same with the orbs. Now I think we should end our little heart to heart chat for now

Melanie. You do realise that for now, my true identity will have to remain a secret." he said seriously, before transforming back into a cat, and winked at her as a firm knock sounded on her bedroom door, seconds before Lynnette popped her head in saying, "Are you never getting up cherie? It is almost 10.30 and we are all slowly starving to death. Get a move on!" and with that statement she slammed the door shut behind her, and there followed the sound of running feet down the stairs. Melanie grabbed hold of the bed covers and tossed them over Austin, burying him completely, before making a mad dash towards the shower room. For several minutes, a tiny yet, highly charged lump could be seen scurrying under the bed covers, trying to fight its way out, and all you could hear was the distinctive sound of an annoyingly frustrated cat.

When at last a small head finally popped out from under the bed covers, its gaze was centred on the bathroom where the sound of running water could be heard. He strolled over to the bathroom door and focused his gaze on the water supply. A smile erupted from the corner of his mouth, as a devilish glint appeared in his eyes and he suddenly heard the beautiful sound of Melanie screaming, as the water turned from a temperate warm to a bone chilling ice cold, 'Sweet revenge' thought Austin, before heading towards the bedroom door.

CHAPTER TWENTY-SEVEN

Later that day on the opposite side of the village near a small wooded area, the air seemed unusually warm and sweet-scented, owing to the abundance of wild flowers, freshly trod on grass and lush vegetation such as Ivy and honeysuckle that had latched onto nearby trees, giving the entire area an untouched feel. It would have had a calming influence on most people, except for Max, who right now had an overwhelming sense of unease and strong stomach churning doses of apprehension, when Taban had approached him unexpectedly, asking him to come on this rather unanticipated walk, that was starting to have all the makings of an incoming revelation.

Having shoved his hands in the pockets of his hooded top, hoping they would stop shaking, due to the uneasy atmosphere, Max regarded the tension in Taban's shoulders with a lump in his throat. While the area seemed unusually quiet, so quiet you could almost hear the Earth moving on its axis, Taban stopped beside a newly erected metal fence, to gaze at what had once been an idyllic scene, close to where the unexpected loss of his sister, had dramatically altered not just him, but his entire future. Taban, after a moments silence, uttered, to Max's surprise, "You felt the connection between us didn't you Max? I could see it in your eyes, you experienced immediate discomfort and unease, correct?" he concluded, pausing for a brief moment before adding, "You have an unusual birthmark on the side of your chest, it's been causing you a great deal of pain, but have you ever wondered why?" he asked trying to appear informally interested, while Max continued to wonder at Taban's unapproachable manner, before daring to utter the words, "How the hell could you possibly know that?" he asked anxiously, while pulling his hands out of his pockets.

Sensing that the boy was about to run, Taban turned slowly to face Max, his eyes seemed cold and unfeeling as he replied, "Your scar is a lasting reminder of the night you were born although, you will not be aware of it, for it was that very night that I took a significantly dangerous gamble with you Max, in order to save your life, all because of a promise I made. An insanely stupid promise." admitted Taban a little too calmly, while his face showed all the visible signs of self-loathing and anger, as the air turned chilly and he added, "It was a promise I should never have kept…I know that now. For an unstoppable chain of events will arise from it, events I will be unable of prevent. But I want you to understand that I was nowhere near well enough to attempt such a thing as saving a life, and now unfortunately, things have gone too far for it to stop, it's out of my hands now." confessed Taban earnestly, having realised just how bad things were going to get, not only for himself, but Max and everyone else. Memories of that awful night came flooding back, as if it happened only yesterday.

He felt the urge to simply walk away and leave her in her own self-induced torment and pain, having heard her cries for help through the darkened haze of his own grief-stricken torture, from within the smashed up remnants of her vehicle. He had cautiously approached the area, with an air of cold insensitivity that almost made him turn and leave her lying there, when suddenly from the darkened depths of his own partially fragmented soul, a tiny part of himself made him go back and help. The need to help did not come from the creature within, for Taban knew it did not care about anything or anyone, only hate, anger and resentment remained, fuelling its putrid, decayed soul against anything with a heartbeat.

It carried a futile need for self-importance and a strong sense of self-gratification, in the causing of pain and suffering, the effect of which, frightened Taban immensely, and he could only just remember what love felt like, what goodness felt like and what being benevolent meant, all of which, was slowly drifting away from him. Suddenly, he heard the sound of Max's voice uttering in an uneasy tone the words "What happened to her?" Max asked, feeling as if he was standing near the gates of hell, conversing with the Devil.

Taban withdrew enough from his hazy deliberations to hear the boys heartfelt plea and replied, "Your mother's car skidded out of control causing her to crash...She was trying to reach the hospital, because she was heavily pregnant, with you." he uttered, taking two steps towards his young friend, but stopped when Max instinctively backed away from him. Taban reached out his hand to gently touch Max's arm, but once again, Max hurriedly backed away, as Taban let out a heartfelt plea. "Max! I need you to understand, before it's too late, I haven't much time left!" begged Taban urgently. An unexpected onslaught of pure anger and frustration arose from within the darkest depths of his shattered alter ego, forcing him to use a stern almost hypnotic gaze to immobilize Max completely. Imprisoned within his own body with no means of escape, Max was forced to witness a little of the horror of what was to come.

A sudden instinctual sense of his own aversion and distaste, shot through Taban's body straight to his heart, while Max tried to free himself from the invisible trap that held him, while Taban felt the sharp overwhelming sense of battle, burning its way inside him, like an everlasting fire, that was slowly gaining strength with each passing day. Only now, the battle was getting harder and harder to win. Taban let in a soothing breath of air, while explaining the rest of this dark tale, realising his time was now limited. "I managed to free her, and carry her to a nearby farmer's hut to keep her warm, but we both knew it was too late. She begged me to save you, almost as if she knew she was beyond saving herself. I tried to save both you and your mother, but I could only save one, you…" Taban paused before adding "I did the only thing I could do, I transferred a portion of my DNA into the unborn foetus…into you Max." he admitted earnestly, seeing the boy's self-loathing and disbelief etched on his face, forcing him to add, "I can see your uncertainty Max, but tell me this, where had the unusual scar come from? A scar you try desperately to hide. Why have you suffered such severe headaches from the age of sixteen?" queried Taban, as he took a step back adding, "Your mother accepted her fate, if you want to call it that, she was a remarkable woman, you should be proud of her." he uttered, showing an unbelievably calm exterior, making Max more uneasy as he never once took his eyes off Taban for a moment.

He shook his head in abject denial, refusing to believe any of Taban's unbelievable confession, saying, "You seriously expect me to believe all this DNA transferral bull shit? You've seen too many TV shows Taban. For all I know, you could have caused the crash, you could have killed her! I think you're a fucking liar!!" cried Max fuelling his pent up rage and anger, while Taban, although wary, took a few steps forward, holding out his hand in friendship, eager that Max should understand and believe, while he listened to the boy's pain and anguish pour out of him like a raging torrent of misery.

On seeing this show of compassion Max was not fooled, clearly wiser beyond his years, and would not trust Taban, "Don't fucking touch me you freak!! Just keep the hell away from me!" screamed Max angrily, with such raw emotion his whole body shook, bringing forth an unexpected outpouring of pain, triggering an unconscious transformation in his eyes that lasted only a moment, but it was enough to transform his eyes from human, to something else entirely. Taban recognised this change for what it was, what it meant, and what it could lead to as did the creature within, and both revelled in this newly found knowledge.

Max tried to curb the surge of uncontrollable anger raging through his entire body, as he shouted, "Lies, they're all lies!

You could have heard about my scar and the headaches from Edna!" he suggested, as suddenly, having found himself free of the restraints that held him, he took the opportunity to escape, with the sound of Taban's voice calling out to him saying, "Max wait! You have to know the rest before it is too late, I have to warn you...Please!" he cried, but Max refused to listen, and replied, "Leave me the hell alone!!" and disappeared out of sight, leaving Taban standing alone at the edge of the clearing. His intention was to follow the boy, when an unexpected attack of pain, caused him to double over, forcing him to his knees in a show of piety, realising himself that the battle he had fought up to now, was only just the beginning, sent a shiver of terror up his spine.

Meanwhile back at the house, Melanie stood rooted to the spot as the sudden unexpected stirrings of something cold, unsympathetic, and deceptively dangerous, moved within their vicinity having only now woken up. As it lay hidden from everyone but her, who had sensed it as you would a childhood nightmare, a nightmare that unnerved her. At first she thought her imagination was getting the better of her, that she could in fact be going crazy, understandable really considering what had happened over the last few months, but that was not the case, not now, this feeling was different, this was more real, making her wonder where Austin was, could he feel this ominous presence, or was it just her?

Meanwhile in a secluded area, close to the stone structures, there was a meeting between Austin and the 'Mafia brothers,' also known as Tarak, Raan and Vian. Austin having transformed, stood with authority in the centre of the clearing waiting for the others to get comfortable. Raan sat on a thick patch of grass lounging against a huge tree stump whittling a bit of wood, Tarak leant against a nearby tree listening for anyone approaching as Austin spoke, "I understand Taban's taken the boy for a walk, do any of you know where?" asked Austin seriously.

Tarak spoke first saying, "He's taken him close to the site of the accident, and is currently telling Max about his mother.

If his intentions are to tell him any more of what happened that night, then I am not aware of it, only time will tell us that" uttered Tarak, as Austin paused for a brief moment before replying, "You've all sensed as I have, Max's unique identity, but should anything be done right now is unclear. My main concern is Melanie, she is my soul priority, especially now, at this crucial time. The boy is in my view, an unforeseen hindrance, and a huge liability to our plans, something we could have well done without right now." explained Austin seriously, to everyone's surprise.

Raan having heard this raised his head, to look long and hard at Austin, as he purposefully got to his feet, and with an incensed barely contained anger said, "Max is no hindrance nor is he a liability, and should never be classed as one. He's in desperate need of help, ignorant of the dangers ahead of him, and at this moment, he's wishing for death, no one should wish that Austin, no one! MY view in this is clear! We are the ones at fault here, not the boy! Do you understand me!!?" explained Raan defensively, trying to control his temper. While Austin looked at his friend in surprise, as did everyone else before asking, "How is it you can sense this about the boy and we cannot? It is inconceivable that you should know this, so explain yourself" ordered Austin, at which point, Raan angrily stepped forward with immediate intent, his emotions highly charged with animosity, as he replied, "Just as it is for a watcher to be so careless and heartless, wouldn't you agree?" He uttered sarcastically, readying for a confrontation in defence of the boy.

The mood within the group altered dramatically, as everyone went into a defensive pose, while Austin calmed the situation with a mere nod of his head, by way of an agreement, having realised his huge error, "Forgive me Raan, the words I spoke were inaccurate." uttered Austin earnestly, noting how his unpredictable friend relaxed somewhat, while Tarak stood by Raan's side with his hand on his chest, both in a meditative state, giving Austin the opportunity to continue by saying, "I assume you've all sensed Melanie now knows who I am?" All three bow their heads, once Tarak had removed his hand to stand a short distance away, "She took it far better than I thought she would, but then she has had a good teacher and mentor by her side." he said blowing his own trumpet, to such an extent that it gave Raan the chance to snigger, and then cover it with an unconvincing cough.

Vian took this opportunity to speak, saying, "The relationship between Melanie and I is not going as well as expected. There are complications. It would've been so much easier on our own planet. Life is a lot less complicated there." complained Vian with a frown. When a voice said, "You know, if things do not work out for you, you could always join the Senan, after all, you practically live in his pocket." Raan uttered, ignoring the look of disapproval from Tarak. Austin continued, "Melanie is part human, and is only now beginning to understand her abilities, I am sorry Vian, but you are going to have to be patient a little longer." he explained seriously.

Tarak took a stroll around the area, while Raan who was still whittling, announced, "You could always try a little romance?...You know; flowers, chocolates, soft music, a candle lit dinner or a romantic stroll along the beach at sunset." uttered Raan casually, generating a stunned silence while several pairs of eyes stared in Raan's direction, who continued to work on his creative project. "Romance!?" They all asked in surprise, as Raan spoke in an all knowing tone "Yes! I read about it in a magazine at Mel's house. I think it was Sarah's, most interesting, and a good source of research material, I suggest you read it." he uttered, as Austin replied, "there is more to you than meets the eye Raan. I'm impressed."

Raan got to his feet with swift intent, having sensed Tarak coming up behind him, and made a sudden grab for him taking him by surprise, while Raan said, "Watch and learn everyone, I've read about these things, so I know what I'm talking about." explained Raan, as Tarak's whole body stiffened with apprehending dread, engulfed in Raan's arms, and lowered to a 45° angle, while his cold eyes looked up to find Raan winking at him saying, "This is how you should hold her, gently but firmly, with your bodies close together. Close enough to feel the beatings of her heart." said Raan, seriously enjoying the moment, before Austin interrupted saying. "We're able to feel the beatings of her heart several miles away, why on the Munastan mountains would you want her that close?" he asked, rapidly losing his patience.

Vian shrugged his shoulders in defeat, clueless as to what to think, when a voice shouted, "Quiet! I'm teaching here." said Raan, feeling good about everything and adding, "Now, as you gaze into each other's eyes, you speak the words of love. Tell her how you feel, how your heart aches for her to be yours. You pull her close and kiss her passionately on her lips, allowing your hands to feel their way around her body." he instructed. Tarak froze with fright as Raan's face moved closer and closer to his own, with their lips just a breath apart and uttered with barely composed menace through gritted teeth, "You go any further Raan, and you will wish you had not. Let me go...Now!" uttered Tarak. "I'm showing them how to be romantic Tarak." Raan explained before letting him go. Vian interceded saying, "We know most of that already, I used to leave Melanie a single rose on her bedside table." Vian offered helplessly before continuing, "Besides I fail to see what good giving her chocolates and sand in her shoes will do…" he suggested remembering the number of times he stood by Melanie's bed watching her sleep, while he tenderly caressed the soft strands of her hair between his fingertips.

Raan gave Tarak another sly wink, as he circled him like a predator with its prey, and pondered on what to say, "Well now, let me see…," he said casually, moving closer to an increasingly nervous Tarak. "First, you take her to a poorly-lit dining area, where you give her an assortment of half dead plant materials in bright colours, wrapped in paper, apparently they like that, and after the meal you give her a box filled with fancy decorated chocolates. Oh! And don't forget the music, plus, I think you should take her out for the day. You know, take her somewhere nice, just the two of you." he explained seriously.

Austin snorted in disgust while he shook his head saying, "I've seen some of the chocolates you speak of. Mel's friends bought her some once, they're disgusting, and I should know I tried one once. So forget the chocolates..." instructed Austin, while he looked about the group saying, "I think it's time to head back." and began walking, Raan quickened his pace to walk alongside Tarak saying, "You're still angry with me aren't you Tarak? I don't like it when you get like this, all broody and serious. You do forgive me, right Tarak? Please say you do." pleaded Raan, whilst looking into his friend's eyes beseechingly.

Tarak having witnessed this disgusting display of persuasive begging, let out a huge heavy sigh saying "Yes...Raan I forgive you, now leave me!" he asked, as Raan put his arm around his friend's shoulder saying with a glint in his eye "Well, that's great. I'm glad you forgive me Tarak, for I'll be needing your help with the next lesson." admitted Raan, forcing Tarak to a complete stop, asking suspiciously, "Oh really? What might that be?" he asked, wishing he hadn't. Raan hesitated in his reply, before running off to join the others saying, "Apparently they call it flirting." leaving Tarak standing there a little confused, before realising what the word meant, when a sudden gust of wind in the form of Tarak, flew past Vian and Austin at high speed. Austin snorted in disgust saying, "Your friend will go too far one of these days. You should warn him." advised Austin, before transforming back into his cat form having approached the edge of the woodland. Vian watched his two friends disappear from view and replied seriously, "Raan might appear unorthodox in his manner and behaviour, but there's always a reason, and besides, Tarak would never hurt him." he explained, as Austin looked up allowing Vian, after a moment's hesitation, to add, "Raan's his little brother." he announced casually, and continued walking back towards the house, leaving Austin with a stunned look on his face.

CHAPTER TWENTY-EIGHT

A familiar aroma invaded Austin's highly tuned nostrils as he reached the house, it was the smell of delicious food being prepared, making Austin's stomach rumble hoping the kitchen window was open, and thankfully it was! The problem he now faced was Edna, for she was doing the cooking. Realising he had to be even more cunning than usual, he hopped onto the window sill and hid behind the curtain, close to the opening without being seen, inhaling the delicious smells while removing his collar, still unable to believe that Raan and Tarak were brothers, waiting for the perfect opportunity to act. The moment Edna's back was turned he slipped into the room like a wisp of air, and hid under the table, that right now, held a delicious selection of food, just waiting for the royal taster to begin his work.

A gentle knock on the kitchen door was followed by Edna's name being called. It was Melanie's voice. Edna rushed over to the door with an icing bag in her hands and unlocked it, before rushing back to finish her ultimate creation, a beautifully decorated birthday cake. For Austin it was love at first sight, the second his wide-eyed gaze captured the freshly iced cake, his mouth watered to such an extent that a small patch of water appeared on the kitchen floor, but he snapped out of it, 'No! No that's a bad idea, Austin' he thought reprimanding himself sternly, 'Mel would never forgive me, and Edna would hunt me down and kill me for sure' he concluded when suddenly, a wicked smile formed on his furry lips, remembering the variety of delicious treats just waiting for him. 'Edna wouldn't miss the odd one here or there, if I spaced them out a bit' he convinced himself, after all, he was an alien from another planet, who could perform the odd miracle or two when needed… And so without further hesitation and in the blink of a cat's eye, he'd somehow managed to gather one of each treats, and cunningly manoeuvre the remains to disguise the theft as he resumed his place beneath the table and gathered his prize collection together in a nice neat pile in front of him with his paw, pondering on which one to try first.

Melanie having realised what Austin had done, positioned herself between Edna and the table, to mask Austin's gratified purring and the smacking of his lips, as Lynnette's head popped around the door offering everyone her best smile. Edna waved her in and stood back to admire the finished creation. "What do you think girls?" she asked cocking her head to one side, "It's magnificent" said Lynnette, looking surprised, Melanie uttered, "Wow! It's fantastic Edna, Max will love it." she said, itching to try a piece. Edna had a glow of satisfaction about her as she lovingly placed the cake in a plastic container for the freezer, along with the other food stuff, with the help of Melanie and Lynnette.

Austin's stomach growled noisily in satisfaction, when suddenly, the back door was flung open, nearly wrenching it off its hinges while Raan flew in as if the Devil himself was after him, and took it upon himself to hide behind Edna of all people, using her as a human shield, and hot on his heels was Tarak, his older brother. Having looked over her shoulder at Raan, then back at Tarak's angry glare she asked, "Alright you idiot, what have you done now? It must be something serious for Terry to get upset, he is never upset, are you Terry?" explained Edna, stepping forward slightly to help herself to a slice of cake, as Tarak's cold hard glare reflected from Raan to Edna, as he slowly and carefully walked towards her saying, in a quiet menacing tone, "Madam, my name is Tarak, not Terry." he replied, before Edna strolled over to him saying,

"That's what I said! Now sit down and eat this, tell me what you think, while I make you a cup of my special tea, you look like you need it." uttered Edna in a placating tone, having managed to pull out a chair, sit him down and shove the piece of cake into his mouth, whilst pouring out his tea.

She then focused all her attention on the still terrified Raan saying, "You!" pointing a wrinkly finger at Raan, "Sit down before I knock you into next week, you bloody fool." and grabbed Raan by his upper arm, forcing him into a chair, as far away from Tarak as the table would allow, "Eat this, it'll keep you out of trouble, while I make you a cup of… ordinary tea." she offered. Raan was about to object to missing out on her 'special' tea but Edna interrupted him adding, "Let's face it kid, you're special enough already, if you were any more special, they'd have to lock you up and throw away the bloody key." explained Edna, gently tapping his shoulder. Raan sank back in his chair and picked at the slice of cake.

Throughout this whole scene, Melanie and Lynnette could do nothing but stare open mouthed in amazement at the way Edna had, somehow, managed to defuse a ticking time-bomb with a simple cup of tea and piece of cake, as Austin crawled out from under the table, to stare at Edna with a new-found sense of appreciation for the old girl, when a voice uttered "I was wondering when you were going to show yourself Austin. I may be getting old, but I saw your flea-infested carcass reflected on the microwave door as you entered through the window." declared Edna with her back turned, missing the look of surprise on Austin's face having realised Edna had got the better of him, and regarded his opponent through narrowed eyes, concluding that this batty old woman was his 'true nemesis', before making a discreet exit through the window.

Sarah popped her head around the door, noticing the cake on the table and said, "Ooh...Cake, can I have some?" she asked, helping herself to a piece before anyone could stop her. "Is there any coffee going spare by chance?" she asked, taking a huge bite of her cake. Lynnette glanced at Sarah asking, "Have you heard from lover-boy yet Sal?" catching Sarah's full attention, who said, while chewing her bottom lip, "No, and I'm getting a little worried. I should have had a phone call, text, email or even a damn letter from him by now, and I've received nothing, I'm starting to think that maybe he's dumped me on the quiet." she uttered dejectedly. Raan interrupted the conversation saying, "I wouldn't worry too much, he's probably been too busy at this so called Observatory, and you know what they say, absence makes the heart grow fonder, personally I wouldn't know what the heart had to do with it, but it fits?" he explained, while everyone looked on in amazement as he noisily licked his fingers of any remaining cake crumbs. Even Tarak paused between sips of his 'special' tea, to gaze at his little brother with raised eyebrows.

A little later that evening Vian entered the front room to find Sarah, Lynnette, Edna and Raan fully absorbed in a powerful period drama. Sarah glanced over her shoulder to say hi, but was given the 'hushing' sound from Raan, whose eyes had not left the screen for a second. Edna wore her fancy TV spectacles for the occasion, and thought it a good idea to bring her knitting as a backup, in case the TV drama wasn't any good, but so far she hadn't lifted a needle. Vian leant against the door frame, when a movement behind him caught his attention, he turned swiftly to find Max standing in the hall staring at him in a troubled manner and quickly closed the door giving Max and himself some privacy, having noted Max's troubled demeanour, Vian while holding the boys gaze, cautiously stepped forward "Are you alright Max?" he asked in a soft gentle tone, as again, he moved closer, waiting for the boy to answer, but Max said nothing, in the hope that if he stared hard enough he would find the answers he so desperately needed, without the need to talk. As Tarak entered the hall from the upper landing, startling Max momentarily who decided a sudden retreat to his bedroom was needed, and mumbled, "I'm ok," for he no longer trusted anyone, and more importantly, he no longer trusted himself.

CHAPTER TWENTY-NINE

The atmosphere in Max's room was far from good, he could not remember coming back, nor did he know the exact length of time he'd walked for after leaving Taban, but right now, he was beyond the emotional wreck he had been in the past, in truth, he felt dead inside. While standing beside the full length window of his bedroom, through which, the full moon cast an eerie glow, giving everything an unnervingly spooky feel, that somehow fitted his mood. Max watched the shadows dancing their way across the valley, while Bats weaved across the night's sky hunting for food, with their eerie silhouette forming a picture of beauty against the full moon.

Max made barely a sound above the deafening silence, while his body felt stiff with tension and animosity, when without warning, he staggered against the window pane, traumatized by the sudden overwhelming wrench of pain from deep within his scarred chest, causing his whole body to collapse against the cold glass for much needed support, with barely enough energy to hold his head up. His note pad and pencil fell forgotten onto the floor, landing by his feet on the soft cushioned carpet, allowing him to clutch at the scar on his chest, as the pain intensified enough to force tears from his eyes, uncertain whether it was the scar on his chest or the breaking of his heart for his dear mother, which was the cause.

Meanwhile partly hidden from view in a nearby tree sat Austin, who having sensed the boys traumatised state, studied

Max's behaviour with close intensity, and had done from the moment he returned. His concern for what he saw was evident, as Max fell to his knees and sobbed with his head buried in his hands, hoping it might smother any sounds he might make, just as he did as a child. Austin's instinctual need to go help the boy was strong, but he, like the rest of the group, was still wary of Max and his questionable bond with Taban, 'For Max was no ordinary boy, but then let's face it' concluded Austin 'the boy's got no one else except Edna, the crazy old bat of the north', looking at the horrific scene being played out by moon light, before deciding to help the boy, if he could, and still be in cat form, for the time wasn't yet right for him to show his true form.

Having silently made his way through the house, by way of the cat flap in the back door, Austin stood outside Max's room, barely hearing a sound from within, as all at once, a sudden flash of light on the landing, (resembling a flickering light bulb) was the only indication that Austin had transported himself into Max's room without any detection, having made sure the coast was clear first before disappearing out of the hallway, for he didn't want another hysterical human on his hands, for he'd got enough with the boy.

Austin stood by the door in Max's bedroom, looking at the emotional wreck huddled on the floor, and kept his emotions in check before slowly making his way over to Max's huddled form, to begin rubbing his furry head against the boys' hand. Max's head shot up to find Austin, looking at him with his unusual cat eyes and whispered, "Austin! How the hell did…" he wondered aloud, while leaning against the glass for support, with all previous thoughts quickly vanishing, as Max continued to stare at Austin, who to Max's surprise winked at him cheekily, before climbing into the boy's lap to begin purring loudly.

Max stared at Austin in amazement having never seen this side of him before, while he hesitantly lifted his hand over Austin's back. Max knew from past experience that Austin never liked being fussed over by anyone, other than Mel, and slowly lowered his hand to stroke Austin's back, and relax against the window pane. Austin purred with contentment which was a surprise, him being an alien who for once, knew he had done a good thing tonight, and stayed there until Max decided to go to bed in a fit of sheer exhaustion, which allowed Austin the chance to uncurl himself from Max's arms and go check on Melanie.

While Austin was with Max, Vian had plucked up the courage to stand outside Melanie's bedroom door holding a bunch of roses he'd snatched from the bottom of Melanie's garden, unaware of the fact that Austin had arranged for Melanie to have a trustworthy bodyguard in the guise of Raan, hidden in her wardrobe, reading a girls magazine with the help of a small illuminating orb he kept in his pocket. Vian felt uncomfortable and completely out of his depth, as he shifted nervously from one foot to the other, before knocking on Melanie's door, having spent quite a few minutes staring at his fist, hovering inches away from the solid wooden structure.

Having heard the knock on the door Melanie set the diary aside, swung her legs off the bed and walked over to the door to see who it was, upon opening the door she was surprised to see Vian standing there nervously holding a bunch of roses. "Vian!" she exclaimed, noticing the flowers he held in his hands, "May I come in for a few moments?" he asked, hoping she would say yes, before anyone saw him looking like a complete fool, standing outside her door. "Of course." "Please come in." she said, stepping back enough to open the door. "These are for you, I hope you like them?" said Vian handing her the flowers.

Melanie produced a genuinely happy smile saying, "They're beautiful Vian. I've always loved roses they're one of my favourite flowers, how did you know?" she asked curiously, as Vian relaxed a little saying, "Intuition, although if I'm honest…These are not the first roses I have given you, my beloved." he admitted waiting for it to register what he had actually said to her. Melanie gazed into Vian's eyes, as if she was seeing him for the very first time, when she said "What? What did you say?" whispered a confused Melanie.

As an influx of memories filled her mind, memories of her waking up to find a rose on her bedside table. "It was you, you were the one leaving me roses." she said, hurrying into the bathroom with the bouquet of roses needing a diversion, a task that would allow her time to think things through, if only for a few seconds. When Melanie returned to place the vase of roses on the bedside table, after moving the lamp to one side, Vian waited for her to say something, while playing with the petals of a single rose, having felt the inner battle she was fighting, while focusing her attention on the velvet like texture of the rose petals, before she had the courage to say "I think deep down I always knew it was you, I just didn't want to accept it just yet. I wasn't ready or prepared for the truth I now know." she confessed, as Vian took a step forward asking, "Why? What were you afraid of?" he asked, needing to be of help to her.

Melanie could hear the silent tread of his feet as he moved closer as she said, "I was afraid of change, the change you were bringing. I knew my life would be so very different after this, I could sense it. It may sound a bit of a cliché but... It's turned out to be more complicated than I could ever have imagined. I know of my parent's life together, which seemed to exclude me by the way." explained Mel whilst fidgeting with the rose petals before continuing, "I mean, don't get me wrong I'm not judging them or blaming them for any of it, I just feel cheated, understandable really." she said before adding, "My mother's true identity and where she came from was a shock, and let's not forget who Austin really is. All these years, I sensed he was special and unique, I just didn't realise how special! He's an alien for God's sake, a shape shifting alien from another planet. Things like this only happen in films, not real life." she concluded, speaking from the heart and it felt good to do it. "I feel as if my life's not my own. I have been spied upon and watched over all my life, until you people thought it was the right time to tell me the truth," she uttered angrily, while her voice shook with emotion as the memories both good and bad came flooding back, prior to meeting Sarah and Lynnette. She felt Vian's hands rest gently on her shoulders realising that they were no longer cold.

Melanie took a deep breath asking, "Why are you here Vian? Please don't answer my question with another question, it really annoys me. I want you to be honest with me," she pleaded. Vian raised his head to stare at the paper covered walls, feeling as nervous as a fledgling, knowing he would have to say something profound, something from the heart. Silence weighed heavy while Vian pondered on what to say and more importantly how to say it, 'She wants me to be honest with her, easier said than done' he thought struggling with his few remaining options, before having the courage to say bemusedly, "I saw you in a vision with Austin, who did, as I remember, his uppermost to cause all kinds of trouble on a daily basis. Even then I knew you were special to me, I could feel the bond from across the stars and I must admit to being a little impatient, but in my own defence, I'd waited a life time for you." he admitted honestly.

Melanie turned to face him knowing he spoke the truth, after all, why would he lie? She could see how uncomfortable he was in telling her. His behaviour was similar to Austin's when he's been caught with something between his teeth, like Edna's best salmon she'd bought from the fish mongers that morning, or the time our neighbour Mr Jessup's steak and onion sandwich went missing, while he snoozed in his garden chair, and his little dog 'Sparks' got the blame. Vian could see Melanie's fruitless attempts at preventing a small smile that quickly disappeared when she said, "I'm finding it all a little too creepy to accept right now Vian, saying you saw me in a vision, a vision of the future, that's way too 'Star Trek-y' for me." and paused briefly before adding, "I can see you're telling me the truth but…" and ended it there as Vian said, "So my sweet Mel, you forgive me?" he asked with a tiny bit of hope in his eyes as Melanie eventually nodded her head.

But before she had chance to say anything, a familiar voice said from inside the wardrobe, "Well it's about time. I'm getting cramp in here." and out tumbled Raan, carrying a small illuminating orb and another of Sarah's magazines. Having got to his feet and stretched his stiff joints, with his arms high above his head, spending several more seconds performing yet more stretching exercises, oblivious to the stunned looks on the faces of his two friends, who gazed quickly at each other before looking back at Raan, who uttered, "I have to pay a visit I won't be long. Oh and by the way Vian you're doing great, all my hard work has paid off, girls like honesty in a man, it said so in this magazine." and with that statement he went to the bathroom, leaving an embarrassed looking Vian, and a disgruntled looking Mel.

When Raan exited the bathroom with a huge smile on his face, Melanie asked hesitantly, "Umm Raan?" You're teaching your friends about human behaviour?" unable to keep the sound of surprise out of her voice, but Raan wasn't at all fazed by this and stated "Well, it's like this Mel my sweet, they were, as you Humans say, 'getting nowhere fast', so that's when I stepped in, and saved the day, with the help of a few magazines." "Oh! And I mustn't forget, Tarak's been a huge help to me as well, I can't say any more than that as he gets a little embarrassed about it. Well come on Vian, you've been in here long enough for one night, it is time to say good night, we all need our beauty sleep. That reminds me, I need two slices of cucumber for my eyes." he said casually as he stood by the door waiting for the two of them to say their good nights. Vian took hold of Melanie's hand saying "Goodnight Mel my beloved, sweet dreams." and impulsively, pulled her into his arms to kiss her passionately in front of his friend, before leaving her standing in the centre of her bedroom feeling light headed and a little breathless.

Listening in on their conversation was Austin, whose ear was pressed against the wood, when an unexpected emotion came over him, and for the first time in his life, he was feeling jealous, knowing he had no right to be. He knew his place, he knew where he stood in regards to Melanie his charge, but he also knew of their long-standing friendship, a friendship that went far deeper than any other. Austin was about to move away when the door was suddenly flung open, and there stood Raan, talking about cucumbers for his eyes, 'The simple minded idiot what's he need them for?' wondered Austin, after Vian had been ordered out of the room by Raan of all people.

Austin lay across the top step with his head hanging over the edge, and that was how Sarah found him moments later, when in search of a glass of water, and despite their frequent disagreements, she took it upon herself to sit down next to him on the top step and wait for Austin's reaction to her presence, before giving him some form of comfort. Austin lay unaffected by Sarah's sudden impulse, although, for the life of him he couldn't think why she would want to, after all, he did ruin her new skirt earlier in the day. Sarah reached out her hand to stroke Austin's back, who accepted this loving gesture before raising his head to stare into Sarah's bright grey eyes, which suggested, "Hey Austin, would you like some milk? Let's go raid the fridge," and she cradled him in her arms while she slowly headed down the stairs in her bugs bunny slippers. 'How she doesn't break her bloody neck is beyond me, they're like barges' looking down he thought 'I wonder if there's any smoked salmon left?' as the kitchen door closed behind them. After their midnight snack Austin was about to enter Melanie's room, as Sarah headed back to her room, but paused for any signs of movement from within Max's bedroom, but could sense nothing, as Max had disappeared.

Max was in actual fact, near the river bank tossing pebbles in the water, watching the starlit night reflected on the water's surface, with what felt like the worlds worries on his shoulders, having made his way out of the house undetected, something he had learned to do as a child with a great deal of success. Finding out about his biological mother was one of many startling turns of events for Max in recent days, for a series of photographically styled images, images of a little boy and girl twins, kept re-appearing night after night in his dreams, from the moment he arrived here.

A strange, disturbing turn of events was starting to happen 'but why? What did it all mean?' wondered Max, as he threw yet another stone into the river, thinking 'The twins always appear happy and although they seem human, they were clearly alien, both had dark hair with equally dark coloured eyes, pale white and grey skin tones, and with it, an inherited number of special abilities, but why show me this?' he wondered, then laughed under his breath having realised the fact that, he actually envied their abilities and their affection for one another. His laugh soon turned to a frown and he shivered suddenly as the night air turned cold, or was it the change in subject matter that caused him to shiver. He knew whose memories they were, but didn't dare want to admit it or accept it, as an eerie unfamiliar thin band of vapour, interlaced its way elegantly and majestically through the trees towards him, resembling a spectral apparition, clearly acting like no ordinary fog, for it had a purpose, a reason for being there.

The fog drifted across the whole terrain, stretching progressively, over a wider area, until it arrived at the river bank, where Max sat gazing into the reflective ripples of water, when the vapour stopped short of revealing itself and waited. Although unaware of the fact that he was not alone, while the vapour hid in close proximity, along with the silhouette of a solitary figure, watching Max's every move with frightening intensity. The only visible feature was a pair of luminous white coloured eyes, filled with an intense fury and resentment, with only one fundamental motive for existing, and that right now, was centred solely on Max, all the preparations, detailed planning and careful observations were at last going to pay dividends, it smirked gleefully, knowing it could almost taste success, as it watched its prey.

Max cradled his head in his hands thinking 'These damned headaches are getting worse, why won't they just go away?' he thought frustratingly as he received yet another disturbing image, it was akin to that of a flash from a camera lens, triggering yet another attack of pain, he pressed his clenched fists against his head. Some images were so dark, so horrifically unsettling, that they would cause him to wake up crying out someone's name, someone called Selemie. The courage to tell anyone had vanished, for they would probably think him mad, after all, he was starting to believe it himself. The unknown intruder continued to watch while Max slowly got to his feet and walked away along the edge of the river bank, with the intruder following him, while all at once, the vapour-like mist mysteriously disappeared.

Max had walked but a short distance, when he came across an unusual group of standing stones, covered in a series of symbolic writings, some of which, seemed oddly familiar, and yet, Max knew he had never seen these symbols before today, and was left wondering what the hell was going on, as thin threads of moonlight filtering through the trees, brushed against the surface of each stone, causing each cypher to illuminate, resembling that of a spectral ghost, in a mirage of faint soft glowing colours. He wondered if his eyes were playing tricks on him due to lack of sleep, as the overwhelming impulse to touch this illusion overpowered him completely. He cautiously reached out his hand to trace the images with his fingers tips, when without warning, a rapid surge of energy travelled all the way up his arm, from deep within the stone structure, triggering a sudden unexpected transformation to his entire bloodstream, causing it to burn and come alive, throughout his entire body.

Max felt the increasing sense of burning as he looked down at his florescent white arm, showing a detailed image of his bloodstream, as minuscule shards of lightning escaped from his hand, causing him to cry out in fear, horrified by what had happened. The impromptu serge of energy reversed back up his arm, giving him a strength like no other, forcing him to hold his breath, hoping it would counteract the effects, while clenching his fists before backing away, eager to escape this horrid nightmare.

The observer glowered at its prey, with hate in its unfriendly eyes, that were afflicted by a series of black veins spreading across the eyelids and face, while Max stumbled away from the area cradling his arm. A sudden rush of immense delight replaced the malicious hate filled eyes, and began formulating a plan, while Max remained oblivious of the horror that followed him. Meanwhile back at home Melanie began to dream once more:

CHAPTER THIRTY

<u>Memories</u>

The soft barely heard sound of running feet could be heard leaving the living complex, while everyone else slept on. The night was warm and eerily still giving the inhabitants an undisturbed sleep. The only sound to break this serene atmosphere was the waterfall as it interlaced its way down the side of the crystal rock face, caressing it as it went. A shooting star soared across the dark pink and mauve coloured sky, before disappearing behind the two moons orbiting their planet, on a solitary journey of discovery. At the far side of the mountain range near the area of the Yoltana waterfall, a series of openings in the rock face were clearly visible. Melanie witnessed a young child, a girl of about seven years of age carrying what appeared to be a heavy satchel styled bag over her shoulder.

The girl stopped to look around her secretively before entering one of the openings. Having seen this, Melanie had to admit the child had nerve being out alone at such a late hour, and so followed her, keeping hidden the entire time. It was dark at first except for the soft glow of an illuminated orb the child carried, which helped guide them further into the base of the mountainside. Melanie watched the child clamber down using both hands to climb deep into the cave.

Melanie continued to follow with a deep-rooted knowledge of who the child was, 'It had to be Arisii' thought Melanie, following the child deeper into the mountain, 'What was she doing, why all the secrecy? Obviously she was supposed to be at home in bed, not going on an adventure on her own' thought Mel, hiding behind a large rock, having realised the child had finally reached her destination and began unloading her bag containing more orbs, placing them at equal distances apart, oblivious of the fact that she was being watched by Melanie, who was inhabiting Amarah's body.

Activating the orbs by a mere wave of the hand, showering the cave with light and colour, causing a host of creatures to shy away from the soft glow. The view Melanie saw was awe-inspiring, a place the universe saw fit to create in this secret haven, forgetting all about the child she was supposed to be keeping an eye on.

Clusters of blue crystallised minerals within the rock face reflected the light on a wall of clear transparent crystal, filling an entire wall, holding back a torrent of lake water that fed the Yoltana waterfall. Around it, an unusual array of plant life grew in bunches, close to a tiny vein of water running down and across the base of the crystal wall, forming a small brook, where a selection of foliage altered in colour, as the light caressed the soft velvety texture, changing it from white and green to a vibrant red. Beyond the barrier wall Melanie could see tiny transparent fish with wings but no eyes gliding majestically through the fragmented remains of a long forgotten crumpled down city, while the sound of soft music echoed around the interior of the cave, giving it an air of heavenly beauty.

Melanie watched as the child removed a number of items from her bag consisting of; a blanket, a variety of food and drink, and a selection of books that were tattered and torn with age and use. Books she immediately recognised from her time spent with Charlie in his book shop. It was an odd mixture of both old and new tales of adventure, Melanie did not know what to think, as she watched the child break apart a piece of what looked like biscuit, and offer it to some of the creatures, who were obviously used to her visits here, several got comfortable on her blanket and fell asleep, to the sound of soft music. Then to Melanie's surprise she noticed movement from the other side of the crystal wall, performed by the sea creatures, who began to weave their way through the ripples of water, performing tricks for the child.

Having seen this, the child walked over to the crystal wall, placed her hand on it before closing her ebony black eyes to meditate, sending them into an immediate haze of eagerness, as they began to brush their bodies along the crystal wall where her hand lay, placing them in a state of euphoric ecstasy, there was no other word for it, they were ecstatic in their happiness. Melanie shook her head in wonder as the child headed back to finish her book reading, which happened to be 'Peter Pan', while eating one of her biscuits. Then in the early hours of the morning after reading books and listening to music, the child gathered together all of her possessions, put them in her bag and left, and the question on Melanie's lips was 'Where had the books come from?' she wondered, watching as the child left the cave and headed home. Melanie followed the child close enough to witness her toss her bag of treasures through her ground floor bedroom window, before clambering in herself, as the early morning dawn began to break, on her home planet of Munastas, casting a rainbow of iridescent colours, as Melanie began to wake...

CHAPTER THIRTY-ONE

Back in Melanie's bedroom, feeling somewhat groggy, Melanie opened her eyes to find Austin hovering over her in his true form, with their faces mere inches apart, Mel pressed her head further into the pillow for a few extra inches of space and took in several breaths of air then asked curiously, "Um... Austin? What are you doing?" He continued to look at her without saying a word while he probed her last dream before saying, "I am reading your mind, and right now, I am more interested in the child in your recent dream, and I can tell you right here and now, that she is in serious trouble, or will be when I get my bloody hands on her!" Austin announced infuriatedly while he tried to calm his temper down several notches, "From the moment she was born, she's been inquisitive, impatient, and totally unpredictable, as to what she may do next? You think Raan's bad and a danger unto himself and those around him, he's timid, shy and withdrawn compared to her! I am as much to blame as anyone, giving in to her like I did, indulging her every whim" admitted Austin, pacing the full length of the room.

Melanie watched in silence for several minutes before daring to ask "I take it the child is Arisii, my Aunt, and that is why you're so upset" she uttered, and continued to watch him pace getting more and more angry with each passing minute, "Upset?...I'm more than a little upset Melanie Rose. I am at the point of an all-out war on anyone that crosses me today.

Where the hell is she? I'm going to ring her damn neck when I do find her!!" promised Austin, whose attitude and talent for earth language had obviously helped his frame of mind.

This was a side of Austin she had not seen before and it made her smile, Austin having caught the smile, stopped pacing and looked her in the eye, as his eyes grew as black as ebony and his wings touched the opposite ends of the bedroom walls, while his feet were apart and his clenched fists rested on his narrow human like hips, it was a frightening sight to see, having never seen it before. "I am in no mood for teasing right now Mel, I'm trying to think, and it's not helping with you smiling at me like that. Now hurry up, and get dressed, breakfast is nearly ready." he instructed, as Melanie with an air of cheerfulness hopped out of bed and into the bathroom humming a little tune as she went, which irritated Austin's mood even more. He took several deep breaths trying to calm down before transforming back into a cat, and waited for Melanie before going down for breakfast.

Melanie stood at the top of the stairs saying, "You go down to breakfast Austin, I'm going to check if Max is up yet, he looked tired yesterday." she said, heading towards his bedroom, knocking several times before entering to find his bed had not been slept in, and on the floor near the window was his note book and pencil. She knew he would never go anywhere without them, 'So where was he?' she wondered, clearly concerned, bending down to pick up the book as it fell open, revealing a detailed drawing of something so unexpected, it caused her to collapse on the end of his bed. It was a drawing of the planet Munastas, and well detailed in every way, for Melanie, it was like reliving one of her dreams all over again, and she spent several minutes looking through the rest of his book, revealing more and more sketches similar to her dreams.

It was as if he had been there with her, sharing the same dream, but how can this be? It didn't make sense. 'This is getting more and more bizarre by the day' thought Melanie worryingly, as she placed the book at the bottom of the bed, making a mental note to have a quiet word with Max later. Her stomach rumbled telling her she was hungry, and she hurried down to the kitchen, as Max entered through the back door, with his head at an angle so his fringe could shield his tired eyes, and paler than usual complexion, looking as if he had slept under a hedge all night. Edna gave Melanie a worried glance as Max mumbled, 'Morning', to those who were still in the kitchen, but not bothering to look at either one of them before heading up to his room.

Melanie eased the atmosphere by saying, "I'm sure he will be alright, maybe he thought sleeping rough for one night was a good idea, maybe it was a dare from one of his mates?", explained Mel trying to sound convincing, as Edna with a glint of hope in her eyes said "Yes....but I've noticed since coming here, he doesn't seem like the same boy, he's changed Mel, and I don't know why. I don't know if this change is a good one or bad", Edna paused before adding "I know it's silly, my worrying like this but, he's my only grandson, he's all I have." she admitted, with heartfelt emotion.

It was then that Melanie saw her opportunity to ask an unanswered question. "You never talk about Max's parents much, or how you and Max found each other, I've always wondered." commented Melanie, as Edna replied distractedly, "Haven't I? Well the truth is Max found me, told me he was my grandson. I remember it like it was yesterday, there he was standing on my door step giving me a nervous yet hopeful smile, hiding a beautiful pair of blue eyes behind that long fringe of his, I would love to get a pair of scissors to that hair, well anyway, he had a tatty old backpack slung over one shoulder and a holdall in his hand, with nothing much in either one. He looked so uncertain, so nervous about meeting me, but offered me the sweetest smile, and immediately won me over. At the time I had little to no doubt that Max could very well have been one of many illegitimate children on this planet, fathered by my son. He never could learn to keep his trousers fastened, the no good louse. But Max, is the shining light in my life, I don't know what I would do without him.", admitted Edna earnestly, before continuing, "None of us know anything about his Mother, but that does not mean we haven't tried finding out." she said scrubbing away at the frying pan.

Melanie could hear a questioning tone in Edna's voice, and thought it time to change the subject, "Any more thoughts on his birthday bash?" enquired Mel curiously excited. Edna's mood changed saying, "I'd like to do something different this year, but I haven't the slightest clue what, do you have any ideas?", she asked Melanie with a glimmer of hope in her tone, as the kitchen door flew open and in walked Raan, wearing the silliest grin on his face saying, "I am glad you asked that, Edna my old pal, for I've got some good ideas." admitted Raan, having suddenly decided to take an interest in the surprise party planning.

Edna and Melanie both looked at each other with a hint of trepidation, as Raan continued by saying, "Why don't we have a fancy dress party with loud music playing in the big dining room, or we could have a camping out beach party, lasting all night long, complete with log fires and loud music like they do in films?", ".....Well, what do you think?" he asked curiously, eager to get started. For a few seconds neither one of them said anything as they stared at Raan in surprise, but it was Melanie who spoke first saying, "They're actually great ideas Raan, and I especially like the beach party, assuming the weathers going to be good. What do you think Edna?", Edna folded away the tea towel saying, "An all-night beach party it is then! Do you want to set it up Raan?", offered Edna, knowing he would jump at the chance.

Raan's eyes lit up like 'Munastan ebony clusters' a rock that glows an unusual dark blue colour when heated as he replied, "I thought you would never ask, dear lady. Leave it all to me." answered Raan gleefully, as he hurriedly left the kitchen rubbing his hands together, with a plan forming in his mind. Melanie's only thought whilst staring at the closed door was, 'Oh dear, what have we done?", "With Raan in the driver's seat anything could happen.' she concluded.

Meanwhile upstairs in Max's bedroom, Max sat staring at his hand trying to come to terms with what had happened at the standing stones, when a knock on his bedroom door made him hide his hand, before telling them to come in, watching Melanie hesitate before entering until she saw the slightest of smiles on his lips, to which she responded with a smile of her own, and then hurrying to sit next to him, causing the bed to bounce. Hey Max, don't you want any breakfast?", "I'll cook." offered Melanie light heartedly. Max merely shook his head saying, "No thanks, I'm not that hungry right now." he said trying to avoid her eye, but Melanie noticed he looked paler than usual, and sensed a heavy burden resting on her friend's shoulders, and in a strange way she could relate to that burden, after all, she carried one around with her the whole of her life, and she wasn't just talking about Austin, who was at this moment hiding under Max's bed eavesdropping on their conversation.

Melanie glanced at Max out of the corner of her eye saying, "I understand you went for a walk with my uncle yesterday. How did it go?" she asked, waiting for Max to say something, but all she got was a single nod of his head forcing her to then add, "He said something to you, didn't he? Something that has upset you." she concluded calmly, for it was plainly obvious that something had happened. To say Max was surprised by her statement was putting it mildly. "What makes you say that?" he asked guardedly, avoiding her eye once again, as Melanie laughed, saying with a flamboyant wave of her hand, "We have eyes everywhere, even Austin, who is right now hiding under your bed." announced Melanie, with a chuckle desperately trying to lighten the mood.

Max looked at Austin in surprise, as he crawled out from under his bed, to give Melanie one of his cold black looks for giving the game away, seconds before his bedroom door swung open and in sauntered Raan with a huge smile on his face, wearing a plain black T shirt with the words 'I AM NOBODIES FOOL' on the front and, with it, an image of a circus clown. "Good morning all." he announced, flicking through Max's sketch book, trying to hide his surprise at what he saw, before sending copies of the images to his brother through their telepathic link, saying 'This is getting more bizarre by the day, something is very wrong here Tarak.' claimed Raan. His brother's reply was short and sweet, 'I know brother.' and ended it there. Raan continued to flick through the drawings Max had done of his home planet, and for a brief moment, felt a slight twinge of home sickness, but only slight, for he was having too much fun here. Melanie smiled saying to Max, "Why don't we go for a bite to eat in town? Just you and me and we can finish our conversation there. We'll take the car and no, you're not coming." she announced, pointing to both Raan and Austin.

As the car headed down the narrow country lane, it had on board a little stowaway. For crouched behind the passenger seat was Austin. After twenty or so minutes of the car swerving to avoid a wild dear, a stray sheep and a family of mallard ducks that had suddenly decided to dart across the narrow lane, Austin suffered irreparable damage, before Melanie at long last parked her car in a public car park close to several shops, including a local café on the outer reaches of the village.

Austin having managed to crawl out of his hiding spot moved with great difficulty once the coast was clear, and for several minutes, all you could hear was the odd moan and groan of something in extreme discomfort, trying to conquer the Mount Everest sized obstacle called the back seat, and flaked out across it. Meanwhile over by the café seating area Melanie offered Max a reassuring smile, and asked before going to place their order. "Would a full cooked breakfast and a coffee suit you? Or do you fancy something lighter?", Max thought for a second and settled for the first option, trying not to think too much about the night before, having noticed his hand was back to normal, 'If you wanted to call it that' he concluded ironically.

Once Melanie had returned, she asked having sat down, "If you want to talk about it Max I'm listening, you can trust me." she said, waiting for Max to make the first move. Max glanced at Melanie through his unkempt fringe saying, "It's hard to know where to start, but when I do, you'll probably think I'm nut's, because I'm starting to believe it myself." he said, tracing the tree rings in the table top with his fingers adding, "The moment I met you at Edna's, I knew there was a link between us, but at the time I did not recognise the connection for what it was, until yesterday, when your uncle told me about my biological mother." uttered Max, while slowly shaking his head still not quite believing it, as the weight of the world seemed a whole lot heavier.

Having sensed this inner torment raging inside her friend, Melanie held her breath waiting for Max to continue. But Max's idea to suddenly open up to Mel was starting to dim, as he said, "He claimed my mother, biological mother, was fatally injured when her car skidded off the road. That was where Taban found her, trapped inside the wreckage, heavily pregnant with me, she was on her way to hospital when the accident happened. Little did she realise how cruel a twist of fate can be." uttered Max, letting out an irony induced laugh, before continuing with his tale, having realised there was no turning back now. "Your uncle had somehow managed to free her and carry her into an old wooden hut nearby, saying a choice had to be made, and apparently she made it. By telling him to save me." announced Max, trying to avoid eye contact with his friend.

Melanie watched Max through tear filled eyes, tears she tried to hide when the waitress arrived with Max's breakfast and two large coffees, giving both a welcome respite, "Eat your breakfast Max, you can finish telling me later." she said in a motherly manner, taking several sips of her hot coffee. Minutes later with the empty plate pushed to one side, Max continued with his story, surprised that he had the appetite to eat any of it, and so without taking his eyes off his cup he said, "My mother insisted he should save her baby, and as you can see he did, but there are times Mel, when I wish to all hell that he hadn't. He tried to save both of us but, it was not to be. She died shortly after my birth." announced Max with a heavy sigh. Melanie pushed her cup away and asked, "What about your dad? Didn't he come and find you?" she wondered curiously, but Max shook his head saying "Hell no! For all I know I am the product of a one night stand or something, because my birth certificate has him as unknown, so no! There is no dad, never has been." he explained, before taking a sip of his coffee.

Melanie watched Max before asking the obvious question, "Umm... Max, where does Edna fit into all this? Is she your grandmother?" she wondered aloud, waiting for the all-important answer. While Max showed signs of guilt or unease, fidgeting in his seat while brushing away his fringe saying, "Not really, I adopted her a few years ago before you moved in, sounds weird huh? but we get on great together, and I would never hurt the old girl, I actually love the silly old bat. To me, she is my grandmother. I was living on the streets when I saw her and followed her home, like some stray dog." and he paused before adding, "You see, the government don't want to know. You're too much of a hand full after a certain age, so you're on your own. I know what you're thinking, I could have been anybody right, a mass murderer or an axe wielding maniac, but she's still alive isn't she?" commented Max with a smile.

Melanie having noticed their cups were empty announced she would go and get refills. Max asked for fruit juice instead of coffee and waited for her return. Eventually Melanie did return and said, "Sorry I took so long, the queue was terrible in there." she said, sitting back down adding, "Are you ok Max?" noticing the faraway look in his eye as he replied, "Yeh, I'm alright, it just feels a little strange talking to someone about all this, but strange in a good way I suppose." he uttered with a slight shrug of his shoulders, before moving his drink to one side, giving him ample elbow room on the table adding, "I can't believe I'm going to say this, let alone believe any of it, but here goes. I hope you're ready for this Mel cos it's a real humdinger. Your uncle claimed that the only way I could have lived beyond that night, was if, ...if he used the power of touch to heal me, transferring some of his DNA into me, and it's because of this, that I now have a scar. I have to say that when he told me, I more or less said he was crazy and a freak. I actually shouted at him, said things I regret now, but the one thing I do know, is that there's more going on around here, more I don't know about and that scares the hell out of me." announced Max seriously.

He started to rub his temples, hoping it would ease the headache, wondering if Melanie thought he was nuts. Melanie could see the immense struggle Max was going through, talking about it, and wondered if it would help if she admitted something of her own, and after a moment's hesitation said "Max...You know the pencil drawings in the sketch book, showing unusual places," she asked, noticing a single nod of his head, "Well...how can I put this?...You see, I visit these places in my dreams, my mother was born there, it was her home, she met my father here on earth." claimed Melanie, hoping Max wouldn't freak out.

But all Max could do was to continue staring into Melanie's violet eyes, with a stunned expression on his face, and a tongue firmly fixed to the roof of his mouth. 'Did I just hear what I thought I heard? Or was it my imagination?' he wondered, coming to a sudden and unexpected decision, he impulsively got up off the bench and headed towards the group of trees at the far edge of the clearing, deciding he had to go take a walk somewhere, anywhere, so long as it was away from here. He needed time to think things through. He could hear Melanie calling out his name, while trying to catch up with him as he continued walking.

Austin, who witnessed the whole thing through the rear side window, made a quick escape and followed them through areas of thick dense woodland thinking, 'Great, just great. This is all we need right now, more complications added to the bloody cooking pot. I need a vacation. How the hell, am I supposed to follow them, when the blasted bell around my neck keeps ringing? I hate this bell.' he admitted, stopping dead in his tracks as an idea so obvious popped inside his head, and he yanked the bell from around his neck, before tossing it under a nearby shrub. He shook his head playfully and even managed several energetic stunts to amuse himself, stopping occasionally, to give another shake of his head listening to the beautiful sound of silence.

While Max's was busy pacing up and down, his behaviour being that of a man attempting to evade his own shadow, whilst unconsciously dragging his fingers through his hair out of shear frustration, as he said, "This is insane. You know that don't you? What you just said is utter madness, you're as bad as your freaked out uncle, I'm sorry Mel but I don't believe a word of it, I can't believe it. Aliens! Next, you'll be telling me you're all bloody aliens, on some package holiday or something crazy like that, or even better, you'll say I'm a fucking alien, your all nuts!" uttered Max angrily, wishing he'd never left Edna's boarding house.

Melanie sat on a nearby log watching her friend, while Austin silently approached the area, listening to Max's raised voice saying, "So, let me get this crazy idea straight! You're trying to tell me that you're half alien on your Mother's side, right?" he asked, as Melanie quietly nodded her head. Then Max added with a sarcastic laugh, "Oh man! This is completely and utterly insane, so insane that it's fucking frightening, for I'm starting to consider it, even believe it." and laughed at his own gullibility, while looking everywhere but at Mel. Time stood still without either one of them saying anything, as Max pinched the bridge of his nose, hoping it might ease the oncoming migraine, when he suddenly lost what little there was left of his tolerance and shouted, "Aren't you going to say anything?!" he asked her frustratedly, adding, "Are you just going to sit there?" he wondered trying to keep what remained of his sanity intact.

Melanie uttered "I know how you feel Max, well sort of, but it's all real Max." she said, with a slight laugh under her breath, noticing the look of complete disbelief on Max's face, as the next words to leave his lips were loaded with sarcasm. "Yeh! Sure you do. You have no idea what I'm feeling Mel!" he uttered angrily, not knowing what to think any more. Melanie offered him a gentle reassuring smile saying, "I've only just found out about my parents Max, so this is all new to me as well. Although, I kinda already knew I was different, I just didn't comprehend how different, until now, we're more or less in the same boat." explained Melanie logically, which didn't seem to help Max's mood at all. Max instinctively burst into laughter while pacing up and down saying, "I feel as if we're in a bizarre episode of the Twilight Zone or something, I'm going to wake up any minute now, and realise, it was all a very bad dream!" Suddenly out of the corner of his eye, he saw something scurrying through the bushes, at the same moment that Melanie saw it, and out trotted Austin minus his collar, and after hopping on a large rock, waited for one of them to say something. He was in such a good mood, having got rid of the bell from around his neck, he didn't much care what happened, as Mel said, "I should've known you would follow me Austin." she said turning her attention back to Max, who was rubbing the back of his neck trying to ease the tension that was slowly snapping his spine in two, and if his body language was anything to go by, then it was obviously not working.

Max turned to face her saying, "So let me get this freaked out version of a fairy tale straight. You're saying that at night while you sleep, you somehow visit these places, the very same places, I somehow manage to draw down on paper without even realising it?" explained Max, trying to keep a tight hold of his sanity, as well as his temper, noticing the slight nod she gave as a reply, before adding, "Right ok. I'll buy that crazy shit" admitted Max generously adding, "Not only that, but you're also claiming to be part alien yourself...Right? So what the hell does that have to do with me! Have you somehow controlled me with your mind, forced me to do stuff through subliminal messages and shit?... Oh great! Now I sound like a badly written script from Star Trek. This is all so fucked up. I shouldn't be listening to any of this. I'm going to end up believing it, and when that happens, I'll be putting the straight jacket on myself!!" announced Max on the verge of losing it, adding, "Your uncle said there was more to tell, and my gut's telling me, that it's all connected to this...this dark side of the moon bullshit I'm hearing!"

admitted Max, with a swift wave of his hand, and a heavy sigh. "Come on let's get back, I've had enough of the unexplained for one day, and anyway, I don't want Edna worrying." he admitted showing the obvious signs that he cared. Austin and Melanie watched Max leave, after which, Melanie merely shrugged her shoulders, hoping to catch up with Max.

On entering the house, Melanie was confronted by Raan who asked eagerly, "How did it go?" waiting for the all-important answer, alongside Vian and Tarak, as Melanie uttered, rather confused, "I don't know...It's hard to say. Let me get back to you on that ok?" she said sincerely, as all three looked at each other, wondering what had gone wrong. While their main topic of conversation was lounging on his bed, busy flicking through his sketch pad, going over all that was said earlier, and inadvertently rubbing the scar on his chest hoping to ease the burning, while continuing to look through the sketches he had drawn. Suddenly he tossed his note pad to the far end of the room, and went to stand by his bedroom window thinking, 'These damned headaches, will they never end?!' he pleaded angrily, whilst rubbing his temples with his fingertips, knowing it would mean yet another night of broken sleep.

Later that same night at around 2am, the door to Melanie's room opened with barely a sound, and out came Melanie wearing a pair of pyjamas with roses on the front, complete with a matching dressing gown, and on her feet, she wore a pair of slippers with a bunch of roses embroidered on them tied with a piece of satin ribbon. They were a gift from Lynnette last Christmas. Having made sure the coast was clear Melanie headed across the landing to gently knock on Max's bedroom door. She was interrupting the work of an unwelcome intruder, busy searching for the answers it so desperately needed, in an ominously lit room. The ominous light was due to an unusual amount of dense cloud, shielding the soft, gentle glow of moonlight, as the shadowy figure worked on Max's unnaturally sedated form. Max having been forced into a coma, so it could begin its work. Malevolent and evil in its objective, irrational in its purpose, and without care, it lunged it's transparent claw like hands deep within Max's chest, causing irreparable damage and yet, even through the coma like sleep, the signs were clearly evident, that Max was in a great deal of pain. Keeping Max sedated while it worked seemed a charitable thing to do, but it was not, as the gentle incessant sound of knocking on the door infuriated the creature, forcing him to release Max and withdraw out of the room, as the door opened.

Melanie popped her head around the door to find Max fast asleep, and was unsure about waking him. She entered the room anyway and slowly made her way over to his bedside. Her hand hovered hesitantly over Max's shoulder, but she concluded, that Max would gain something fundamentally positive from what she was about show him. Melanie shook his shoulder saying, "Max! Max wake up, its Melanie." she insisted, before turning on the lamp by his bed. Max's eyes fluttered slightly before opening, to find what he could only describe as an angel standing over him wearing rose covered pyjamas, "Mel, what's wrong?" gasped Max with an immense amount of effort, due to the excruciating burning pain erupting from within his chest, while Melanie placed her hand over his mouth urging him to, "Shhh" before adding, "Do you trust me Max? I mean really trust me?" she asked firmly. That didn't sound like Mel. At first he didn't answer, simply because he wasn't quite sure if he was still a sleep or awake, but eventually, after managing to sit up said, "Yeh sure!","Why do you ask?" he uttered with a groan, feeling the after effects of the nightmare, as Melanie beckoned him to follow her, still indicating that he should keep quiet, as both headed down the staircase, and into the panelled room.

She turned on a table lamp and shut the door, "What's going on Mel? Why all the secrecy?" asked Max curiously, whilst glancing at the uniquely painted wall panels. Melanie faced him saying, "After our talk today, I wanted you to see something, something that will open your eyes to the bigger picture, but before you do, you have to give me your word that you won't tell anyone about it?" she asked seriously. Max was so intrigued by all the cloak and dagger routine that he agreed to her request, as his curiosity got the better of him. She took hold of his hand, led him across the room, and stopped, saying, "Oh wait. I'd better bring you a chair to sit on first, just in case." she explained in a matter of fact way that puzzled the hell out of Max.

After sitting down in the seat provided, Max watched curiously, as Melanie closed her eyes and waved her hand across the entire panelled wall in front of them. Max looked puzzled as he leaned forward, having seen sparks of raw energy escape from the palm of her hand, similar to his own experience, only this caused the entire panel to be engulfed in a soft glowing white light, that lit up the entire room. Max watched, remembering what had happened earlier, when the need to touch the stone pillars was so alluring. His hand began to tingle, forcing him to clench his fists, producing deep lacerations in the palms of his hands from his finger nails, while images began to form from within the panelling, strange mysterious landscapes looked frighteningly familiar.

A warm scented breeze drifted in through the opening in the wall to gently caress his face and hair, as it circulated around the room, and he breathed in a deep restorative breath of air before closing his eyes to savour the moment. A sudden rush of euphoric bliss fed the frantic need for serenity and calm that his body craved so desperately, replacing the fear and trepidation that haunted him like a ghost on a daily basis. His headache had suddenly disappeared, and the scar no longer burned as fiercely, causing Max to wonder why? Melanie smiled noticing the positive effect it was having on her friend, as Max opened his eyes to watch the vision slowly take shape and come alive. It showed both the Amarii and Orianas Moons acting like guardians of the night, reflecting their landscaped surface on the planet below.

The last remaining rays of sunlight bounced off its surface before disappearing, leaving a gradual stream of dark blue-purple hues, against the star speckled universal sky, reflected on the surface of a nearby lake, surrounded by lush plant life and large rock formations. Growing amongst the vegetation were clusters of delicately formed flowers that seemed to illuminate with each whispered touch from the breeze. Melanie took hold of his hand, having sat down beside him to share with him a small slice of heaven, and for the first time in his life he felt at peace.

Logically they were still in the panelled room, and yet for Max, it was as if they had been transported to another biosphere, in another as yet unknown galaxy. As Melanie pointed to the centre of the lake, an infusion of bubbles appeared, before fish the size of salmon, shot out of the water like missiles, their yellow scale-covered bodies speckled with a series of turquoise dots, they soared higher and higher, then miraculously transformed to become large birds, complete with feathered wings a long feathered tail and a pair of long legs. Their heads were similar to those of lizards, but instead of having beaks, they had mouths and razor sharp teeth. Melanie saw the look of disbelief on her friends face and said, "They are known as the Acipti." she claimed, as every single Acipti landed on overhanging tree branches nearby. One turned to look inquisitively at the two observers through the open vortex, and they saw hidden just under its wings, a pair of claw like hands.

Some Acipti performed a series of mid-air dance routines, while others gathered a meal consisting mainly of green and yellow porcupine tipped beetles that have elongated antennae folded neatly over their backs. Meanwhile hanging beneath the tree branches were large cocoon like nests the size of basketball hoops, made from a mixture of mud and vegetation, and nestled within each one, were chicks eagerly anticipating their next meal. Max stared in amazement as he shook his head in wonder thinking, 'Never in a million years would I have imagined, anything like this, but my God, I'm starting to believe it, cos I'm damn well looking at it! What a buzz!' He concluded, as for the first time ever Max actually smiled.

For the next three hours they continued to absorb the scenery and the daily life of the wildlife living nearby, one being a 4 inch long creature with razor sharp teeth and a nasty attitude, looking similar to an eel, known as a 'Culus', that without warning, shot out of the water to grab an unfortunate insect gliding majestically across the lake. The arrival of a group of inhabitants, hidden within the tree line opposite the lake, caught Max's immediate attention. The new arrivals made their way to the water's edge to wash their meagre collection of food, and gathered in family groups. They were known locally as 'the Grinlun', an intelligent creature reaching an average height of about 5ft, extremely shy of others and living in isolation. It resembled an evolved panda only without fur, slimmer in stature, with skin a faint reddish brown colour with traces of yellow here and there. It has large intelligent dark yellow/ green coloured eyes, and appears more comfortable walking on two legs instead of the usual four as a panda would.

A young Grinlun pop his head out from behind his father, and walk over to the water's edge carrying his small bundle of food. He sat down with a thud and began imitating the others in the group, in the art of cleaning before devouring his food enthusiastically. Another youngster joined him, and began a playful water fight, soaking everyone in the group, but instead of preventing it, the whole group joined in. Having heard the unwelcome noise, the Acipti popped their heads out of their nests to see what all the fuss was about, but they soon went back in and went to sleep, just as the Beliasis flowers, growing nearby, closed their petals until the end of yet another day. Having noticed the sun rising on this alien planet, Melanie decided to end the surprise saying, "We should stop now Max. We don't want anyone seeing us. But we could do this again sometime if you like?" she suggested.

Max appeared disappointed, but soon jumped at the chance of a repeat performance saying "Oh! God yes! How about tomorrow night and the next two nights after that, and if possible the whole of next week as well." he said in a jovial tone, and offered her a cheeky smile, while wiggling his eyebrows, causing her to burst out laughing saying, "I'll let you know when the next one will be ok? Don't worry, I will not attend one without you Max, I promise." she said, as an unusual looking bird called the 'Tulion' with its red, blue and yellow coloured feathers, and small down-curved beak and large eyes, watched them curiously, while perched precariously on the end of a tree branch. Melanie waved her hand over the panelled wall, leaving behind an ordinary hand painted panel, only this time it had an image of a Tulion bird posing attractively on the canvas, with an impish glint in its eye. "Come on, time for bed I think." said Mel with a suppressed yawn, with Max following close behind her, who decided to take one more look at the panelling on the wall before closing the door.

Having reached the top of the stairs, both whisper their good nights before heading to their own rooms. Melanie found Austin waiting for an all-important update. "Well, how did it go? Was I right?" he asked from his position on the bed, lounging against the headboard and a stack of pillows, with his legs crossed at the ankles, and his arms folded behind his head. He was tapping his foot to the beat of the music he was listening to on Melanie's iPod.

Melanie hurried over saying, "Yes, I think so. I could see a positive difference in Max the whole time we were there." she said excitedly, noticing an immediate nod of confirmation from Austin as he then said, "Good. I thought so. I wasn't too sure at first, whether it would work but..." and he paused having noticed the yawn Melanie was trying very hard to hide. "Bedtime for you young one, and don't give me any lip about it either." he said, pulling down the bed covers for her. "You will be able to help him won't you Austin? Max I mean." she pleaded, as Austin leaned close to her ear. "I will do my best" he said with gentle authority, and watched her drift into a deep sleep before going over to the window, to gaze out across the valley and letting out a heavy sigh, with his arms behind his back.

CHAPTER THIRTY-TWO

By mid-morning the following day Melanie, Vian and Max were busy checking out the bird boxes Mel had set up weeks earlier, but found not one of them had a nest in them, "I don't understand it, why aren't there any birds nesting in these things? I did everything correctly, I know I did." she complained, looking down from high up the ladder, the very same ladder Vian held steady, while Max and Austin looked on from a safe distance. "Have you ever thought that it could be due to a problem a little closer to home" commented Max casually, with his hands in his pockets, as three heads turned suddenly to face him, all with blank expressions on their faces. Max shrugged his shoulders saying, "Austin, your cat? They'll not nest if there's a cat nearby." Melanie's expression turned from blank to downright annoyed, as with each rung of the ladder she climbed down, she stomped her feet saying, "All the pain and anguish my poor hands went through, was for nothing. Well that does it! The birds can go to bloody hell for all I care. Hmm...There's nothing wrong with my dear sweet Austin, everyone knows he is as gentle as a lamb. Aren't you Austin? My little babykins!" she proclaimed to the world, making a sudden grab for him before he could make a clean getaway.

When at last the four super heroes of the bird nesting world entered the house through the front door, they heard verbal warfare being committed from inside the living room, as a voice said, "Do ya feel lucky? Well do ya punk?" announced Edna gleefully, closely followed by another voice saying, "In my experience there's no such thing as luck." It was Raan's voice. Edna immediately replied, "You're dog meat pal!" but Raan just laughed. "You've got all the leadership qualities of a cold rice pudding, old woman!" he claimed, enjoying the moment. Edna chuckled out a swift reply saying, "This old woman will send you into the next world old man, so get ready!" Raan erupted into bouts of laughter saying, "The next world and I are good friends old woman, so bring it on!" and laughed at his own joke. Meanwhile out in the hall Melanie, Max and Vian all glanced at each other, before going in to see what was going on.

Edna was having the time of her life as the verbal sparring continued with her saying, "You're about as quick as a spaced out slug. Why don't you surrender now old friend." "Make it easy on yourself." she suggested with a chuckle, as Raan replied, "You should know by now old woman, I don't believe in surrender. So get used to it!" he said smugly. Max, Melanie and Vian all entered the room with Austin still in Melanie's arms, all of whom, were stunned to find them playing a game of chess. Edna was wearing her lucky hat, and had a flask of her favourite tea by her side. She watched her opponent with eagle-eyed intent, who wore yet another of Max's T-shirts along with a bandana around his neck. Where he got that from nobody knew, but it looked good. "Hey guy's! What's happening?" asked Raan, taking his eyes away from the board for a split second. "We were just wondering the same thing" said Max curiously, before sitting down on the sofa opposite the board game. "We're having a serious game of chess, with a sharper edge" explained Edna, pointing to the two guns on either side of the table.

The sight of which, caused a horrified gasp from Melanie, as Edna said. "Relax for goodness sake, their only water pistols." "Get a move on Raan you useless toad. I want to win." announced Edna gleefully, while rubbing her hands in eager anticipation of winning. "I am not a toad, a frog yes, but never a toad." answered Raan with a raised eyebrow and a superior look on his face, whilst making his move. "My flask of tea's smarter than you, fool." claimed Edna laughing at her own joke. "Who's the more foolish? The fool, or the fool who follows him?" replied Raan, clearly amused at his own reply, as his next move caused an eruption of joy from Edna. She quickly made her move, shouting, "I win! Its check mate pal, you lose!" picking up her water pistol, without taking her eyes off her opponent, and rewarding him with the entire barrel load of water. At the first sign of water Austin shot out of Melanie's arms and into the hallway, closely followed by Vian. While Raan having realised he was cornered, tossed his water pistol at Max saying, "Here Max, I need backup, quick!" he said urgently, as Max lifted the water pistol, but didn't fire.

Sarah and Lynnette having made their escape early during the chess game, were busy sharing a pot of coffee in the kitchen, listening to the slow cooker preparing a vegetarian casserole, when Melanie walked in. "Ooh, coffee I'd love one." she said, sitting down at the table before helping herself. adding "Edna's won the chess match." Sarah shook her head saying, "We weren't getting involved with those two crazy eccentrics. Right Lynni? So we thought we'd hide here and prepare dinner, didn't we?" explained Sarah, when Lynnette caught Sarah's eye. "Yes you did, didn't you cherie? And I did all the work!" announced Lynnette folding her arms across her chest.

Sarah's retort to her friend was obvious. "How can you say that Lynni! I helped a little, didn't I?" she suggested, stretching the truth a little more, sending Lynnette into uncontrollable bouts of giggling saying, "Oh she helped! She'd eaten a good portion of the vegetables before they'd even got anywhere near the pot" she spluttered, and chuckled a little more. Sarah snubbed her long-time friend declaring, "If you're going to be like that Lynni, then I'm not going to help you ever again!" she said, imitating a spoilt child. Edna walked in carrying her empty flask, with Max following, who, having glanced over his shoulder, smiled at the sight that followed him, which was a very wet but happy Raan. Austin hid under the table listening to their conversations, and thought, ‘This is one crazy place I’m living in. They’re all raving mad. I’m going outside, before I go crazy.’ and with that, he hopped onto the window sill and out through the open window...

CHAPTER THIRTY-THREE

Owing to the sudden unannounced thunder storm keeping everyone awake that bit longer, Melanie waited for as long as she dared, before getting Max for their regular cinema visits to the other planet. She was quick to conclude that, 'Austin had been right, the visits were helping Max.' she didn't quite understand the how's and why's, but whatever it was it helped Max. He was eager to ask Melanie a question, a question that had been bugging him for days, and so, without taking his eyes off the scene that was becoming a vital part of his life he now asked, "Have you told any of your friends the truth yet?" he wondered aloud, as Melanie watched a Zinie dart playfully across a tree branch, before diving off the end of it, to catch a bunch of falling berries, saying with a heavy sigh, "I've wanted to tell them for quite a while, but I need to be sure they won't freak out or anything. You're in the same boat as I am, and as we're only just finding out the truth ourselves, there's no real point...Yet. We'll cross that bridge when we come to it, ok?" advised Mel sensibly.

Max tried to ignore the loud cracks of thunder from outside the window before daring to ask, "There's something wrong with me isn't there. You don't have to deny it Mel, I know there's something wrong, I can feel it, the pain I suffer isn't normal is it? And if I'm honest, it's gradually getting worse, and yet, when we come here, to our secret get together it does make a difference. I must admit that the pain's been bad lately, so that I don't sleep much any more, or at least I can't remember sleeping." admitted Max confusingly, and paused before adding, "Whenever you look at me I sense you know more about what's going on, but your reluctant to tell me, so I think it's time I knew the truth don't you? I think I can handle it Mel, how about you tell me some of it now." he asked in a way that surprised Mel. A sudden flash of lightning followed by a loud crack of thunder sounded outside, when another voice spoke saying, "Are you quite sure you can handle the truth Max, because when the truth's been laid out in front of you, you'd better be ready for the next step, cos it will be a real doozie." explained the voice earnestly.

Max suddenly shot to his feet and turned towards the voice saying, "What the..." as another flash of light along with a crack of thunder sounded, turning the whole scene into a poorly written horror movie. Max stared at his worst nightmare come to life, while staggering dangerously close to the partly open vortex. Melanie made a grab for him while he continued to stare at whatever it was that was staring right back at him, when Melanie spoke saying, "Austin, what were you thinking, you could've killed him scaring him like that." she said, keeping a tight hold of Max, who looked as if he was about to pass out. Austin's reply was understandable, "You forget child, I hear your thoughts, yours and everyone else's in this crazy house. I knew what he was about to ask, so there was no time for soft-soaping him, or getting out the Kleenex." announced Austin taking several small steps forward, hoping the boy did not fall head first into the bloody vortex. "Don't you think Max ought to sit down before he falls down." he suggested before adding, "Mel sit him down for goodness sake" advised Austin as Mel guided Max into the nearest chair, while giving Austin a look that told him it was all his fault that Max was in such a state, not hers.

All Max could do was look at Austin in slack-jawed amazement and Melanie rubbed his hand, as he asked, "What the hell is that thing?" unable to tear his eyes away from the sight in front of him. Austin replied, clearly offended "Thing?! Thing?! You cheeky little...The name is Austin, Melanie's guardian and protector." explained Austin in a sharp tone, while he carefully unfolded his wings. Another loud crack of thunder echoed outside, before he made himself comfortable on the small settee, opposite the boy, whose lips twitched having seen the quirky fringe hanging over one eye, but didn't dare laugh, after all, he'd seen enough horror films to know, he could very well end up a dead man if he did. Melanie stared at Austin saying "I'm surprised you didn't offer Max a glass of brandy, after all, you did me." while Austin looked Max in the eyes saying, "There's no need for that, Max is strong enough to handle the situation, aren't you Max?"

But Max was unsure as to what he could handle, when he replied nervously, "Yeh sure! ...I think." looking from one to the other. Austin continued to look Max in the eye saying, "Tarak was right the other day, when he said you'll get to know the truth when we know it, but I can give you some of the basics now? But I'll keep it short otherwise we will be here all damn night." All Max could do was nod his head in agreement, wishing that the bloody thunder would go away, when Austin added, "We know about the headaches, and the pain you suffer due to the scar on your chest, that started around the age of 16. The moment we met you, we identified you as one of us, as we did Melanie, but the problem for us was that Melanie we knew about, but you...Max, you were a shock, we had no idea you existed." admitted Austin seriously, sensing the boys heart beating faster and faster by the minute, as a question left the boys lips asking, "Are you telling me that like Mel, I'm part alien?" asked Max, eager to know the truth, wondering if his mother was alien.

But Austin having seen the thoughts buzzing around the boys head replied, "Don't be an idiot Max! This is real life not a science fiction film." "Try and focus your mind for goodness sake!" instructed Austin, while Max looked with raised eye brows, saying rather bravely, with just a hint of sarcasm, "Ok Einstein, I'll take that as a no then shall I?" Mel's lips twitched, as she continued to watch the interaction between Max and Austin, noticing how well Max was taking it, when Austin added, "There's no other way of saying this Max, so

I'm going to have to tell you straight, ok?" he announced, while interlocking his fingers across his chest. "On the night you were born, Taban tried to save…" uttered Austin, as Max interrupted him saying, "I know all this Austin, that's old news as far as I'm concerned, so get on with it!" instructed Max, with a sharp edge in his tone.

Austin raised an eyebrow, due to Max's sudden show of temper and answered, "I know you do boy, but that's only half of the story, the only way Taban could have saved you, was by transferring himself into her body, making the transfer more potent" explained Austin, in an almost dead pan tone, when the boy asked curiously, "Is that why I have the scar?" and Austin replied, "The fact is, Taban was and still is very ill, and as such, the energy levels in the transferral intensified to a dangerous level, hence the scar" announced Austin seriously. Max looked somewhat alarmed and he asked, "There's something you're not telling me...What is it?" Austin didn't bat an eye when he replied "That's the part we don't know...yet. I know it's frustrating Max, but we're not exactly overjoyed about it either. Put simply, we don't know. We're going to have to be patient, until we do." and with that, he transformed back into the cat we all know and love.

Max had to blink several times, wondering if what he had witnessed was real, as Austin gave him a sly wink, before leaving as Mel asked, "Are you alright Max" she wondered aloud, as Max replied, while still in a state of shock, "Yeh, I think so, but I'm more in the dark now than I was before. He hasn't told me anything new has he? Making me wonder if it was deliberate." he admitted, listening to the heavy rain lashing against the windows, feeling as if he was living in a nightmare, before saying goodnight to Mel and heading off to bed.

CHAPTER THIRTY-FOUR

The forecast for the following day was good, so sunbathing and Margaritas were a 'must', according to rule No Six of Lynnette and Sarah's do good things list. Both were reorganising the back garden. The music was playing, the sun loungers were out and the umbrellas were up, "Hurry up Mel with the ice!!" shouted Sarah, busy making cocktails, mostly non-alcoholic. Lynnette hurried out carrying a tray loaded down with snacks, and placed it within arm's reach of Edna, who looked as if she had just stepped off a Hollywood Movie set. Max sat in one of the vacant chairs nearest the house, with his book and pencil working frenziedly, recreating a host of characters he'd seen a few nights before.

Melanie hurried outside with a bucket full of ice for Sarah, before sitting on a lounger in the shade of a huge umbrella. Just then a voice shouted, having just exited the back door, "Hey! You lucky people! I'm here at last!!" announced Raan enthusiastically, wearing yet another of Max's T shirts. Austin vacated the area by climbing the nearest tree thinking, 'The idiot gets worse with each passing day. I think we ought to ban him from watching TV programs, they're obviously a bad influence. In fact, we ought to ban him from doing anything.' he concluded. Max recognised the top Raan was wearing, was about to say something, but decided not to, thinking, 'Oh! What's the point' and he carried on listening to the music on his iPod.

Later while snoozing in her chair, listening to the sounds of a steam train and a farmer's tractor echoing across the valley, Sarah's sleepy voice asked "Would someone rub some lotion on my back? Before I burn." she asked, as Raan flew across the garden. "I'll do it!" he offered generously, taking Sarah by surprise. Within minutes of his hands touching Sarah's back, a spark of mischief emerged in his eyes, and he whispered something in her ear. Suddenly Sarah leapt to her feet shouting, "Right! That does it!! Mel!! Raan's causing trouble again, stop him or I'll start lashing out with my fists!!" promised Sarah, with her fists already clenched. Raan appeared the epitome of innocence asking, "Was it something I said?" having seen Melanie heading his way with Max in tow. Once Mel had left Max asked, "Umm Raan, can I ask you something?" Which caused all the visitors ears to prick up.

"What is it?" mumbled Raan with closed eyes, having laid back against the sun lounger Sarah had vacated. Max sprawled across the grass, "What do you really look like?" he asked, unable to hold back his curiosity any longer. Raan opened his eyes, "I couldn't show you yet, after all, we wouldn't want to frighten anyone." he announced calmly, as Max responded by asking, "Why not?" "You're not terrifyingly ugly are you?" he enquired with a chuckle. Raan paused before adding, "Well, it depends on how you look at it, I take it you've watched the film Aliens? So naturally, you will have seen the weird looking alien creatures, correct?" enquired Raan in a calm tone, giving his young friend enough time to look suitably horrified, as Raan then added, "Well...We look nothing like that so you can relax" and closed his eyes.

Max then asked, "How long have you been visiting Earth? Can you at least tell me that?" he asked feeling a little frustrated, which caused Raan to smile saying, "You're an inquisitive little monkey, aren't you?" he said before replying, "It's difficult because, from our point of view, we've only just begun exploring, but from your perspective, we've been here quite a while, so it depends on how you look at it." he concluded seriously, knowing how frustrating it must be for his young friend. Max was left feeling annoyed and somewhat put out about the whole ordeal and remarked, "That was the most vague, inaccurate load of bull I have ever heard, thanks a lot Raan, you've been a joy!" and headed off towards the house for a snack.

Listening to a host of musical greats being played on the radio before a classic U2 song, entitled 'Original of the Species' was chosen, Sarah hurried to turn up the volume. Max leaned against the kitchen door eating his sandwich, watching Vian guide a surprised Mel into a dance on the lawn. "What are you doing?" she asked, having never seen this side of him before. Vian's reply was an obvious one, "We're dancing, I think." he remarked, trying to remember all he had learned on the internet, while Melanie's laughter echoed in his ears. The dance started slow and clumsily at first, but as the momentum changed, so did the dance, causing everyone to laugh. A sudden high pitched squeal of an animal in pain caused an immediate halt. Austin very nearly fell out of the tree he was sleeping in, Raan shot off the sun longer so fast, it landed right on top of him, before realising it was Sarah who screamed and not some great hairy monster, because she had seen Tristan running towards her with a huge smile on his face. "Did you miss me?" he asked, as Edna, on the spur of the moment, announced she was going shopping, and instructed Lynnette, Sarah, Tristan and Tarak to go with her.

CHAPTER THIRTY-FIVE

The group waved goodbye, with their fingers crossed behind their backs, having realised it was Edna doing the driving. Vian gave Raan the signalled nod, while Max and Austin, who had transformed into his true self, guided a somewhat confused Mel into the panelled room, closely followed by Vian and Raan, who carried with them a picnic basket. "What's going on?" she asked clearly puzzled by all the cloak and dagger routine, when Raan smiled, saying in an overly hushed tone, "Shhh, it's a surprise, but a nice one, I promise." and winked at her, while Max waited in eager anticipation for what was about to happen, having been made part of the planning team.

With the door to the panelled room firmly closed, Vian guided Melanie over to a chair and sat her down, and placed a finger over her lips indicating that she should "shush" and left her staring at him open mouthed, as he went to join the others. Austin with an air of authority turned to face them saying, "Right, you know what to do? So let's get started before the others get back. Hopefully your grandmother will unknowingly keep them busy for a while, the crazy old loon", explained Austin, with a hope and a prayer, while he glanced at Max, who was ignorant of the fact that this was to be a test for him as well. To see what abilities, if any, he had inherited through the DNA transfer with Taban.

Raan turned to Max saying, "Now, remember what we told you Max, and everything will be ok. You will not be harmed in any way, or at least you shouldn't be." stated Raan, putting on a show of looking worried, as Max stepped away from the panelling asking "What?". "Stop teasing the boy Raan, or you'll be the one going through the damn thing, and you'll not be coming back!" announced Austin with authority. Raan merely winked at Max saying, "Sorry Max, I couldn't resist teasing you." he claimed, giving his young friend a hug. Melanie leaned forward in anticipation as her friends linked hands, with their palms flat and their eyes closed, and what surprised her the most was the fact that Max was involved, making her wonder what Austin was up to, hearing him say, "Now focus your thoughts on the vortex Max, and you will begin to see it opening in your mind's eye. As soon as that happens, you must break the link with us, ok? We'll keep it open for the time needed" explained Austin, as Max nodded his head saying, "Ok, got it." Almost immediately an amazing vision materialized in his mind's eye, a vision so effervescent, so vibrant and full of life, it made him stagger back in surprise. Nothing could have prepared him for what he was seeing, sensing and experiencing, but most of all wanting, needing and craving. He could feel himself being pulled both physically and mentally into the vortex, almost as if the very essence of his life force was being sucked into it. He had neither the strength nor the willpower to prevent it. His whole body moved towards the vortex with a will of its own, when suddenly the sound of Austin's commanding voice, echoing inside his head got his full attention, 'Max! Focus your mind boy, do not lose yourself in the open vortex. Come on, you can do it, now focus!!!' shouted Austin, giving Max enough time to gain control, as Raan announced, "You can release the link with us now Max" and let go of his hand.

Max slowly opened his eyes, to see what they had created, and boy, he was not disappointed! He thought, the visits with Melanie were something special, but this...this was something else entirely, this was beyond miraculous, the intense pleasure of it made his heart sing. Max stared at the vision in front of him, saying, "Oh my god...This is amazing!!" he uttered, when a sudden touch of a hand on his shoulder forced him to look away, to find Melanie standing next to him. "My God Mel this is, what can I say? It's fantastic!! exclaimed Max with a hint of awe in his voice. Melanie turned to Vian and asked, "Are we going through the vortex?" she wondered with a flash of excitement. "Not all of us, just you and Vian" explained Austin, as Raan interrupted them by saying "Yeh, you're going on a date, isn't that exciting!" he said with a silly smile on his face, giving Vian the picnic basket loaded with goodies.

Melanie turned to ask, "What about Max, wouldn't he like to come as well?, I'm sure he would" she said generously. "Hell Yeh!" admitted Max, giving Austin a cold hard look. Vian took hold of Melanie's hand and guided her carefully through the vortex, taking her to another world. Max watched and shook his head in wonder as he took an inquisitive step forwards, for the urge to follow was powerfully strong, when Raan said, with a huge smile on his face, "Come on Max! I'll treat you to a walk through the woods." he offered generously, as Max turned to give Raan his full attention saying "Oh Joy, a walk through the woods, I can hardly contain my excitement." feeling as if he had just been punched in the stomach, watching in heart felt misery as the vortex closed. Raan replied "I'll even show you my collection of unusually shaped rocks." acting as if he was giving away one of his biggest secrets. Max stared in disbelief saying, "You have got to be kidding me, you are joking right! Raan...Raan!! Please tell me you're kidding ...Raan?!" shouted Max.

CHAPTER THIRTY-SIX

Meanwhile back on Vian's home world called Munastas, a planet situated in a far off Galaxy, Melanie was for the first time, euphoric and as giddy as a school kid, mesmerized by everything around her as she hurried on ahead of Vian, eager to explore, touch and smell everything within arm's reach, every tree, leaf, flower, stone and blade of grass, you name it she went ahead and touched it. The air appeared lighter, fresher and sweeter to the human senses, an experience she revelled in. Vian could not believe any one person could get so excited over a visit to his home world, that so simple a thing could bring his beloved such joy and happiness. He felt foolish for not thinking of it sooner, and after an hour of exploring, Vian decided it was time to eat, and chose the perfect spot near the lake, surrounded by vibrant colours and lush vegetation, with the Yoltana waterfall sparkling all the brighter, thanks to huge shards of crystal that had penetrated the planets natural bed rock.

Melanie looked up to find the Orianas and Amarii Moons watching her, welcoming her, protecting her in their own special way, as she impulsively spun around in a circle with her arms out wide, feeling a sudden rush of euphoric bliss coursing through her veins, before glancing over her shoulder to find Vian watching her, while he laid out the food and set down the music player, pressing the play button. She went to join him, but the music chosen for them made them laugh, forcing them to utter just one word "Raan?" while Vian sat by Melanie feeding her an assortment of berries and mixed salad, and she did the same for him, in between the odd experimental kiss or two, being one of the most memorable days of her entire life, one she would never forget.

From the moment Melanie had stepped into this new and unexplored world, she was unaware of the fact that she was being watched, for just a short distance away, a couple stood, tall, regal, yet nervous and apprehensive. Both wore shoulder length jet black hair, and had a pale white-grey skin tone, and a transfixed expression, due to the young girl before them, who right now fulfilled Vian's every waking dream. That recognised her as their only granddaughter, named Melanie Rose. Attempting to say her name had been difficult at first, after Austin had passed on the information all those years ago, along with images of her growing up on the farm, feeding their frustrations at having to wait until the time was right, before they could meet her, and at last that time was now.

Tenzin, Melanie's grandfather placed a reassuring arm around his wife's waist, guiding her closer to him, knowing it would help his beloved Amarah find the courage needed to introduce herself to her new granddaughter. He looked down to see tears of joy and immense happiness filling his beloved's eyes, as Amarah linked hands with her husband saying, "She's more beautiful than I had ever imagined her to be, but I am afraid Tenzin, I'm afraid it might be too much for her if we face her now, what do you think? What should we do?" Tenzin smiled at his beloved wife before kissing her on the lips, bringing a little colour back to her pale cheeks, saying 'If we do not go out there now and introduce ourselves, then I will never hear the end of it, and besides, I thought you were the strong one in our bonding?' he announced with a smile. But Amarah looked even more nervous as she replied, 'Right now I am not.' she uttered, allowing Tenzin the opportunity of guiding her out into the open.

Vian knew the instant Melanie's grandparents had arrived, and the fact that Tenzin had to forcibly guide his wife out into the open made Vian smile. He turned to face Melanie saying, "I have a surprise for you, I would like to introduce you to some people I know." he uttered, offering a helping hand before turning her to face... her grandparents. Melanie's heart leapt into her mouth and almost choked her, having recognised who they were, while the couple made their way over to her. Melanie could feel Vian standing right behind her with his hands on her shoulders reassuring her. Amarah's hands shook slightly as she clutched them to her chest, with Tenzin's arm around his wife's waist, this was confirmation enough that Amarah was as nervous as Melanie was, giving her the courage to slowly walk up to them, offer them a shy smile, saying hesitantly, "Hello." "..I'm Melanie..." she uttered nervously, as her throat was seized with a wave of emotion.

But courage gave her the strength to go up to her grandmother, and gently wrap her arms around her, giving her a loving embrace. Melanie could feel Amarah's body shake moments before her own body was enfolded in an equally loving embrace. Tenzin smiled at Vian noticing his wife's immense joy caused an explosion of wild flowers around their feet before Melanie pulled away, as Tenzin and Amarah then uttered aloud, "Hello." but before saying anything else, Amarah placed her hand on Melanie's saying, 'Did we say it right?' she asked, as Melanie replied "Yes, you said it perfectly" turning to give her grandfather Tenzin a welcome hug, but found herself being lifted into the air and spun around in circles, causing everyone to laugh. Within minutes they were sitting on the blanket eating what Max and Raan had packed in the way of food, while Tenzin inspected the music player, finding it a highly amusing toy, while the afternoon became more of a success, they talked, laughed, joked and had a wonderful time, but just as the sun began to set behind the Munastan planet, casting a glow of soft effervescent colours, Vian announced it was time to leave, much to Melanie's disappointment and regret. "Austin's rallied the others, apparently he has Raan performing one of his best acting roles, claiming to have received a call from

Max, whose had an accident somewhere in the woods and needs help, when in fact, Max is upstairs in his bedroom hiding. Edna's forming a search party as we speak." claimed Vian who wondered how Edna would react when she found out the truth.

Melanie and Amarah did not want their time to end, as Melanie impulsively removed her favourite necklace and placed it around her grandmother's neck, kissed them both on the cheek before returning to Vian's side. The teary-eyed smile from her grandmother was all Melanie needed to get her through the next few days, until she could visit them again, as she reluctantly waved goodbye. Melanie and Vian looked back to see a moving image of Tenzin and Amarah waving to them, as the vortex sealed itself. Melanie continued to look at the image for several minutes before Amarah turned and walked away, holding the precious gift Melanie had given her in the palm of her hand, with her head resting against her beloved's shoulder. Tenzin was not left empty handed, for tucked under his other arm was the music player, an intriguing device he was most reluctant to part with.

Meanwhile back on earth an angry voice shouted, "Alright!! Where is he!! I'm going to ring his dammed neck when I find him." said one voice, when another said, "I am going to slowly marinade him in a barrel of French wine, while he's still alive." and the final voice uttered "Get in line girls, I'm going first, some may call it murder, but I'll call it extreme self-defence." announced Edna. Raan uttered nervously, "I think it's time for me to leave." and as if by magic he disappeared, as three women walked in. Following them in was a rather bemused Tarak who, having willingly volunteered to help them in the search, found it the highlight of his visit here.

CHAPTER THIRTY-SEVEN

Later during dinner, Edna noticed the dark rings and almost pure white complexion of her grandson, and asked, "Max, are you alright?" looking a little worried, worried enough to gain everyone's attention. Max having been suddenly pushed under the spot light, which he hated, glanced across at Edna saying, "I'm ok...why?" he replied dubiously, causing her to add "I ask because you have dark circles under your eyes and a complexion a ghost would envy, that's why!" she announced adding, "I want to know what's going on, and I want to know now." giving everyone a do not mess with me look. Max knew that look, he'd seen the poor Reverend Hislop receive it on more than one occasion, when his sermon had taken too long, or his song choice had been wrong. Max caught Edna's eye saying, "Umm... You see, basically. It's like this. I'm er..." But before he could finish, Tarak interrupted him saying, "He goes night fishing with me?" Everyone looked as if he had suddenly grown an extra head, including Max, and it was obvious to all that Edna was having a hard time believing it.

Melanie and Vian had decided to take a romantic walk together along the river bank, Vian wore a dark T shirt and jeans while Melanie wore a sequin encrusted Indian style top over a pair of light coloured jeans with her hair down, so the breeze could ruffle her curls. She glanced furtively at Vian and asked "Umm...Vian, this may sound odd but, do you age as we do, you know humans, or are you a lot older...Say in your fifties or something like that, I don't mind if you are because I like older men although, now that I think about it, you being a hundred plus might give me second thoughts." she replied a little too honestly. After all, she'd seen enough X-Files and Sci Fi films to get her wondering all kinds of stuff. Vian stared at Melanie as if she had suddenly turned into a 5ft 8inch tall Zinie, and burst into uncontrollable laughter, and he continued laughing for quite a while before he could say anything. "Sorry Mel, I couldn't help myself, that was the funniest thing I have ever heard, and believe me, I have heard a lot from Raan over the years." he admitted. Melanie stood with her hands on her hips and her foot tapping, a sure indication that she did not see the funny side of a genuine question. Having regarded Melanie's somewhat annoyed stance Vian replied soothingly, "We age as you do, I am about 33 Earth years old" he admitted, and gently took hold of her hand, having just guided her across the old wooden bridge 'minus the troll'. Melanie spotted the first of many stone columns positioned around the area and while reaching out her hand to trace them with her fingers, noticed them tingle and gradually come alive with a sudden burst of energy, causing her to step back as Max had done. She asked curiously, "I know you recognise the symbols carved in the stone, but I have to ask." "How did they get here?" she wondered curiously, as Vian answered saying, "They symbolise our language, the Escenii language. They are a stored conduit of raw energy we brought here to supply the vortex, without which, we would not be able to stay here for as long as we do".

Melanie was intrigued by this vital piece of information, and said "They came by space ship right? And you have it hidden somewhere, protected by a cloaking devise of some kind...Oh! Wow this is great! Can we see it? I'd love to see an alien space ship!" She asked with the eagerness of a child. Vian having never seen this almost immature child-like excitement in her before, did not want to spoil it by telling her that there never was a space craft... Well not here on earth, and and said, "You think the silliest things Melanie," "Come on, let's continue with our walk shall we?" he suggested, leaving her standing there feeling utterly bereft, with her hands firmly planted on her hips, "How can you walk away like that!" shouted Mel before adding "Are you saying there isn't one hidden away somewhere Vian! Vian are you even listening to me?" she yelled, as he disappeared, giving Melanie no option but to hurry after him.

But the moment she was by his side, Vian replied, "No Melanie that is not what I am saying. There is a space craft hidden away... But not here." he admitted, walking several more steps with Melanie beside him. Melanie thought for a moment before saying, "You mean, it's hidden in another country right" she asked before letting out a gasp saying, "You don't mean to say it's hidden near...Area 51?! It is isn't it? It's near Area 51, right?" and paused briefly before adding "Why hide it there you idiot," but Vian shook his head replying, "Wrong again my beloved, when I said it wasn't hidden here, what I meant to say was that it wasn't hidden here on this planet." he established seriously, as Melanie's temper exploded and she said "Why didn't you say so in the first place? Why all the song and dance?!" "Right now I don't know whether I should be angry with you or laugh about it." commented Melanie heatedly, while walking up and down in an agitated state, trying to make up her mind. This gave Vian the opportunity to turn and face her saying, "Would you settle for a kiss as an apology instead?" he offered, hoping she would say yes.

But what he expected and what he got were two very different things, for heading straight for him at high speed was a dark auburn-haired, violet-eyed missile that very nearly knocked him to the ground. He carried her over to a patch of lush green grass, and laid her down with his lips still firmly pressed against hers, while he held onto one of her hands, so together, they might experience the full onslaught of the love he had for her, while his other hand travelled slowly over her body committing every loving inch of it to memory. He ended their kiss so he could gaze deep into her heart, which shone so brightly through her eyes, as Melanie lifted her free hand to cradle the side of Vian's face, and asked with a curious beguiling smile, "What is it?" Vian merely shook his head saying, "I want to remember this moment, and tell you that I do love you Melanie Rose. I love you more than it is possible to love anyone," he admitted earnestly with a slight hint of embarrassment. Melanie gazed deep into his eyes with tears blurring her vision saying, "I think underneath it all, you're a sweet romantic trying to get out, you know that don't you, and I love you for it." declared Mel having realised for the first time, that he really did love her. Vian laughed and admitted saying "I borrowed Max's computer and did some research on 'romance' using a thing called the internet." he confessed awkwardly.

Melanie laughed out loud saying, "You did all that for me! What else did you find?" she asked curiously. Vian having caught her gaze, held it and said seriously, "For you, I would do anything, and as to the other question I would rather not say." and ended it by kissing her passionately, pulling her nearer to him as his need for her grew with each passing second. Suddenly she stopped and pulled away to cup Vian's face with her hands saying, "I've just realised something. You haven't answered my question, have you? You changed the subject." she said accusingly with a hint of humour, while Vian traced the delicate contours of her cheek, eye brow and lips with his fingertips before saying playfully, "Didn't I?...Well my inquisitive one, they used another hidden Vortex as a core conduit" but before she could utter a reply he covered her lips with his own, and continued kissing her, until a vital source of oxygen was needed, forcing them to separate briefly.

Vian was as close to being in paradise as anyone could be, for an alien. Melanie concentrated on Vian's soft gentle voice, speaking to her telepathically, telling her over and over again just how much he truly loved her, while she sent her own words of love, knowing that at long last, her uncertainty had disappeared, thanks to a surprising visit to Munastas and an introduction to her grandparents. Intimately they showed their love for each other, a love that will no doubt, continue for as long as there are stars in the night's sky.

CHAPTER THIRTY-EIGHT

Later that night, the time was fast approaching 2am, and at the top of the stair, a small creature was spotted lounging across the top step, it was Austin, having concluded that this was to be the beginning of a new era for him as a guardian. For that task now rested on Vian's shoulders, for their relationship had moved onto the next step, and even now they were sharing a bedroom. But the one thing Austin would miss the most would be the morning play time together, they were special moments, one of many actually, and the possibility of being someone else's watcher did not appeal to him, not after his sweet Mel.

Austin continued to listen to the rain hitting the roof top above his head, concealing the unending silence he hated so much. 'Why does it always rain on this damn planet, and does it have to sound so loud?' he asked aggravatedly, when his thoughts were suddenly interrupted by a different sound, a more nerve shattering unearthly sound, coming from inside Max's bedroom. A desperate voice was crying out for help, saying over and over again, "No!! No more I beg you please!! When will it end! Why won't it end?!" yelled the tortured voice to an empty room, adding after a brief pause, "Why did you leave me? Am I to be forever plagued by the monster within? Please? Help me?!" yelled the persecuted voice. Austin wasted very little time in getting inside Max's room, and was standing by Max's bed in his true form within seconds, looking down at a boy who was in dire torment, suffering an inflow of feelings that were obviously not his own, but were in fact, a product of Taban's.

Austin meanwhile, having never dealt with anything like this link between Max and Taban before, wondered how long the abuse had been going on for, and continued to watch while the young boy unknowingly cradled his head while he slept, hoping it might ease the unending suffering, while at the same time, protect him from the invisible forces that were hard at work, destroying what remained of his fragile sanity. Having realised that the boys sleep pattern needed improvement, to be strong enough to survive what lay ahead, which could cost the loss of not two lives, but quite possibly three, Austin knew of only one temporary solution to this problem, a solution he had not done in a very long time. He glided effortlessly onto the bed, scarcely making a bounce, and stood with his legs on either side of the boy's body with his wings fully open, and entered a meditative state, ignoring the agonising cries of the person he was desperately trying to save.

Then suddenly with a rapid surge of energy, causing his entire body to glow and levitate above the bed, Austin's eyes transformed in colour, from a bright green to a molten black, while his wings expanded to double their normal size, glowing an effervescent blue/green, as several items of furniture toppled over onto the thick shag pile carpet. Austin knew he had to act fast, as his wings began to envelope them both, to resemble an unusually large chrysalis-styled pod, that emitted a sequence of shimmering brown, green and orange colours.

Now securely housed inside the almost impenetrable pod, Austin waved his hand across Max's face, sending him into an even deeper sleep, having noticed the boy's eyelids start to flutter and begin opening, "Rest easy Max…Sleep." instructed Austin in a hypnotic tone, and Max did exactly that, while Austin let out a sigh of immense relief. The temperature inside the chrysalis was moderate and comfortable for both occupants. Both were able to see quite clearly as a volume of energised light filtered in through the thin membrane of the fleshy wings. Max began to settle down and sleep more peacefully, and the unsettling images vanished, it was a huge blessing for Max, but a great relief for Austin.

However for Taban, the mood was far from being good. He staggered suddenly as the link between him and the boy was brutally weakened, severed by a stronger source of power, causing him to snarl and grit his teeth in a fit of frustration, trying to ignore the annoying sound of the car radio, whose occupants were busy celebrating an anniversary. Taban wondered who could be strong enough to sever such a link between him and the boy so effortlessly, but realised the source immediately, and uttered a cold and malicious curse, the name "Austin!!"

The mere mention of Austin's name caused the Demon within to lose control, fury, rage and resentment fired his almost cold dead emotionless heart, before feeding the rest of his hosts body, turning this once kind, gentle being into a dangerous and highly unpredictable predator, while it uttered with the briefest of whispers the words 'so close' producing a series of ugly black veins in and around Taban's eyes, spreading progressively across the whole of his face, neck and chest, resembling the tentacles of an evil looking monster. Deciding it shall wait no longer, it forced the strongest power of persuasion towards Max, bringing him back to its will, forcing the young captive to witness, the sudden birth of this horrific new transmutation, while it slowly and purposefully approached the couple in the parked car.

The sudden distorted images and sounds flooding the boys mind, that had somehow bypassed Austin's defences, caused the vulnerable young captive to become more unsettled, as the distorted sound of music, intermingled with a couples terrified screams swamped the boy's head, and along with it, a lingering sound of a laugh, a laugh so frighteningly evil, it caused Max to cry out in utter terror. Almost immediately the lingering migraine that had haunted Max all these years doubled in strength. Austin quickly subdued Max's flaying hands and fist's, preventing him from attacking his own head, hoping it would stop the pain and unwelcome images flooding his mind.

Austin positioned his hands on two strategic areas of Max's body, one hand settled over the boy's heart preying its energy might protect what is hidden there, and likewise strengthen its defences. His other hand was placed against the side of Max's head near his temporal lobe to see what the boy was seeing, Austin's whole body jerked violently when the link between them was established, as a multitude of flashing images flooded his alien mind. Most were of people, places and familiar landscapes, that appear almost blackened and distorted, similar to that from an old movie camera that had been singed by fire. The images of an old book shop where Melanie used to visit caught Austin's full attention, as did those of a parked car, Austin's first thoughts on seeing this were, 'No, Taban, don't do it' but it was too late, for the nightmare had already begun.

Austin turned his attention to Max, and tried communicating with him through the link, "Max, please listen to me, you must listen to me. Do you understand? Focus on my voice and only my voice, do you understand me? Forget everything else, just focus on my voice do you hear me boy?" instructed Austin to his young friend. Austin's familiar voice reverberated inside Max's head, almost as if he was speaking down a long tunnel. "Austin?" asked Max with a slurred and somewhat confused voice, adding, "What's going on, how the hell are you doing this?" wondered Max aloud through a haze of pain, Austin could not have been more pleased if he had won the lottery, once the connection with Max had been established. "It doesn't matter how I'm doing this boy, just accept it alright? Now! Pay attention to what I'm going to tell you." explained Austin, taking Max's silence as acceptance, before adding with a sense of humour, "Look I wasn't Dracula's accomplice for nothing you know, so live with it and besides, it goes without saying that I'm a creature of many talents." admitted Austin smugly.

Max wasn't fooled for a second by this show of humour, he knew there was a valid reason for Austin's presence inside his mind, so he got straight to the point and asked, "What I just saw was real wasn't it, they're not all dreams are they? They have to be…" to which Austin replied, "They're real up to a point, the images you see are memories, some of which appear warped and distorted over time." explained Austin reassuringly. Max was left feeling somewhat confused and asked "I don't understand, they're obviously not mine, so they must belong to someone else, who?" but before he could get a good enough answer, Edna's commanding voice was heard shouting at Tarak, whose immovable body stood between her and her grandson, "Get out of the bloody way you long-haired spaniel!" she instructed sternly, but Tarak was unfazed by Edna's insults and calmly replied, "Please return to your room Edna, everything is alright" advised Tarak, with a 'I shall not move' look in his eye.

Edna straightened her thin shoulders and said, "Really? Well I don't think it is. So if you don't get your bony ass out of the way in the next ten seconds I'll..." But before she could finish her reply the door behind Tarak opened, and there stood Max with Austin. "What's going on out here?" asked Max scratching his head. Edna looked at her grandson as if he had just grown another head "I came to see if you were alright but this, this sorry excuse wouldn't let me in." explained Edna in a quarrelsome tone, Max hid a grin saying, "I'm ok, it was just a nightmare. Sorry if I woke you. Go back to bed. I'm fine really." he replied, with his fingers crossed behind his back, knowing he wouldn't normally lie to her.

Edna was unsure whether to believe him or not, after all, she'd been aware of his disturbed sleep patterns ever since he first arrived on her door step, but reluctantly, she went back to her room, but not before kissing Max on the cheek, followed by a full-on black look for Tarak, and she hesitated in closing her door, to offer Tarak yet another of her world renowned dark glares. The moment Edna had disappeared, Tarak turned to face Max and Austin, who immediately transformed back into his true form before beckoning Tarak into the room. They were about to shut the door, when Raan popped his head in saying in a secretively hushed tone, "Wait for me!" and shoved his way through the opening before laying on the bed with his arms behind his head, smiling as if all was right with the world.

Nevertheless things were quite the opposite for Taban, whose malicious gratification for what he had created filled his heart, as he inhaled the deep invigorating aroma of burning flesh and scorched earth, intermingled with engine oil and burnt rubber. An uncomfortable nerve shattering silence filled the air instead of an anniversary celebration, while Taban carried an air of delight, planning yet another ill-timed meeting between him and the boy known as Max. He left behind him the twisted pile of charred metal and smouldering remains, of what had once been a car and its occupants.

Back in Max's bedroom, Tarak stood to full attention as he stared at Austin asking, "You're not planning on telling him are you? Now is not the time Austin, you know that!" explained Tarak seriously, as Austin turned and replied, "You think you have a say in this do you Tarak?" asked Austin objectively, and just as Tarak was about to reply, Austin held up his hand, indicating that he should shut up, as he glanced across at Raan. "I suppose you agree with your older brother?" enquired Austin, never knowing what Raan thought from one moment to the next. Raan opened his eyes and with a serious expression remarked "I wouldn't say that exactly. Most of the time we don't agree on anything, so I'm willing to hear your point of view Austin." he replied, ignoring the look he got from Tarak, while Austin gave Max, who hadn't moved an inch from his position near the window, his full attention. Austin paced the full length of the room with his arms behind his back, having collapsed his wings to a more manageable size, and did some reflective reasoning, before he lifted his head saying, "I agree, the boy should not be told. If we tell him now, then it would only complicate matters, making the situation worse than it already is." knowing full well Max wouldn't like it. Tarak breathed a sigh of relief, while Raan merely nodded his head, closed his eyes, and waited for the storm to hit, and it did, from Max, who having taken two paces forward uttered determinedly, "Well I disagree! I insist you tell me what the hell is happening to me, and tell me now! I know there's a connection to Taban. I also know the memories I see are his, and it has something to do with this sister of his, what's her name umm...Selemie, right?" decided Max, looking straight at Austin before adding "I'm not a child Austin, so don't treat me like one" he stated seriously.

Austin had to admit he was impressed and it showed from the look on his face, but Raan did one better, he shot off the bed grinning like a Cheshire cat on space dust, giving Max a swift pat on his back "Well, well! What do you know, our babies all grown up and ready to leave the nest!" he said in an over expressed tone. Austin took a deep restorative breath of air and looked skywards, while Tarak could do nothing but stare at his brother saying, "Raan be serious and stop scaring the boy, you idiot." which caused Raan to reply in his own defence, "We are...Umm, I mean, I am being serious Tarak, it might not look it to you but I am, and as for Max, well, he's not the least bit scared are you?" he asked curiously, but Max merely shook his head, trying to get as far away from Raan as he could possibly get, and still be in an arm locking embrace with the crackpot alien.

Suddenly without any warning, having taken all he could stand, Max's calm reserve snapped, having reached its absolute limit, enduring endless nights of broken sleep through no fault of his own, tolerating scores of images, images that would undoubtedly haunt him for the rest of his life, and the thought of having to put up with these crackpot aliens any more than he had to, was the end for Max. He broke free from Raan's hold, and backed away from all of them, saying with pent up frustration, "Damn it, enough of this!! This is no game we're playing here! This is my life, my sanity for God's sake! I'm slowly losing my mind here, and no one seems to give a shit!! All you people care about is Melanie, well I've had enough!! Tell me the fucking truth...Now!! Or so help me, I start walking!" he announced, pointing towards the door and adding, "There's nothing keeping me here, and I know Edna would come in a heartbeat. We owe you people nothing!" announced Max sternly, meaning every word, obviously putting his anger management lessons, learned from Edna, to good use. Raan was the first to reply saying, "He's serious Austin...Tell him or I will." Austin looked at Max and after a moments pause said, "Sit down Max, you as well Tarak, we may as well get comfortable." and he let out a heavy sigh.

CHAPTER THIRTY-NINE

Raan decided to get the ball rolling by saying, "You've probably got a load of unanswered questions Max?" as Max, with a hint of sarcasm replied, "You could say that!" but Raan merely shook his head saying, "Total waste of time worrying over them, for most of what Taban told you was fact Max. You know abou..." but before he could say anything else, an impatient voice interrupted him saying, "Who is supposed to be telling this bloody tale? You or me?" asked Austin standing with his hands on his hips, looking extremely annoyed. "Oh right, sorry Austin" remarked Raan sheepishly, while relaxing on Max's bed. Austin shook his head in despair, as Tarak's well-timed cough interrupted them, and he said, "Can we please focus on why we are here, in the middle of the night, with this fledgling." he uttered, pointing in Max's direction. "Fledgling?!" replied Max, feeling somewhat offended at being called a fledgling, when he was in actual fact approaching his mid-twenties...Well nearly, give or take a week or two, but who's counting?

Austin held up his hand, initiating a form of order, as you would in a court room, and said, "You already know about the DNA transferral and the reason for the scar on your chest. Correct?" Austin asked with a hint of superiority in his tone, while Max gave a slight nod of his head. Austin continued by saying, "We know what occurs while you sleep, the flashing images, the memories that, on occasion appear distorted and dark in nature. You're not stupid Max, you've realised yourself that these memories, images, are Taban's, and the reasons are simple..." Austin paused before adding, "Taban did more than just transfer some of his DNA to you Max, he unknowingly or knowingly, we don't know which yet, exchanged a small portion of his own consciousness with yours. He can control this at will, whereas you, you cannot because you're merely human." announced Austin, leaving Max somewhat insulted at being called merely human, before continuing, "Taban must have realised early on, the benefits of this link, and has managed to tap into its source, i.e. you, successfully, whenever the opportunity was available to him. We're not clear on how he's able to do this, and keep it from the rest of us. But the one thing I do know, is that a fully opened vortex would help curb the headaches, and marginally ease the chest pains, so I'd arranged for Melanie to take you down to the panelled room at a time when the others would be asleep." Austin explained calmly, adding, "I will admit that the last thing we needed right now, was more complications at this sensitive time. None of us were fully aware of your condition, and when we were, we needed to test your abilities Max, see what you are capable of, and the only way we could do that was by having you attend a fully opened vortex, which gave Melanie and Vian time enough to visit our home world, and her grandparents." Once again he paused briefly before adding, "I think it's safe to say you surprised us Max, and may yet surprise us even more, with what you're capable of." "We may have only just scratched the surface of your capabilities, so you must be aware of this. Ok?" added Austin, as he sat in one of the upholstered chairs nearby.

Max glanced at the others saying, "Is that the reason you wouldn't let me go on a visit to your planet, because of this link?" he asked, already knowing the answer. Austin was the first to reply, saying, "In a way yes. You see, it was through the link I'd formed with you earlier that we realised just how ill and dangerous our friend has become, not only to you, but to everyone else as well. The link itself did not escalate until you'd reached over the age of 16 years old, which is a good thing for you," concluded Austin seriously, but Max was curious enough to ask, "What would've happened if the link had developed earlier?" Austin did not sugar coat it, he looked him straight in the eye and replied, "In basic terms Max, you'd have gone insane and taken your own life! Obviously you wouldn't have been born with it, which would be impossible. Right now, we need to stop him before it's too late, and unfortunately he's already one step ahead of us. Your headaches have got worse over the past few months? Correct?" he asked Max, who replied, "Yes. Some have been painful beyond words. Before coming here, I was able to subdue some of the pain myself quite easily, but not any more" admitted Max earnestly.

Austin gave an understanding nod of his head, saying, "Taban's been visiting you while you sleep, or attempting to sleep. I've seen him myself on the landing, hidden within the shadows waiting until the time was right to visit you. He's preparing you for what will be the final step of his plan." explained Austin instructively, while Max tried to restart his heart that had suddenly stopped working, managing to ask in hushed tones, "This final step you're talking about, do you have any idea what it might be?" wishing he didn't need to know, feeling the insides of his gut twisting into knots. Raan and Tarak sat forward, as the sudden change in atmosphere electrified the room, as Austin replied, "We have, as you people say on this planet, a rough idea, but the question we would most like an answer to is... Will you be strong enough to live through it Max, should Taban eventually manage to hold you long enough to..?" but he left the sentence unfinished.

Austin watched Max's blue eyes widen expressively, as the last fragment of colour in his complexion disappeared, before he collapsed against his chair, rubbing his hands over his face, while he attempted to process what Austin had just told him. Austin leaned forward saying, "I'll be honest with you Max, prior to tonight I didn't think you were strong enough, but there is a way for me to help you, just as I did tonight, if you would allow me? But in order for me to do this,

I will have to sleep in your room every night. Do you agree to this?" he asked, as Max lowered his hands from his eyes to look at Austin suspiciously, and eventually ask, "How will that help me? You're not going to use any mind probes or anything like that are you?" "Because I'm telling you right now, the answers no! You're not turning me into a science project." remarked Max earnestly.

Austin leaned back in his chair, trying to ignore Raan's hilarious laughter concerning mind probes, as he replied, "Basically, we will be joined together in a chrysalis styled pod, with our minds continuously linked throughout the night. By doing this I will, in effect, shield you enough for you to gain the sleep you need. Sleep is your body's way of refuelling, gaining much needed strength to heal. Unfortunately, you haven't been sleeping, Taban wouldn't let you, he didn't want your subconscious mind strong enough to fight back. That's what he feared the most, do you understand?" he asked with a slight worrying frown.

Max shot to his feet and began pacing the room clearly in an agitated state, while dragging his fingers through his hair, wishing he was anywhere else but here. This went on for a good few minutes before he went to stand in front of the window, to gaze over the dimly lit landscape with his arms behind his back, trying desperately to focus on the shadows moving under the moon's spotlight, thinking, 'I'm living a hellish nightmare here with a bunch of crackpot aliens. I must be one of the unluckiest people on the damn planet.' thought Max. Raan, Tarak and Austin all glanced at each other, clearly feeling insulted at being called 'crackpots', although they were not clear what that meant.

Silence stretched like an elastic band about to snap, before Max without turning round, said, "You know if you weren't being so dammed serious right now, this would've been a hell of a joke you're pulling. But right now, I don't feel like laughing, stuff like this is usually imaginary, the kind of shit you find in books, on TV or in a computer game." he said "You don't hear of it happening in real life do you? And to suddenly have it thrust in your face, making it as real as any nightmare could ever be, was not what I wanted out of life ya know. This is so fucking crazy what I'm about to say, but ok, I'll do it...I'll do as you say." He continued "But first, I'd like to know something. One of the images I saw tonight was of a burned out car, with the smouldering remains of two people in it. I've been hearing music from their car radio for most of the night, it's been driving me crazy. My gut's telling me Taban's responsible, that he cold bloodedly killed them, that he took his anger out on them, because the link between us had been severed. Am I right?" he asked bravely, while everyone else got to their feet, as Austin strolled over to Max "Yes, but you shouldn't dwell on it Max, it's not your fault" he said reassuringly.

Max eventually asked, "If you people are all part of an advanced alien race, then why the hell can't you find him and stop him? You're sitting around doing nothing, and putting other people's lives at risk, namely mine, I might add! You're allowing a maniac free reign on my planet by doing nothing!" he announced angrily, defending his own planet and himself. Tarak was the first to speak saying, "we are doing a great deal Max, the majority of which, is done in secret, as you would expect. We're not going to tell you anything, due to your link with Taban remember? We have to be cautious Max, now more than ever. I think you should go back to sleep now. Austin will help you relax enough so that you sleep. Ok?" he instructed, sensing their young friend's uncertainty.

Max turned and said, "Umm... Austin? About that, don't take this the wrong way, but... after giving it a great deal of thought I've decided that I can't accept you sharing my bed every night, it would freak me out. I'm sorry, but that's how it is, couldn't someone else do it?" he asked, trying to avoid eye contact with Austin, ignorant of the plan being formed in Austin's head, sending a message to the only one he trusted enough to do this task, and replied, "Rest easy Max. I have just the help we need, they're on their way." he said kindly, knowing the boy was in for one hell of a surprise. Raan and Tarak wondered who this remarkable person was, when as if by magic, and a trick of the light, the visitor appeared near the window, startling Max half out of his wits, and he had to blink several times, for he couldn't quite believe what his blue eyes were showing him.

Max was held captive by a pair of the greenest coloured eyes he had ever seen, and thought, 'Wow! She is some sleeping partner!' coming to terms with the idea fairly quickly, and liking it. Her luscious long dark hair fell half way down her back, that sported a hint of green to it whenever the light hit it, and he only word to describe this creation of beauty was 'exquisite', most definitely 'exquisite'.

Feeling a lot happier about the whole idea, Max watched while Austin and the newcomer embraced using a single wing, they elegantly wrap around each other, while a hand placed on each other's shoulder formed a more intimate greeting. Austin turned to face the others with his guest standing alongside him, as he said, "I'd like to introduce my sister 'Zennia'. She has agreed to stay with Max while he sleeps." he announced with a hint of pride in his voice, leaving everyone feeling a little shell shocked.

Raan, stood near enough to Max to give him a few playful nudges with his elbow saying, with a sly wink and a cheeky grin, "Heeey!" sending Austin the worst possible impression. His eyes turned a ferocious black, due to the adrenalin fed anger that was getting the better of him, leading to Raan falling to his knees, begging for forgiveness, having sensed his life was about to end. Only the slight touch of his sister's hand on his arm calmed Austin enough to beckon a rather nervous Max closer, as Austin said, "Zennia. I'd like you to meet Max." Zennia held out her hand in friendship, and along with it, gave an amazing smile that very nearly made him pass out. The warmth from her hand progressed all the way up his arm, and straight into his heart, and if that was not enough, her voice stimulated him in ways a man could only dream about, in the privacy of his own bedroom, when Zennia spoke saying, "Hello Max. I hope we will become good friends." she said in a sultry, yet husky tone, that made him go weak at the knees, as he thought, 'Her voice should be outlawed!'

From that moment on, he was putty in her delicately formed hands, as he thought, 'I'll do anything you say. I'm all yours, do what you want with me you sexy thing.' remembering the fact that Austin could read minds, and apparently, so could Zennia who was laughing behind her hand, while her eyes held a twinkle of mischief. Max tried to save what little he had left of his dignity by saying "Umm...Sorry about that...I lost my train of thought for a moment, I err, wasn't thinking clearly." and broke eye contact. Austin decided he would remain here having witnessed this little show. While Raan turned to Max saying, while heading towards the door with his older brother, "I doubt you'll suffer claustrophobia tonight Max, or any other night." when Austin said "get out you idiot" he ordered, enjoying the moment.

Alone at last, Austin guided Max back into bed, before helping his sister into position next to the boy, who had a sudden bout of unease and a terrified look on his face, until he gazed into Zennia's bright green eyes, which sent him into an immediate state of relaxation, while her wings extended to twice their normal size, before moulding themselves around the two of them. Max found himself inside the chrysalis with Zennia by his side.

Her small, delicately formed hand settled over his heart, moving sensually, preventing the need to scratch his way out of this enclosed tomb. But it caused him to think such suggestive, inappropriate thoughts, 'Oh man! Get a grip Max, they can read minds remember.' he told himself sternly, as the faint glow of light emanating from within the thin membrane of her wings, made it possible for Max to turn his head, gaze deep into Zennia's soulfully seductive eyes, and forget why he was here enclosed inside a confined fleshy tomb.

Zennia lifted her hand to gently caress the side of Max's face, and spoke with barely a whisper in that sexy sultry tone of hers saying, "It's alright Max. I'm going to send you to sleep now, and before you know it, it will be morning." she uttered, and smiled softly with a pair of lips made for kissing. Max had managed to utter the words, "Wait a se..." before he was sleeping like an angel. Zennia breathed a huge sigh of relief, knowing she had a job to do. For Austin had taught her well, but even at the tender age of 102, she still had a lot to learn, and if anything, she was a fast learner. As this was her first task as a would-be watcher, she did not want to disappoint her older brother in this most serious of tasks, that of protecting this young fledgling known as Max, who she noticed, had a pair of the most expressively emotive deep blue eyes, behind which was hidden a lot of hurt and loneliness, in one so young. She impulsively lifted her hand to caress the side of Max's face while he slept, before she too, closed her eyes and began meditating.

CHAPTER FORTY

The following morning Max woke up to the sound of an all-out war being fought on the back lawn between a black and white tom cat and a group of birds, who suddenly decided to play a game of swooping past the annoying cat. For Max it had been the best night's sleep in a long while, as his stomach growled noisily, indicating how hungry he was. He dived out of bed, straight in the shower, got dressed, and headed down stairs for breakfast, where he heard an all too familiar voice saying, "For goodness sake Terry, anyone would think I'd asked you to amputate the limb of a live animal, when all I've asked you to do is whisk the egg mixture." complained Edna, while instructing Tarak in the intricate workings of cooking breakfasts.

Tarak stiffened like an ironing board, while holding the whisk at arm's length by his fingertips, focusing on the contents in the bowl. His expression was one of extreme disgust. "Morning all! What's for breakfast? I'm starving" announced Max with a huge smile on his face and a bounce in his step, as Austin came in through the kitchen window, gave Max a look of understanding before concentrating on his food bowl. Melanie and Vian were not up yet, neither were Sarah and Tristan, so it only left Edna, Tarak, Raan, Austin and Max, eager to start the day. Edna hurried over to give Max a kiss on his cheek saying, "We'll not be having any breakfast if Terry doesn't get a move on", she announced, as Raan shot to his feet saying "I'll help. Tarak didn't get much sleep last night." explained Raan sympathetically, and began beating the living daylights out of the mixture, while humming a happy little tune.

Edna leaned close to Max asking, "Are you alright? You had me worried last night, when this great buffoon wouldn't let me in your room, It's no wonder he's tired, he spent most of last night stood outside my your bedroom, the idiot." as Max replied, "I'm fine honestly, I'd had a bad nightmare that's all." Edna turned to Max suggesting, "How about we go out for the day? Just you and me. We haven't spent a lot of time together, and while we're out we can buy your birthday gift. What do you think?" Max could feel every pair of alien eyes burrowing into the side of his head as he replied, "Ok, why not. We'll have dinner together somewhere." he suggested, when a sound from Austin's direction caught his attention. He was thinking, 'The boy's obviously lost his mind poor kid, this is far more serious than I realised.' he concluded, wondering why anyone in their right mind would want to spend the day with a crazy old bat like Edna.

When the day trippers eventually returned, loaded down with goodies, they were set upon by Raan, who cornered both Max and his shopping bags, and within minutes, Raan had tried on every item of clothing that took his fancy, before badgering Max into trying them on as well., He especially liked the dark tailored jacket, as it would go well with both suit-trousers and jeans, he announced with a flare of professionalism, while parading up and down insisting the new jacket had been bought for both him and Max. Edna on hearing this gave Raan a quick glance saying, "You're a solid gold idiot, you know that don't you? If I could, I'd have you kidnapped by a tribe of mini sloths, although saying that, they'd probably give you back." commented Edna, knowing Raan had watched an 'Ice Age' film on DVD and had never stopped talking about the damn mini sloths. Raan was so busy looking through the rest of Max's shopping bags, he missed Max rolling his eyes and shaking his head in exasperation.

"Hey Max! Are you alright? We heard what happened, I've been so worried, haven't we Vian?" claimed Melanie genuinely, having found Max as Vian laughed under his breath saying, "Yes you have, haven't we?" prompting her to laugh while hitting him for teasing her, before turning to ask, "What happened? You know ... with Zennia. Did she help you? Can you tell me, or have they told you to keep quiet, because they do that sometimes, especially Austin, he can be a real spoil sport." she said frowning. Max merely shook his head. "There's nothing much to tell really, I was asleep for most of the night, sorry Mel." he concluded, while heading back into the kitchen, where he found Austin sat on the window sill, gazing out of the window, who turned, having heard the door open, and hopped onto the counter top to look at Max, while the boy helped himself to a drink saying, "You know, it's a lot easier talking to you when you're in cat form. Your sister's probably back home. Right?" as Austin nodded his head, Max laughed saying, "I'd like to know what a shrink would make of all this, they'd have strait jackets for all of us." he said with a chuckle, as Austin offered him a sly wink.

Later while everyone snuggled under the bed covers due to the chilly night air, all except Max, who was safely housed inside the chrysalis pod with Zennia, Melanie once again began a journey to the land of dreams, only this time, the dream was quite different.

CHAPTER FOURTY ONE

Memories

She found herself standing near one of the many lakes on Munastas, with an image of the night's sky reflected on the surface of the water, with clusters of illuminative flowers brightening the entire area, due to the breeze caressing their petals. Melanie looked down to see her reflection in the water, only it was not the reflection she expected, but that of her mother Selemie, as suddenly Taban hurried to her side, and took hold of her hand to guide her to a secret area, where a huge curiously formed rock as black as ebony, stood alongside a dead remnant of the Altaroo Volcano.

With an air of foreboding, Taban navigated her carefully through an opening, using an illuminated Orb as a guiding light. Dark brown naturally formed rock formations, encrusted with a multitude of meridian-blue coloured shards of crystal, sparkled when touched by light, while they journeyed deeper into the cave. Even under these unusual conditions, life still seemed to flourish in abundance. Various creatures of many descriptions have undoubtedly evolved, to thrive in total darkness, creatures that have adapted by having no eyes or skin colour pigments, similar to Trilobites, some have tubes protruding out of their heads covered in masses of minute hairs, and visible endoskeletons, which detect the vibrations of both movement and sound of oncoming prey.

Strange and unusual plant life were everywhere, most of which, would shy away from light, and retreat into small holes in the rock face, but would soon reappear once the light had dissipated.

Taban having finally arrived at his destination, showed his sister the surprise, a surprise so spectacular in its creation that it alarmed Selemie enormously, for she knew its meaning, a fully established completely independent Vortex leading to another world, but this was outlawed. Having realised this, Selemie hurriedly backed away, knowing what it meant, but Taban stopped her, using nothing but gentle persuasion, by convincing her of the possibilities of it, but Selemie violently and adamantly shook her head, unwilling to attempt such a feat as this. Images of an alien world stared back at her through an unauthorised Vortex, a Vortex Taban himself had created without the knowledge of the high Senan. She tried convincing him to close it down, threatening to tell their parents of it, but he would not listen to any reason or common sense, the device he had created was too important to give up now.

He was adamant bordering on obsessive in his behaviour, in that he would not shut down his creation, and so released the seal enabling a person to go through to visit the other planet, after making sure he had a portable stabilizing orb, in which to secure the opposite end for the return journey. He regarded Selemie and smiled knowing only too well, that if he goes, she would naturally go with him, for she was after all, his twin, and they were bound together.

Taban's unnatural hunger for knowledge overwhelmed most of his ingrained sense of logic and intellect, sending them on one of many unauthorised visits to this planet. It was here that they came across a building called the ROE (Royal Observatory in Edinburgh), 'Where my parents met.' concluded Melanie, the thought of which, made her cry out while she slept. Vian opened his eyes to find tears splattered across his chest, and turned towards his beloved, wrapping his arms around her as the tears continued to fall, due to the emotional onslaught of her parent's doomed relationship flooding her mind. As a sudden change of image caused Melanie to shudder slightly, her Mother pointed towards an unused part of the cave, 'She obviously wants me to go and take a look.' she concluded, for this part of the cave was dark, damp and gloomy, but luckily she had an illuminating Orb.

Sooner than expected, she came across a container in the shape of a large incandescent egg, and opened it to find a small book, realising straight away that it was Taban's journal, containing fragmented notes, comments and precise snippets of data, from most of the experiments he had been working on, leading to present day, 'Why show me this?' wondered Melanie curiously feeling a little confused. Then suddenly within a blink of an eye, the image transported her to the far side of the complex, far away from any recognised location. Melanie watched while her mother hid the journal, in a hidden sphere-shaped storage box behind a large cluster of rocks for safe keeping, before scurrying away, making doubly sure she was not followed. Leaving Melanie with the secure knowledge of its whereabouts, in the hope that she would know what needed to be done.

CHAPTER FORTY-TWO

Melanie awoke with a start to find Vian looking at her while he gently caressed her cheek. She impulsively cupped the side of his face saying, "Did you share the memory with the others?" she asked, as a plan started to form in her mind, Vian nodded his head saying, "Yes, and I know what you're going to suggest." he said trying to hold back a grin. Melanie's answering smile was radiant, as she quickly kissed him on the lips saying, "I need to visit your planet Vian, and it has to be tonight! But we may need the others. Ok?" she said diving out of bed. She was washed and dressed within minutes, "hurry, we may not have much time." announced Melanie anxiously, while hurrying towards the door. But all Vian had to do, was click his fingers, to become fully dressed and ready to go, having seen this amazing magic trick Melanie said, "Oh very funny. Come on funny guy, let's go." and quietly hurried out of the room.

Meanwhile inside Max's bedroom, Zennia and Austin were monitoring Max's sleep pattern, and so for the moment, they were staying where they were most needed, having vowed to protect the boy no matter what the cost. Meanwhile the rest of the group headed through the vortex, journeying towards the far side of the Yoltana waterfall, an area least visited, and all they could hear above the serene sound of the Munastan wildlife, was the unending chatter from a highly neurotic Raan, who said, "I never used to go in these places

Tarak, you know that, but you did." he said, pointing a finger at his older brother adding, "you were always in there, but I never was, so why now, why is it always me?" complained Raan nervously, as he suddenly took a hold of his brothers sleeve in a vice like grip saying, "please don't make me go in there Tarak, can't I stay outside? You know, stand guard? I'd be good at that." he admitted hopefully, grasping the last remaining ray of hope he had left. Tarak released his brother's hold saying, "Calm down Raan, you'll be alright, you won't be going in alone." he replied and carried on walking.

Melanie having listened in on the conversation asked, as her curiosity had got the better of her, "Raan? What happened that frightened you so badly?" Tarak rolled his eyes in exasperation, while Raan gave an over theatrical reply saying, "Yes my dear sweet innocent," he announced with a heavy sigh before adding "I was very young at the time, full of daring and fledgling bravado, but the moment I entered that dark and gloomy place, I got chased back out by a huge ugly great thing with glowing eyes and sharp teeth, I'll never forget it! It was horrifying Mel, truly horrifying!" he admitted with a shudder. Tarak stopped, turned to face his brother and said "Raan, I have a confession to make," he admitted, as all turned to face Tarak, who to everyone's surprise announced "it was me, I was the monster, I did it as a joke, but the joke went too far, I'm sorry." he confessed in that monotone voice, before resuming his walk through the Munastan landscape, with Vian and Melanie following, both wondering if it was true. Raan was in an obvious state of shock and disbelief, questioning why his beloved sibling would do such a horrid thing to such a beloved younger brother.

Having reached a bare sandy terrain, covered with a scattering of dark black boulders, one such rock had an opening leading deep into a cave. Raan wavered somewhat, pulling nervously at his T shirt, "You look a little nervous." stated Vian holding back a laugh, as Raan replied, "Well thank you Captain obvious." he said sarcastically, before being dragged inside. After an age of endless walking, climbing and scurrying through narrow gaps, listening to the incessant whining from Raan, a blood curdling scream echoed off the walls of the cave, startling everyone half out of their wits, to find Raan cowering behind his brother's back for much needed protection, saying, "It flew straight at me Tarak! I swear it did, it nearly had me!!" shouted Raan on a full hysterical meltdown, causing Vian to turn and say, "Take him back outside Tarak, he's of no use to us in here." and both brothers headed outside.

Eventually after many minutes of exploring Melanie, found the vessel left by her mother, and inside she found Taban's precious journal, and instigated a quick exit home, where upon Raan headed straight to his room, having suffered a traumatic experience, and indicated that he would not be getting up until about three in the afternoon, or quite possibly four, just in time for the children's T V channels.

Later that day, Austin was secreted away in Max's bedroom, busy decoding Taban's manuscript, having first sealed the room so he could change into his true form. It was an odd sight to see, sat in one of the two upholstered high backed chairs with his feet up on a leather foot stool, wearing a pair of narrow designer reading glasses to help him read, for he was after all, 200 years of age, so his eyesight was not as good as it once was, and beside him on a small card table lay an open packet of his favourite pork scratchings, a glass of wine and a slice of Edna's light fruit cake, he cunningly stole the second her back was turned, in the hope she would blame Raan. After a lot of hard work and brain power decrypting the writing, he eventually succeeded.

He closed his eyes and pinched the bridge of his nose, hoping to prevent a migraine, clearly affected by the seriousness of the situation, and thought 'I have to arrange a meeting with the others' and went to find Melanie, to tell her of his plan. A short while later Melanie ran into the house shouting, "Austin's gone into the woods after a wild rabbit, we have to go find him, are there any volunteers?" she asked, knowing all too well that Edna, Sarah or Lynnette wouldn't willingly help in the search, but then, that was the whole idea.

Later on in the day, at a secret prearranged location, the air was heavy, filled with tension and concern, as Austin took the stand saying, "I think we have a problem, a serious problem, and no, it doesn't involve the cooking of tonight's dinner." he stated with sarcastic levity. Max burst into laughter saying, "That was funny, I like it." but soon lost his funny side having caught the look in Austin's eye, realising he was in no mood for humour. Raan slapped Max on the back saying, "It's all show really, he's as gentle as a lamb honest." when Tarak interceded by asking, "What have you found out?" noticing the look Austin gave his younger brother, before taking a deep breath and saying, "Taban's been working on more than just the vortex. What that is, I do not know as yet, and as informative as the journal is, it doesn't tell me anything of his more recent work." announced Austin with a sharp edge in his tone adding, "There are hints of other inventions, but he won't say what they are. He's a gifted scientist, and since the death of Selemie, his current work could very well be anything, there are hints of more than one journal." he declared, and in a fit of anger added, "I should have noticed the signs, been there for him, helped him, guided him." he announced in a fit of self-loathing.

Melanie was quick to rush over, stand directly in front of him and say, "Don't blame yourself Austin, it's not your fault. You had other things to worry about, remember?" she said, giving him a gentle hug and kiss on his cheek, then whispered in his ear so no one else could hear, "You did the best you could Austin, you were there for me, you protected me, all because of a promise, a promise I will always love you for." she admitted earnestly, while Austin went a little red faced, saying softly, "It's times like these I see your mother in you, child." Melanie cupped his cheek saying, with a wealth of love in her tone, "And it's times like these I get to say I love you, you old softy." and finished with a gentle kiss on his lips before walking back to her seat.

Raan stood up suddenly in defence of his friend, taking everyone by surprise, and said with a degree of tension in his voice. "You all think the very worst of Taban, and already find him guilty, but I do not and never will." he announced defensively, on behalf of his friend adding, "even if he was riddled with grief due to the loss of his twin, he wouldn't do the things you all think him capable of. I know there is far more going on here! Is it obvious only to me? Am I the only one seeing the truth here!!?" he shouted, while shaking off his brother's attempts to restrain him, before continuing "I know Taban, I know him better than any of you, and as ill as he is right now, he is not capable of doing these things! The fact that you're ready to condemn him disgusts me!! We are reputed to be a noble race, how noble are we now!!" accused Raan, to the whole group, putting everyone more on edge.

Tarak wasted very little time, and hurried over to his brother and spoke in hushed tones, with his hand resting on his shoulder, while Austin looked on anxiously hoping he would succeed in calming him down. It was a side of Raan people rarely got to see, Max did not know what to think neither did Melanie, if the look of confusion was anything to go by. Austin watched with an eagle eyed intensity, before catching everyone's attention saying, "I think it's safe to say that there are others at work here, that something has been cleverly planned, something that could rock our entire way of life, and it's because of this, that we may need the others. I've already sent word ahead of us, along with the possibility of off-world guests," he instructed, as Vian and Tarak voiced their objections saying, "Are you sure that's wise Austin? Taking the off-worlders with us? After all, we never allowed James and he was Melanie's father." forgetting who was present. Melanie's ears pricked up at the mention of her father, and waited for a reply, as Austin said, "That is where we went wrong, it is the reason we lost Selemie, she would not leave James, we lost a great many things that day, you all know the truth, so there is no use in denying it. It will not happen again, not a second time, I will not have another person's life on my conscience, and quite possibly two lives." he declared, looking squarely at Max as did everyone else in the group.

Max felt all the more nervous and thought, 'Well that's made me feel a hell of a lot better, thanks a lot.' knowing every alien in the area could hear it. The chance of stepping through the Vortex had been a chance of a life time, but right now, he was having second thoughts about the whole idea, as Austin said, “Before we all go through the Vortex, I have one more task to perform.” he announced leaving everyone puzzled as to what the task was. Raan was curious enough to want to know and made huge efforts to find out the truth, but to no avail, leaving Raan feeling decidedly put out about the whole thing, for he hated secrets.

CHAPTER FORTY-THREE

Having arrived back at the house, with Austin nestled in Melanie's arms, they entered through the front door shouting "We're back, and we found Austin!!" Several doors flew open and out popped several curious heads, as Mel announced "How would you all like to go on a trip? Even Austin, what do you think?" asked Melanie with excitement in her tone. Max stood rooted to the spot and had difficulty breathing, as the stirrings of anticipation outweighed the heavy sense of foreboding, when a voice close to his ear whispered, "breathe Max, breathe." Max turned to find Raan smiling at him as he placed a reassuring hand on the boy's shoulder, while Edna spoke saying, "Of course I'll have to change first, but where exactly are we going, may I ask?" she wondered aloud, as Vian stepped forward trying to appear relaxed and at ease with the whole silly idea, but with a distinct feeling of tension in his manner which gave the game away, as he said, "It's a surprise, a big one, but we think you'll like it." he uttered sincerely giving Tarak a quick glance of unease.

Edna did an immediate gathering of the troops, issuing out orders left right and centre, while heading to her bedroom saying, "Terry go and prepare me a flask of my special tea would you? Oh! And Ron, get the container of homemade cookies out of the cupboard...Now!" Tarak and Raan were both thinking the exact same thing, which was, 'Help somebody, anybody!' while a heavy sense of impending doom stifled their excitement of going home, both wondering how the high Senan was going to survive the uncomprehending Edna, as suddenly above the hushed din of enthusiasm, a voice from the very depths of hell shouted out "Lynnette, Sarah! Get a bloody move on, we haven't got all day! Come on all of you shake a leg!" ordered Edna authoritatively. Max merely shoved his hands in his pockets and smiled indulgently at his grandmother, knowing this was going to be one interesting ride. Raan and Tarak hurried past him to the kitchen, both wondering what 'shake a leg' meant?

Later after everyone had warily entered the panelled room, Raan gave Austin the thumbs up sign, while Max knowing what was about to happen, watched Edna closely as Austin transformed into his true self without any prior warning. Luckily Melanie was in a position, which enabled her to see everyone's reaction, especially Lynnette's, Sarah's and Tristan's, who it seemed were coping rather well, considering they were now looking at a five and a half foot tall humanoid bat-like creature, with dark blue-grey fur, wings, and a cute little fringe hanging over one eye.

Edna on the other hand did one better, she boldly walked up to Austin pointed her finger at him accusingly saying "I always suspected there was something not quite right about you Austin, so it's a relief knowing that I'm not going mad in my old age." she then took it upon herself to give him the once over, by walking around him, and faced him once again, saying, "Well, you're not terrifyingly ugly Austin, otherwise I'd have misgivings." she uttered, offending Austin, who straightened his shoulders, and was about to say something when Edna then added, "Well out with it then? What are you all doing here?" she asked with her hand resting on her narrow hip.

Austin was taken by surprise, looked her square in the eye and replied, "I was assigned here to protect Melanie." he explained seriously, as Edna nodded her head asking, "And where are you from? Because you're not from around our neck of the woods, that's for sure. It's obvious to a blind man that you're alien," Austin merely nodded his head clearly amazed, by the old girls calm acceptance of what was going on, of all the people here, he thought Edna would be the most difficult. Edna turned to face the others in the group and asked, "You're all aliens I take it? Because it would explain quite a lot about some of you." giving Raan a meaningful glance, who merely shrugged his shoulders, trying to look as innocent as anyone could at a time like this.

But Sarah while in a state of hysteria said, "I knew it! I just knew it, it wasn't my imagination that night, you all thought I was raving mad, that I'd dreamt it, and yet it was here all along, living amongst us, spying on us, watching for the perfect moment to act out its evil plan. It's an alien invasion!!" she shrieked, on a full on melt down, while Tristan did his best to calm her down. Edna having seen this disturbing show of hysteria went and sat down on one of the chairs close to Max saying, as she tapped her walking stick on the wooden floor several times, "Pull yourself together girl for goodness sake, or I'll come over there and slap you silly." before she turned her attention back to Austin and asked, "So, what now? I take it there's a reason you've exposed yourselves like this, so what is it?" watching while the others set to work in opening the Vortex. Melanie turned to Edna saying, "It's kinda complicated, but I can reassure you, that you're in no danger, please believe that. You're all in safe hands right Max?" she said giving him a clear signal saying please back me up or else, "Oh Yeah! We have the good and bad in equal numbers here." he replied in a dead pan tone, laced with sarcasm, while dodging Melanie's well aimed punch to his shoulder, "That's not helping much Max" she announced with annoyance.

Edna having faced her grandson asked, "I take it you've known for some time then?" she concluded, witnessing his attempt to hide the guilt before adding, "Never mind, don't answer that, I'm not going to bore you with endless questions Max, I'll grill Austin later." and gave Austin a look that promised a lot, as the room was suddenly filled with gasps of astonishment as the vortex came to life, releasing a sweet scented breeze that flooded the entire room, and their senses. Edna looked stunned for a moment as she very slowly got to her feet and stepped forward in eager anticipation of such a visit, but Max's restraining hand on her arm stopped her, as he whispered, "Shhh wait." in hushed tones, and followed his gaze to watch the scene unfold.

Austin with an air of authority turned to face everyone and announced, "Before we go any further I would like to say one thing…Arisii!! Show yourself now! I know your here, so stop wasting my time and everybody else's." he insisted looking at all those in the room, waiting for one of them to transform, leaving everyone else wondering which one of them could be the illusive Arisii. And one of them did indeed step forward, to transform into their true image, leaving behind a lot of stunned faces, especially Melanie. For standing before them in all her glory, was a tall pale white skinned young woman with grey colour pigments, wearing shoulder length black hair to match her jet black eyes. Her gown was a full length creation of the colour lilac with the slightest hint of pink whenever the light hit it, and a gem stone covered belt hanging around her slim waist.

Arisii having been found out at long last, stood with her head held high looking regal and majestic, while she continued to look Austin in the eye saying, "I am not ashamed of our actions Austin, we've been curious about these people for some time now. We'd gathered enough data over the years to safeguard ourselves. I was perfectly safe living with my niece." announced Arisii who up until a short time ago, had been living as Lynnette. Edna while looking somewhat puzzled, turned to Max and asked, "We? Who is she talking about?" she whispered softly, but Max merely shrugged his shoulders.

Austin stepped forward, saying, "If it hadn't been for Melanie's dream, showing me your degree of inquisitiveness, spanning from an early age I might add, I would never have known. But I would however, like an answer to a very important question. How did you get hold of the objects you have hidden away on our planet, you know the one's I speak of, who got them for you?" asked Austin taking a firm stand. But Arisii was not the least bit intimidated by Austin's temper, and replied, "You think me incapable of such tasks? Me being a French Troll in your eyes Austin." she stated, holding back a laugh, while Austin's cheeks glowed a beautiful red, before clearing his throat saying, "Don't change the subject Arisii, I want to know..." he announced authoritatively, with a hint of displeasure in his voice, while everyone else stared at this new stranger standing before them, who somehow stood up against Austin with a bravery that was all her own, for Austin was a creature, they never dared intimidate before.

Never in a million years would any of them have guessed that Lynnette was an imposter, and not just any imposter, an alien. It was going to take some getting used to for Melanie, not seeing Lynnette, and she wondered how Sarah was taking it. She found her dearest friend a crumpled wreck on the floor, in a state of disbelief saying, "My God! It's worse than I thought." she uttered. Tristan tried desperately to calm her down, when a voice suddenly announced, "It was me."

Everyone turned in surprise to stare at the last person on the entire planet suspected of committing such a crime, as the culprit said, "I could never say no to Arisii" admitted Tarak guiltily, whose eyes gazed at Arisii with more than just a look of friendship in them, adding, "I never once allowed her access here Austin. You have my word on that. Anything else she did on her own without my knowledge." declared Tarak, with a degree of annoyance, "Oh please!" stated Arisii bravely with her hand resting on her hip. "What's the big deal, we were eager to experience life here, and by making contact with my niece Melanie, it gave us a chance to become more acquainted with her, and help soften the experience. We have had a great time here, I only hope you can all forgive me for deceiving you" begged Arisii to her friends and niece.

All Sarah could do was nod her head as she looked around her in bewilderment. Melanie on the other hand was more concerned as to what punishment Austin would subject Arisii to, and looked up at Vian, who offered in his own way, a soothing suggestion "Umm...Austin we have no doubt that Arisii may have broken several of our old laws and quite a few new ones, but as for handing out punishment I don't think now is the best time." he said, as Edna, having glanced up at Max, said in a loud hushed voice, "this is far better than daytime TV, we ought to come here more often." before turning back to Austin saying, "Austin, can we please get this show on the road, you can punish the poor girl later if you wish, but right now, I want to get moving…" she said, before stopping in mid-sentence, having remembered something, and shouted out, "Wait! Nobody move! We may have a serious situation here!"

And began emptying the contents of her carpet bag, handing out various objects to the people closest to her, the contents being; 1 hairbrush, 2 head scarves, 1 tape measure, 1 flask of special tea with cup attachment, 1 thermal vest and a pack of Kleenex tissues, plus the item she was looking for, which was a camera complete with a spare film, and an item belonging to Max, "Ah this is yours Max, put it in your bag." and handed him a bottle of men's deodorant, which Max put hastily in his bag, while trying to hide his embarrassment.

Having reloaded her bag Edna hooked her arm through Austin's saying, "Cheer up Austin you old fossil, you're getting way too serious in your old age, or I'll make you turn back into a bloody cat." she said with a chuckle. Arisii having heard this, inched closer to Max whispering "I love your grandmother Max, she's a darling." and was about to lead Max through the Vortex, when Max caught the steely- eyed look from Tarak, that almost stopped his heart beat. But luckily for him, Raan came to the rescue, saying. "Hey! Wait a minute, if anyone should go with Max then it should be me, his number one pal, he did after all, give me this new jacket." declared Raan, with a flourish that was all his own, as Max glanced over his shoulder saying, "I did! When?" knowing only too well that he did no such thing.

Raan was at Max's side in an instant saying, "I'll do the guided tour bit Arisii, anyone got a flash light handy?" he asked jokingly to lighten the mood a little, when all of a sudden, a flash light was shoved under his nose, from within Edna's Tardis-sized carpet bag, which produced a laugh from everyone, due to the look on Raan's face. While Max having slung his bag over his shoulder, walked towards the edge of the Vortex, and hesitated, as fear and uncertainty knotted his insides. Raan could understand his young friends concerns, and turned to Max saying reassuringly, "Don't worry Max, you will be alright, I promise." he promised his young friend. Max glanced at Raan with a hint of doubt in his eyes and said, "If you say so." before being ushered through the Vortex to a whole new adventure.

Edna being the least nervous, watched in eager anticipation as Max entered another world, and immediately linked arms with Austin, acting as if she was just nipping to the shop for a bottle of milk, while at the same time, giving Austin a lecture on how to handle Arisii and her wild disobedient nature. Austin sighed deeply, wishing it had been anyone but him, who had the rare privilege of guiding Edna to Munastas.

Melanie hurried over to her friend Sarah and asked, "Are you alright Sal? I know this is a lot to take in all at once but..." and paused when Sarah looked up at her friend saying, "You don't look alien....Well half alien. Did you always know that you were different?" asked Sarah, who paused briefly before adding, "never mind, it doesn't matter, forget I asked. I'm not going with you Mel I'd rather stay here on familiar ground, if that's ok with you. I'm not brave like you, and anyway, you have to go, they're your family after all? Tristan's promised to stay with me." she said with a hint of relief in her voice. Melanie offered Tristan a smile of thanks before replying, "You're sure you'll be alright? I'll stay with you if you'd like" she offered, but Sarah shook her head saying, "No you won't. Now go, that's an order." waving her friend goodbye, who with a degree of reluctance, walked through the vortex with Vian by her side.

The moment Melanie and the other visitors disappeared through the Vortex, on what was to be an amazing journey of adventure and discovery, Sarah, having managed to gather what was left of her wits, got to her feet saying with an embarrassed laugh, “I think I need a drink, something with alcohol in it. It isn’t every day you find out that two of your best friends are aliens...Well one is part alien actually, but it still counts right?” she said, still not quite believing it. But before she could say any more, a hand was waved across her face, and a voice whispered, “Sleep!” causing her to collapse on the floor, in a coma induced sleep, while Tristan stood over her, staring at her through a pair of cold, detached and unsympathetic eyes, before making his way through the vortex to Munastas, leaving Sarah on the panelled room floor. While the real Tristan remained on the opposite side of planet earth, in Mexico, thus leaving an unanswered question:

Who had just stepped through the vortex, if it wasn’t Tristan...?

To be continued…